Devil You Know

Nicole Dixon

Copyright © 2021 Nicole Dixon

Lucky Thirteen Publishing, LLC

All rights reserved.

ISBN: 9798520793595

ACKNOWLEDGMENTS

I've always heard it takes a village. I couldn't write these books without my tribe. So, I need to give them a shout out for dealing with my extra special version of crazy.

Jacob – aka hubby Dixon. To the man who has to deal with me 24/7, bless you. Thank you for keeping the littles occupied while I meet the impossible deadlines I set for myself. Thank you for providing me with endless sexy material and not caring that I use it in my books. Lastly, thank you for ignoring the numerous pictures of shirtless men on my phone while I search book covers and the weird text conversations, I have in my dirty book club. I love you big, Jacob.

Mom. My constant support, and biggest fan. The woman who introduced me to "the other" side of the library. Thanks for being my sounding board and proofreader. Also – thanks for not telling Dad the full extent of the content of my writing. *wink, wink*

Beth. To the woman who listens to me speak of the voices in my head and doesn't call the crazy home on me. Thank you for keeping my secrets. Thank you for always being willing to be my beta and for calling me out on my inability to get my grammar correct.

My children. You have no idea the "scary books" Mommy writes on her computer aren't really scary at all. Not really. I just can't have you reading sexy things over my shoulder. One day you will be scandalized by your mother and I'm not even sorry. Not even a little. Love you babies.

My readers. Thanks for hanging with me. Writing is my creative outlet and I have so many people chatting in my head whose stories demand to be told. Stick around, there's more to come.

XOXO, Nicole

Devil You Know

DEVIL YOU KNOW

REID CHAPMAN
AGE – SIX YEARS OLD

"Reid, honey, it's time to come inside." I leapt over a crater and darted my eyes around the perimeter looking for the evil that I knew lurked around every corner. Evil, it's always there. You just have to find it. Then defeat it.

"Five more minutes Mom, the bad guys will get away if I don't protect the Empire." I ran for cover behind the big oak tree that holds our headquarters and readied my shot, waiting – waiting for the evil to reveal itself.

"Alright, honey, five more minutes. But stop pretending to shoot people, you know how I feel about guns."

Movement.

Get ready. Get set.

Pew. Pew. Pew.

"Reid! Stop it with the stick guns!" Her mom voice carried through the back yard, the one that says she means business, interrupting the galactic battle of the century.

Moms are stinking scary when they use the mom voice.

"Mom!!!!" I groaned as I threw my gun down after a battle to the death, defending the Galactic Empire against the evil forces of the universe once again.

"Get up Alex, it's over, you can stop pretending you're dead now." I pushed my thick glasses up my nose and kicked my best friend in the leg as he rolled over from his spot in my backyard.

"Ah man, they got away again." Alex climbed up to his knees, covered in dirt and mud, just like me. It's dirty work, but somebody's gotta do it.

"They live to see another day. We'll get em' though, don't worry. Good will always triumph over evil." I put my hands on my hips as I threw back my black cape. My mom made it especially for me. It has a giant red R on the back. You know, for Reid.

I'm going to be a superhero when I grow up.

The real-life kind.

"Be careful walking home Alexander, tell your mother I said hello." My mom spoke up from her perch on the back patio as she watched us. Alex lives next door; we've been brothers since forever even though we have different parents.

"Come inside baby, supper is almost ready."

"Is Dad home yet?" My dad works all the time, mom says it's because his job is super important.

"Not tonight, maybe by bedtime." She gave me the look that she gets when she has sad eyes. Moms worry too much.

"One day Mom, one day I will defeat all the evil in the world. You just wait and see!" I walked the steps to our back patio as I followed her inside.

"I know baby, I know."

REID CHAPMAN
AGE – FOURTEEN YEARS OLD

"Alex, dude, let's go. Some kids from school are meeting down at the new café that Uncle Bill and Aunt Shelia just opened. It's in that old bank everyone swore was haunted, and my mom said I can stay out until nine since Uncle Bill's there." I stood in the doorway to my best friends' bedroom as he hovered over his desktop computer. He wore a pair of old faded blue jeans with holes ripped in the knees and a solid black hooded sweatshirt. His dark hair hung down in his face, too long and in serious need of a cut, and his room smelled like rotten socks and two-week-old dead goldfish.

"I don't know man, I just don't feel like it, you go ahead." He didn't even bother to look at me, just continued to stare at the screen, using his hand to push his greasy hair up and out of his face every time it fell forward.

"Hey, Alex, are you okay? It's been what, six months? And you haven't left the house, not once. I get it, but we used to do everything together. I just want my sidekick back." It's been six months since Alex's mom was killed coming home from work by a drunk driver. Six months since I saw him leave this room for something other than for school.

"Reid, my mom died. Some asshole killed my mom. And what? He just sits in the county jail and awaits a court date that may or may not ever come? What do you think, they give him five years? Eight? I lost my mom, man. She's never coming back." His voice broke, but he still didn't turn to look at me.

"I know, I'm sorry. But that's why we're going off to college after high school and then to the Academy after that. Only a few more years and we're going to be the good guys. We'll get the assholes like the one that killed your mom off the streets, we're going to make a difference. Right?" Ever since I can remember Alex and I have wanted to be cops, and not just any cops - FBI. The good guys – the best of the best.

We've watched almost every single episode of *Law and Order*. Well, until the accident.

My dad, he runs our family insurance agency, and yeah, maybe they have expectations that involve me joining in on the family business, but I have other plans. Plans that don't involve boring contracts and dealing with complaints and nagging adjusters. I want to make a difference in the world. I want to do something meaningful with my life.

"Yeah, sure, but what if I told you I could get to the bad guys now? What if we didn't have to wait?" I watched Alex's knee jump with nervous energy as he spoke, sitting at the small desk against the wall in his bedroom.

"What are you talking about Alex?" I walked further into his room so that I could see what he was doing. I don't even have a computer at home. Sure, my dad has computers up at his office, but I don't have access to anything like what Alex has. His parents got him the new Apple Macintosh for Christmas. It even has dial up internet hooked to it. He can watch porn on this internet thing and won't get caught. He doesn't even have to hide his dirty magazines.

"Check this out. It's called code. I'm teaching myself, but people are idiots. They're putting all their information out here on the internet for anyone to find. And these websites? Watch this." I watched Alex click around on his keyboard as names and numbers appeared all over the screen. None of it made any sense to me.

"What is that?" I asked.

"It's a bank, I'm inside their accounts. And I can hack other things too. Why wait on the Academy when I can get to the bad guys just sitting here at my desk in my bedroom?" I stepped back and took a good look at my best friend. My ride or die. I was losing him.

"I don't like this Alex, what if your dad finds out? Or worse, what if the police find out? What if we can't get into the Academy?" I asked as I ran my hand nervously over my neck.

I'm no goody-goody, but I know enough to know that what Alex is talking about could get us into some serious trouble, and I don't have time for trouble. Not the felony kind of trouble.

"I'm going to get so good no one will be able to find me. Just wait. I'm just testing the waters right now; learning. I've been doing my research. But I won't get caught, and I'm going to make the real bad guys pay."

I took another step back trying to make a decision. I

can't nark on my best friend; he's already been through so much. But I also can't stand here and go down with a sinking ship, no matter how much I love my brother. My hands twitched nervously at my sides as I tried to choose – my best friend or my future?

"Yeah, well, I don't like it. I'm going to the café, meet up with us later if you feel up to it. Julie's going to be there. She's been asking about you. I think she wants you to ask her to the Winter Formal."

I really don't know if that last part's true, but I'm willing to say anything to get my best friend to come out with me instead of staying in here and digging himself deeper into a hole that I don't know how to get him out of. I've never dealt with anything like this before. My grandma died when I was eight, but she was old. I don't know what I would do if something happened to my mom.

"Whatever, you take her. Later dude." He dismissed me with his hand, never tearing his eyes from the screen.

My mom didn't die, but I kind of feel like my best friend did. It's not fair.

I took the stairs down from the second floor of his house two at the time, stopping at the door to look back into his kitchen. His dad sat at the dining table, his back to me, with his head in his hands, completely oblivious to my presence. He wore sweatpants and an old t-shirt, and his shoulders shook as he stared at the round oak table.

"Hey, Mr. Straton. Um, maybe check-in on Alex if you get a minute." I spoke up, worried about my friend but not wanting to get him into trouble.

"Yeah, Reid, thanks. Night." His voice was raw as he

spoke; broken. That was it.

I spent as much time in this house over the last fourteen years as I did my own, but it doesn't feel like home anymore.

REID CHAPMAN
AGE – TWENTY-TWO YEARS OLD

"Your muscles are so…big. You said you start the Academy next week? Like, the real FBI?" My blood buzzed with Jack Daniels as the pretty blonde I met no less than five minutes ago leaned into me close enough that I could smell the fruity drink she was sipping on her lips. Her blonde hair hung down her back in big loose curls, and her boobs were pressed up high, nearly falling out of the skin tight red dress that may as well have been painted on her body.

She's not too drunk, just bordering over the line of tipsy, and she's already half naked as it is. She's perfect. For tonight.

I graduated with honors with my degree in Criminal Justice two weeks ago, having already been granted pre-admittance into the FBI training academy. I've been riding a high since that day. My entire life has been leading up to this moment.

No distractions. It's been my mantra since before I can remember. Anything or anyone that threatens to derail my goals, I cut them out. It may sound harsh, but it's the way it has to be.

But I'm not a saint. And the women, well they love a

man with a badge. Even if I don't technically have one yet. They practically beg to be fucked by an aspiring FBI agent, and who am I to deny them that? It's a win, win. They tell their friends that they spent the night handcuffed to the bed of an agent, and I get a quick release.

They don't question me when it's rough, they beg for it because I'm a good guy by default, so they trust me and scream for more.

I fulfill their fantasies, and they go back home to fuck their boring ass husbands/boyfriends - whatever, and I move on. If you think about it, it's kind of like a public service, really.

I'm an arrogant son of a bitch and believe me – it works. Every. Single. Time.

I felt my phone buzz in my pocket just as I was sliding my hand around her plump ass. Dammit. It's after midnight. I pulled back and put a finger out in front of my face, indicating I needed a minute. I pressed the button on my cell phone and put it to my ear.

"Incoming collect call from Jefferson County penitentiary. Select one to accept."

I groaned as I hit one and walked away from a sure thing. I sobered up in an instant as my gut turned knowing who was on the other end of the line. The one person I've never been able to bring myself to cut out of my life.

"Reid, man, you there?" His voice carried through the phone, it was slightly muffled, like he was leaning into the phone and trying to cover the background noises.

"Yeah Alex, I'm here. What the fuck man?" I ran my

hand over the back of my neck and walked out on the street to grab a cab back to my one-bedroom apartment.

"They found it. They confiscated everything. Raided my apartment. Shit, I'm in deep." Climbing into the back of one of the waiting cabs outside of the bar I frequent, just down the street from my apartment, I ran my hand over my face. Feeling the stubble on my jawline under my palm that I would have to shave off when I report to the Academy next week.

"Dammit Alex, what did they find? What are you talking about?" I spoke low enough that the cab driver hopefully couldn't overhear what we were talking about, not that he cared.

Alex and I were always supposed to graduate high school and head off to college together. It was always supposed to happen that way. Until it didn't. Alex was never the same after his mom was killed. His dad became a recluse, pulling further and further away from his son, and leaving him to basically finish raising himself.

Alex skated by in high school, barely graduating. Not because he wasn't intelligent, he's the most intelligent guy I know. No, he became obsessed with the hunt. His computer was a living and breathing entity for him and revenge was the fuel for the fire that burned inside of him.

I've always asked Alex to keep me in the dark, I would rather not know than know something that I felt put me in a situation where I had to make a choice. So, our relationship was strained, but I felt like I was the only person holding the tether on the end of his rope to reality. I held tight, keeping watch. But apparently, I failed, and my "don't ask don't tell" policy is now biting me in the ass all the way from the Jefferson County Pen. Where the fuck is Jefferson County anyway?

"I can't say much. Pretty sure they record these calls."

"They do."

"Right, but I need your help. Anything you can do. I don't think I'm going home anytime soon, Reid. And my dad, he'll be alone back at home. I don't trust him by himself. I've been keeping tabs on him, had him all wired up with surveillance, but hell, I think they took that too. I can't keep my eyes on him anymore. Can you check in on him? Just make sure he doesn't kill himself or some crazy shit." I could hear the fear in his voice. My trusty sidekick. We were always a team, and right now I can't help him, and he knows that.

"Yeah, I'll keep an eye on him. How long, you think?" I questioned as I stepped out of the cab and shoved some cash toward the driver.

"Years. I gotta go, Reid. I love you man." A dial tone rang through the line as I stepped onto the sidewalk outside of my apartment building.

REID CHAPMAN
FIVE MONTHS LATER

"Reid, honey, come get a picture with your father and I. Just one more." My mom ushered me towards her in the crowd of people swarming around each other at my graduation from the FBI training academy. Twenty weeks of absolute hell, but I was handed a badge about thirty minutes ago that made it all worth it.

A badge and orders to report for assignment next week. Sex and human trafficking. FBI as a Division of the Department of Homeland Security. I'm going undercover. My first assignment is meant to put my training to the test, but if I pass - when I pass; I'm going in deep.

I want to come face to face with the devil and tell him to go fuck himself.

"Ok, ready, smile." My mom stood next to me, and my arm easily wrapped around her shoulder. I've been taller than her since the day I turned twelve, and I didn't stop growing. My father stands to my right and is just shy of meeting me at eye level. I imagine that has less to do with my height and more to do with his age. My parents had me later in life. They struggled to conceive. I was their miracle baby, and they were forty before I was born.

Having older parents had its pros and cons. I never had to watch my parents struggle like many of my friends did. My father inherited the Chapman Group from his father, and his father before him. A business that has been in our family for generations. A business that I was destined to take over from birth, except I didn't. I think my father has come to terms with it at this point, but it wasn't always a topic of conversation you wanted to have over family dinner.

But, on the flip side, my parents were always older than the parents of all of my friends. They had more responsibilities, were further along in their careers. It was just the three of us, and to be honest, my dad wasn't around half the time.

Then there was Alex.

After Alex's mom died, I was kind of a loner. Not that it mattered, my goals were bigger than Friday night football games and underage drinking parties. I didn't have time for that shit, even then. Still don't.

"I'm proud of you son but remember – if you ever get tired of this lifestyle, you've got a career back home. Your desk will always be available at Chapman." My father placed his hand on my shoulder and congratulated me in the only way he knows how – conditionally. I'm used to it at this point.

"George, let him be." My mother leaned in to kiss me on the cheek, rubbing it in and smearing it around with the palm of her hand, like only a mother can do. Ever my biggest supporter, even if I know the thought of it scares her half to death.

"Reid, please be safe. You know how I feel about the

guns."

"Mom, I'm fully trained. I graduated in the top five percent of my class. I'm ready."

It's true, I am ready. The minute I left home for college I joined a group of guys at a shooting range and began perfecting my shot. Pistols, rifles, handguns, even machine guns. You name it, I've trained on it, spending countless hours perfecting it. In addition to that, I began Krav Maga training and have been honing my skills for the last five years. Not to mention, the rigorous training the FBI put us through the last twenty weeks. This is the pinnacle of everything I've been training for my entire life.

"When will you come home?" She asked, her eyes misting over as the call came over the loudspeaker that we were wrapping up.

"I don't know, mom. But, I promise, I *will* always come home." I kissed her on her head and threw an arm around my dad, who stood next to her stiffly – his face impassive before turning to head back to the Senior Special Agent I've been training under for the last few months.

This career is something I was born to do. It's my destiny. I'll be damned if I get killed before I fulfill it. I will always come home.

REID CHAPMAN
AGE – TWENTY-FIVE YEARS OLD

"Special Agent Reid Chapman, good to see you again."
I stood in the back of a dimly lit room in our headquarters building at Quantico. My shoulders broadened on instinct, and I stood taller. I twitched with the urge to head back into the field, but I was called in from my current assignment for this meeting which means something big is happening on the case.

I'm rarely called in because one slip and my cover is blown. People die. And in my line of work that's usually women and children. That's not something I take lightly. So, while I'm standing here, my mind is back there. Back in the damp storage shed off of a main interstate that houses twenty or so young girls readying for shipment. I know they're there. I've seen them. I've touched them. I've played my damn role, and if we don't break this case open before we lose another group, I might lose my fucking mind. So, whatever the hell I've been called in here for better be damn good.

"Director." Respect. It doesn't matter how pissed I am, how much I hate the fucking chain of command in this place and the red tape that keeps us held back more often than not. The red tape that kills innocents every damn day. I will keep my mouth shut and listen. Because if I lose my temper, if I slip up and get pulled, there's no telling what will happen to those girls. There's not a damn agent in the field right now that cares for those women and children as much as I do. That fights for them. I am their hero, and I will play my part and be a puppet when need be so that I can save them when no one else is even in the damn ring.

"We need a specific skill set." He paused.

"I'm already assigned to my mission, sir."

"Let me speak." His voice rose another octave. "We need someone with a specific ability and level of intelligence that we don't currently have available to us here at the agency. We need someone that can think like a criminal. Get inside their minds. It's my understanding you might know someone that fits that description."

"I don't understand, sir. Permission to ask for clarification."

"Alexander Wyatt Straton. Does that name register with you?"

Alex.

"Yes sir."

"Alexander Straton is currently serving time at a high-profile state penitentiary after being sentenced to ten years for hacking into our National Defense Database."

"Excuse me?" I spoke out of line, but National Defense? I thought Alex was just doing some basic Robin Hood hacking shit. Stealing from the bad guys and funneling to those that needed it. I didn't go to his sentencing because I couldn't, and he knew it. I had to keep my distance or risk damaging the future of my career.

"Alexander Straton was in the back door of the Department of Defense for almost a full year before we found him and put him away. But now we need him. We're looking to offer him a deal. Your case, the transactions are all being done electronically, and every time our cyber security group thinks they have them something goes haywire, and we lose them again. You know as well as I do, we can't afford to lose another group before we shut these assholes down. Someone is screwing with us, and I think your friend can figure it out. We damn well can't count on those monkey's sitting over in the Cyber Intelligence Unit right now."

"Have you made the offer?" His iron-clad features turned up into what I think may be a smile, but lack of use is causing it to come across as more of a grimace.

"He spit in Agent Bennett's face and told him to…go fuck a unicorn." A unicorn. Dammit, Alex. I fought to keep the laughter that threatened to breach my lips locked down.

"You need me to talk to him?" I asked, knowing how much Alex hates the system. A broken system that allowed the man that killed his mother to walk free after only six months. Alex resents authority, and I can't say that I blame him. We're best friends, brothers by choice. While our approach is very different, we are still very much the same.

"I need you to get him to sign the damn contract. Yesterday."

Dismissed.

CHAPTER ONE
HOLLY – PRESENT DAY

"Listen, Holly, just one date. It doesn't even have to be a real date; you could just go grab coffee one afternoon or something. It would do you some good to put yourself out there again, you're not getting any younger." I rolled my eyes so hard they nearly fell out of my head as I leaned back in my office chair. I held my cell phone between my shoulder and ear, balancing it as I continued to make adjustments to the digital mock-up of the layout I was working on for my latest project. I guess I could put her on speaker phone but considering as I'm currently debating on whether or not I'm going to hang up on her, it may be a waste of my time anyway.

"Well, that was a bitch thing to say, you sound like mom. I just turned thirty last year. I'm not ancient, Tilly. And I definitely don't want to be set up with one of Kris's golfing buddies, no offense." Tilly is short for Mistletoe. Yepp, our mother has a thing for Christmas. Tilly is my oldest sister and is thirty-seven, happily married to her high school sweetheart with three kids. She wears an apron to cook dinner every night, and probably only has sex in the missionary position – if you get my drift.

I have another sister, Noel, she's thirty-four and writes sexy romance novels for a living, or you know, porn with a storyline as our mother likes to refer to it. She has an affinity for tattoos and is kind of the black sheep of the family – I think Tilly has given up on trying to tame her, and our mother definitely isn't sharing her work with her friends down at the Country Club.

"Holly, language. I've got you on speaker and the baby is nursing. All I'm saying is that your fertility clock is ticking down by the minute. Not to mention, Chet was an asshole. I can assure you, there are other men out there. Men that don't shave their arms. That was weird, Holly."

I snorted through my nose at the reminder that Chet shaved his arms regularly because he swore that it highlighted the definition in his muscles. Gag me. Show me a woman that likes day old prickly man arms. Exactly.

"I am fully aware that there are other men on planet Earth besides Chet, Tilly. Also, can I just point out that my foul mouth isn't going to spoil the mind of your infant while she sucks on your boob. She's not even listening to me, she's too busy getting milk drunk on your tits. Remind me again, how are we related?" I teased.

My sisters and I have an interesting relationship, the age gap between us is rather large and throw in the fact that our personalities are all so vastly different, sometimes it makes it hard for us to relate to each other.

For a while there, after Chet somehow swindled me into a borderline abusive relationship, I didn't see them or talk to them. I was segregated from my entire support system, and if it weren't for my group of girlfriends, I don't think I would have been able to pull myself out…without having to bury a body. Not gonna lie, there were a couple of times I considered sneaking some arsenic in Chet's morning protein shake. Sue me.

"Jesus, I ask myself that question every day. Have you talked to Noel lately?" Oh boy, have I talked to Noel lately. I talked to her last week. She was shacked up with an Italian guy somewhere in Europe. Apparently, he doesn't speak English, and she doesn't speak Italian, but there is one language they both speak and well, let's just say that's not something I'm prepared to share with Tilly tonight.

"Yeah, did you read her new release? It's still hanging on tight to the number one spot in Kindle Unlimited for the erotica genre. That scene with the guy and the other guy and the girl. Holy hell." My sister is a lot of things, but damn that woman can write some steamy sex.

"Shhhhhh….yes. Yes, I read it. Don't talk so loud, Kris is in the office with the door open."

"Tilly, it's a book, woman. It wouldn't kill Kris to take a few pointers, I'm sure. I mean, not that his swimmers aren't obviously working fine. I'm just saying. Live it up a little, take a walk on the wild side. When was the last time you did it in the middle of the week? When, Tilly?" I gave up trying to work, having too much fun playing with my sister. I know her face must be beet red right this minute.

"Now who's being a b-word? Talk to me when milk leaks from your boobs if your husband so much as looks at them the wrong way, and you have a three-year-old that screams and beats on the bedroom door the second they sense the lock is turned. The very second. Bunch of cock blockers. Oh my gosh. I can't believe I just said that. You and Noel both are bad influences. This is why Cousin Margaret is the godmother of my children." Blah, Blah, Blah…Cousin Margaret, she may as well go ahead and send her kids off to boarding school instead.

"And thank God for that really, Til. I love your little devils, but if something were to happen to you or Kris, heaven forbid, I just don't think I could do it. I'm not cut out for the parenting thing. And Noel, we won't even go there." I hate to even admit this out loud, for fear that my ovaries may actually shrivel up and fall out of my vagina – you know on the off chance I change my mind one day, but I've never wanted children. Never even had the slightest inkling that I would one day want to suck snot from a baby's nose with my bare mouth. Yes, it's a thing, I watched my sister do it. I prefer to spend my time with my one true love, design; specifically historical properties. Give me a building that has some history behind it - walls that have seen centuries pass - over dirty diapers any day of the week.

"We won't even go there. Right. Anyway, if you change your mind about the coffee thing, text me. I'm telling you, Kris has some really good-looking friends, and successful – they all have jobs, and none of them live with their parents. Well except the one, but I wasn't even going to suggest him. You don't need to stay holed up in your office for the rest of your life, Holly. Because I know that's where you are right now. I can smell you through the phone, smells like caffeine and a graveyard of ink pens." She's not wrong.

I looked around my desk at the scattered black ink pens, half of which I've discarded because they no longer roll as smoothly as the new pens do. At some point they start to skip, and if one of my pens even think about skipping, they are trashed. I only buy one specific brand and it has to be the black.

Technology has its place, and I don't know how I would do my job without it, but when I'm truly designing – when I'm feeling the stories of the people that have walked the halls of the worn and haggard architecture before me – I will always go back to my ink.

"Give the babies my love, Til. And tell Kris I said hello, and might I suggest that sex on Tuesdays is fun too."

"Night, Holly." I could physically feel her tired through the phone as I hit end on one of the longest phone calls I've had with my oldest sister in over a year. Having three children all under the age of five is killing her. Not that she wasn't a total bore before, but now she's extra vanilla.

-o-

My parents are the upper crust of the upper class, old money, handed down generation after generation. I'm not even entirely sure what my father does for a living. Investing? Trading stocks? Real Estate? I really can't be sure, but the money – there was always plenty of it, and my mother made sure everyone knew too. Her career consists of hosting dinner parties and social gatherings, thus her love for all things Christmas. *It's the most wonderful time of the year, darlings.* I can hear her now, as she spends enough money to fund a third-word orphanage on a nine-foot-tall Christmas tree for the entrance in the grand hall.

We were raised to be debutantes, even had a coming out ball on our consecutive 16th birthdays. In case you were wondering, that's kind of like an auction for your fancy virginity. My mother put us in etiquette classes from the time we could walk, and we spent our summers swimming in the pool at the Country Club while my mother sipped cocktails and gossiped with her fake friends and my father played golf with his associates – or fucked one of my mother's friends in the locker room.

Not that she cared, she fucked the pool boy every Thursday at precisely three o'clock in the pool house. That's when I was supposed to be practicing my piano, but what my mother didn't realize was I could see the entrance to the pool house from the windows in the conservatory. Ms. Sicily, my piano instructor, bless her two-hundred-year-old soul, was totally oblivious to the scandalous activity I was privy to every week.

Tilly, being the first-born, was a people pleaser. She followed the rules, dated within the pre-approved circle and married for money – er, love – when she turned twenty-six. She had to wait for Kristopher to finish his doctoral program, of course. Kris is a good guy, but the man's a podiatrist. He couldn't go to medical school for something cool like cutting people open. No, he looks at crusty old toes for a living.

Anyway, I'm sure my mother thought she was golden, raising Tilly to perfection. Until Noel came along and dropped a stick of dynamite in her evening bourbon.

Noel was hell on wheels straight out of the gate. Her favorite pastime was sneaking her boyfriends into our three-story home in the coveted cul de sac of our gated community – don't even ask me how they scaled the fortress we lived behind, because those boys weren't from our side of the gates, that's for sure. And then the time she forged my dad's name on the form for her first tattoo – at sixteen and we won't even talk about the time her phone synched up to the Bluetooth in my mother's luxury SUV and began playing hardcore porn through the speakers on our way to ballet class. I was ten.

By the time I came along, well, they were just glad I preferred drawing over writing. I kept my nose stuck in history books and stayed quiet. Noel was so busy being a distraction that it was easy for me to slip by under the radar.

That was fine by me, because I didn't care for their high-class, society. The gossip and the fake smiles. Maybe that's why I fit in so well with my girlfriends now. They are crass and loud, but they're real. And sure, maybe I'm the odd man out now and they push me to date just like Tilly. But their men, the men they lean towards…well, maybe I wouldn't mind getting trapped into having a cup of coffee with one of them. Or trapped under them, I never said I was an angel.

CHAPTER TWO
REID

"Twenty-seven seconds. Twenty. Dammit, Reid. Get the fuck out of there." The muscles in my legs burned with the fire of a thousand suns as I ran, ducking for cover and then sprinting to safety. My clothes were drenched in sweat, the humidity suffocating as I gasped for air.

"Hell yeah, you beat your record by three seconds. Good work Senior Special Agent." Alex walked up behind me decked out in all black with a headset on, his voice echoed through the microscopic earpiece I wore in my ear as my chest continued to heave, searching for air that I couldn't get to process through my lungs and into my bloodstream fast enough.

"Was the rubber bullet necessary in that third room? Really, Alex? It hurt like a bitch." I rubbed my leg where a rubber bullet shot me in the thigh just as I was rolling under a synthetic fallen tree.

"Quit crying, pretty boy. How many times have we gone over this? You have to expect the unexpected, even in the simulation rooms. If you let your guard down in here, you let your guard down out there. And if you let your guard down out there, you're dead." He's right, but that doesn't make the purpling that I know is currently bubbling up on my thigh feel any better.

"The new weather control devices in here are legit, this humidity will kill me if the bullets don't." I pulled my soaked t-shirt off over my head, revealing my state-of-the-art bulletproof vest. I train in my gear, but when I'm undercover I don't get luxuries like flame retardant clothing and bulletproof vests, I just get shot. And it wouldn't be the first time. I've taken my share of bullets, but nothing I haven't lived to tell about later. And I *always* got those fuckers, so it wasn't for naught.

"Right, we're tweaking the simulators every day, and every day they get better. We train you guys harder, push you further. I was worried about you there for a second, thought you might be getting too old for this." Alex can poke and prod all he wants to, but I know where his train of thought is. I'm in my thirties now, and in our world that makes me an old man. The young guys training up behind me, they are counting the days until I'm pushed to a desk and told to sit down. Alex wants to see me settle down, find a wife, have kids, and buy a puppy or some shit. News fucking flash: It's not happening. I will die first.

Seventeen missions. Hundreds of women and children. Hell.

I've seen it.

I've lived it.

And I'm still here.

Every day.

I close my eyes at night and the screaming, the crying, it's all I hear. Their pleading voices echo throughout my dreams. My entire childhood I wanted to be a superhero – Batman in the flesh. I wanted to save the world. But we lose them. I've watched shipping containers full of children leave the damn harbor and I was the one that turned the lock. All because I had to maintain cover and damn it if we didn't have what we needed yet to lock the evil away.

The evil, I always knew it was out there. I could feel it, still can. It's buried in my bones, nestled against my soul. Right beside the lives of the women and children I've lost.

But I won't stop. I will not stop fighting, because each time we save one. Or we put a bullet through the skull of one of the bad guys, on accident, of course. Because you know, we're supposed to arrest them or some shit. Each time we save a life, I can breathe. Even if only for a second.

Some might call me a hero, I'm one of the good guys. Right? But I live a life of evil, and I pray when I lay my head down at night that I will be redeemed by the souls that I save in return. I'm fighting for me just as much as I'm fighting for them at this point. It's my own personal war, and I won't be defeated. I dare them to try me.

That's why I'm here today, training with Alex. I've been given notice that I've been assigned to a new leg of the case we've been building for years. I'm supposed to report next week. It's been a few months since I've been undercover. Some shit about me needing R&R. I'm itching for a new assignment. I can't sit still knowing what happens when the lights go out and most people are warm, and cozy snuggled up in their beds. I need to work. I need to fight the evil that threatens to swallow me alive.

-o-
HOLLY

"LGM Décor, this is Holly Adkins." I grabbed at the phone on my office desk as I chewed on the end of one of my ink pens. My black high heeled stilettos hung over the ledge of my desk as I balanced on the rear wheels of my office chair and tempted fate every time I rocked, and the wheels threatened to give way underneath me. Only new clients call our direct line, all of our established clients have my cell number, and they usually prefer to speak with me personally.

"Ms. Adkins, this is Laurel Chesire. I'm with Wilks Luxury Automotive." Wilks, why does that sound familiar?

"How can we be of assistance, Ms. Chesire?" I asked as I released my pen from my teeth and prepared to take notes.

"Mr. Sylvester Wilks would like to employ your services." Sylv, my gut rolled, he's friends with my father. That's why the name sounds familiar, I remember he and my father sitting on our back patio smoking cigars and laughing on many occasions over the years as I was growing up.

He's a slimy old man. He's been old for as long as I

can remember. His oversized gut protrudes out over his dress slacks, and he always had the creepy eyes; you know the ones. You can feel them following you, and you just know the things going on behind them are pervy and disgusting.

"And specifically, what services does Mr. Wilks need?" I'm curious, but I'm at the point in my career that I don't have to take every single client that calls. I make enough money that I can be selective.

"He recently acquired Anderson House. Are you familiar with the property?" I felt the gooseflesh rise on my neck as an awareness washed over me. My senses tingled with those words alone.

"Anderson House. But, it burned six months ago?" I questioned, remembering being engrossed in the news coverage that enveloped the historic property. The property is so much more than its name implies, the history surrounding it is dark and mysterious.

Anderson House is an old plantation house on the outskirts of Carlton. Untouched by the revitalization efforts that have been sweeping the city over the last few years. My entire life I heard the stories that surrounded that house. Left abandoned for years, the rich history of the home discarded and left to rot. The property sat back behind tall iron gates that have been padlocked for as long as can remember.

As teenagers we would dare each other to run up the long, wooded drive and touch the gates. Only no one ever made it that far without running back screaming, the tall tales of what they saw swarming through our young minds and fueling our fear.

Hubert Robert Anderson II, second generation plantation owner. Raped and murdered countless women and young girls in the three-story-mansion as he forced his wife to watch on. Until one day she broke, unable to live with the horror of all she had witnessed any longer. The staff at the time saw her leave his room with a bloody knife in the early hours one morning before the sun rose, sheltering a young girl under her arm. Old man Anderson was found tied to their grand four poster master bed - naked, covered in blood, with his genitals shoved in his mouth. His eyes were taped open. Rumor has it that his wife wanted to watch him bleed to death, wanted to watch the evil from his soul cross over into the depths of Hell.

According to the legend that surrounds the mansion, the young girl was brought to safety just before Mrs. Anderson was found with the same knife in the clawfoot tub of the master bath, just down the hall from her husband. Both wrists slit as bright red water flooded the floors.

The house is said to be haunted by her ghost and the ghosts of all the women and children that died before her. After their deaths, the house was abandoned and has remained untouched up until a few months ago when it mysteriously caught fire in the middle of the night.

According to the news reports, the arson investigation surrounding it found no cause, but they did locate secret tunnels beneath the house that ran under the property and out to the train tracks. Those train tracks lead directly to the harbor. The newspaper article insinuated it might have been used at one time as part of the underground railroad, but there was no solid proof to back up that theory.

According to the article, the shell of the house remained, but the inside – which had remained untouched for nearly a century – had gone up in flames.

"Mr. Wilks understands that you have a specific skill set. Historical restoration. The property does have some damage from the fire, but there was an insurance policy already in place at the time of the incident. The damages and restoration effort will be fully covered by the policy. He would like for someone with your level of expertise in this type of restoration to handle the renovations." I'm intrigued, I've worked on numerous historical properties over my career, but never have I worked on something with such a vibrant past.

"Who is the point of contact for Mr. Wilks?" I'm curious enough to want to take the project on but I'm not sure I'm willing to work with Mr. Wilks, the man makes my skin crawl.

"You will have free reign on the project Ms. Adkins. Mr. Wilks specifically requested your undivided attention on the matter. Let me reiterate, budget is not an issue."

Free reign.

No budget.

Haunted, historical property.

"I need four weeks. I just got started on a project in downtown Carlton, but it's a simple renovation of a historical bank, I shouldn't need longer than that. When this project is complete, I can personally handle the Anderson House renovations. I will have my assistant call back and iron out the specifics. I look forward to working with you, Laurel." I immediately clicked my computer to life and began researching any and every piece of history I could find on the old plantation house.

"Please, call me Ms. Chesire. Holly, there is one other stipulation. Mr. Wilks has asked that you stay on the property for the duration of the renovations. There is a guest house that also has historical significance that was not damaged in the fire, it should be sufficient for your stay. Should you need anything, I will leave you with my direct contact information. Should you need to speak to Mr. Wilks, please contact me, and I will arrange a meeting." I paused. Um, what? She wants me to stay on the property? Like some modern-day ghost hunter.

"And this stipulation, how firm are we talking here? I can easily commute to Anderson House from my apartment, and I can assure you this project will have my undivided attention."

"Take it or leave it Ms. Adkins, it's non-negotiable. We will see you four weeks from today."

Dial tone.

I wonder…

Can you buy ghost hunting supplies on Amazon?

Also, might need some holy water? Garlic?

CHAPTER THREE
REID

"Senior Special Agent Reid Chapman, it's been a while." I sat in a cold metal chair across the table from Director Alan Reynolds, Senior Director for the Sex and Human Trafficking Division of the Federal Bureau of Investigation. The room was cold and barren with the exception of the clock hanging on the wall behind my head, that I could hear ticking in the background. I mentally catalogued the exits in this room - two, one directly behind me and one to my right. I scanned the room, unmoving, always aware of my surroundings, always on. I can't turn it off, and I wouldn't want to. The moment I turn it off is the moment I die.

"Director, that it has." I don't have time for pleasantries. I see the folder that sits under his hand as his thumb moves up and down in a slow tapping motion. The folder that I know contains pictures of women and children that have gone missing; ones we don't even know are missing yet. The hundreds unaccounted for, their lives matter. And yet we sit here, wasting time, looking at each other as another shipment moves out.

And then there are the pictures of those that hurt them. The ones that consider themselves Gods; that think that they get to determine who lives or dies, and fuck if they care as long as the money gets wired to their accounts at the end of the day. They've lost their humanity and have sold their souls to the devil.

"We've been doing this together for…how long? Almost a decade. And in all that time your record has been impeccable. You have laid your life down for the women and children of this unit. This assignment, this isn't going to be easy. It's going to test every skill you have worked to hone over the last ten years, mentally and physically." His thumb hovered over the file as he stopped tapping momentarily and paused, looking me in the eyes, evaluating.

"We considered putting someone else on this mission, but this is the culmination of your work, and if you can pull it off, well…this is one case we will be able to close. Understand, this assignment is unique in that if you review the file and you don't think this is something you can manage, you do have the option to pass; you can walk away. Special Agent Bennett is chomping at the bit for this assignment, but the agency feels you are the best fit and our best bet in catching these assholes."

"No. Under no circumstances will I pass on the assignment." My jaw locked as I ground my teeth together and bit back the words I wanted to say. Fucking Bennett. This career, we hover the line of good versus evil, and sometimes we have to cross that line to accomplish our ultimate goal. But, Bennett, he likes to cross the line for funsies, it's a joke to him, and I have my suspicions he's not living the high life off of his shit pay from the Bureau.

Director Reynolds nodded slowly, pushing the file across the table to me as he flipped it open.

Sylvester Wilks, owns a luxury auto company that in reality is a shell company for international trade. Late sixties, Caucasian, he specializes in young girls and virgins. We've been trying to nail him down for years, but every time we get close, he disappears on us.

Victor Adkins, old money. Selling sex is big business for his family. We have reason to believe that his grandfather was part of the original mafia. He hides behind his stockpile of dirty money and a shell trading company that dabbles on Wall Street to maintain relevancy.

I remained stoic and held the tremble in my hands that threatened to give me away as I flipped to the third photo. Director Reynolds watched me intently, waiting for my reaction.

"My father, what does he have to do with this, Director?" I forced my voice to remain even. My father owns a fucking insurance company, as did his father before him. I don't understand.

"We have reason to believe he's indirectly related to this case. While there is no indication that he is directly involved with the trafficking of these women and children, we believe that he is assisting these men in a money laundering scheme filing fraudulent insurance claims. He's cleaning their dirty money for them and getting a hefty slice off the top in return." I let my guard slip, if only momentarily as I ran my hand over my face.

"When was the last time you went home, Chapman?" Director Reynolds stared at me, his eyes narrowed as he tested me and looked for a tell. I don't have one.

"Years." After my first assignment, I was changed. They try to warn you in the Academy, I underwent numerous psychological exams and am constantly being re-evaluated every time I come out of the field off of an assignment. I pass with flying colors, because I'm damn good at my job. I can fool the best of the best doctors.

But my mother, one look at my eyes, and I will break her heart. She will see the devil. The devil I fight against every day. I can't live with the knowledge that I broke her. So, I've stayed away. I call home regularly, but I spend the majority of time on assignment, and they understand. It's my calling, and while I've always known that it eats away at my father, my mother has been supportive. Now I'm questioning whether or not I should have stayed away for so long.

"Well, pack your shit. You're moving back, and I hear there's an opening at the Chapman Group. Get ready to join the family business, you're going under as Reid Chapman – Claims Specialist and Adjuster. Can you handle this Special Agent Chapman? If your father is found guilty, charges will be brought against him. We might be able to work out a deal, given the circumstances, if we can get to Wilks and Adkins through him." The rush of adrenaline I'm all too familiar with flooded my system. My knee bounced, and my blood raced through my mind.

I can't let Bennett touch this case. Dammit.

"I'm in."

-o-

"Oh, Mr. Chapman, right this way." I followed behind my young twenty-something-year-old administrative assistant that was assigned to me the moment that I mentioned my early retirement from the Bureau to my father.

Last night, I sat next to him on the back patio of my parents' sensible upper-middle class home in the same neighborhood I grew up in as he lit a cigar in celebration of me finally coming to my senses, as he so nicely put it. I couldn't help but glance around and wonder about the money laundering. Wonder what my father was involved in and how deep. I'm a fucking federal agent, and my father was involved in this shit under my nose the entire time.

I did, at one time, have an apartment here in Carlton. I sold my penthouse in the Shaeffer building when I realized I was on assignment more than I was at home, it didn't make sense financially for me to keep it. The Shaeffer building, it was my investment property, my future – if I lived to see it.

As part of my trust, I was allotted certain funds on my twenty-fifth birthday. I used those funds to invest in an old shoe factory when I saw the potential in the revitalization of Carlton. I turned that property into upscale apartments and a boutique hotel. The revenue stream from that venture feeds into a savings account that I keep as my nest egg. I've never had much of a reason to touch it, and now hell it may have been funded with dirty money to begin with. I never questioned my father when he told me about the trust. He mentioned it was family money, from the business, and I didn't ask questions. I was twenty-five and never intended on receiving the other half, which had a stipulation in it that I take over the company. Which I still have no intentions of doing, even though by every outward appearance currently, I am.

So instead of moving back into my apartment, in the building that I own, I'm moving into an apartment building not too far from here, that, funnily enough, Alex has already wired up. This apartment belonged to some friends of his. There was an incident involving security at the apartment a couple of years ago. I was out on assignment at the time, but I heard the stories that filtered through the Bureau.

Ryan Walsh, CEO of Walsh Inc. and an old friend of Alex, almost lost his, then girlfriend, now wife, in a kidnapping and attempted murder situation that was mere seconds from ending badly. If Alex had not been involved, and not been able to tap federal resources quickly, things would have probably ended differently. After the incident, at the request of Ryan, the apartment had a full security detail done on it. So, other than some job specific details that Alex has already secured there for me, I should be able to easily move in and settle into my assignment.

Being in our cyber security division, Alex has more flexibility than I do. He can come and go as he pleases because the work that he does is hiding behind a computer. He's not easily recognized on the street. He doesn't have to worry about walking into the corner drugstore and taking a bullet to the back of the head.

I'm taking a huge ass risk coming home for this assignment and going undercover as myself. I risk having to go into a protection program permanently depending on how this all goes down. I'm risking my life, the lives of every single innocent these men have left their mark on, and I'm risking my family. It will never be the same after this. None of it will.

"Amanda, is that what you said your name was?" I asked as I watched her ass bounce from side to side in the tight black pencil skirt she wore as we stepped off of the elevator onto the twenty-first floor of my father's building.

"Yes sir, but you can call me Mandy if you want." She giggled; the sound only slightly annoying as she turned back to look at me. Her bottle-dyed blonde hair was pulled up into a sleek ponytail, up off of her face, making her big blue eyes stand out amongst her other features.

"How old are you Amanda?" I ignored her request and closed the door behind us as we walked into my office. My father has been holding this office for me my entire life. I used to play in here as a child while he took phone calls, and my mother ran errands. Growing up, I did my homework at this very desk. Floor to ceiling windows overlook the city, but we're so high up in the clouds that no one can see in, and that's what I'm counting on as I hear Amanda giggle again from behind me.

"Twenty-two, I'm really excited about this job, you know. I was answering the phone at the front for ages, but when Mr. Chapman, you know, your dad, asked me if I might be interested in a promotion, I had no idea he meant I would get to be your assistant. Is there anything at all I can do for you while you get settled?" Her eyes scanned my body, not even remotely hiding her intentions, stopping on the semi-hard bulge that pressed against the zipper of my dress slacks, and I considered my options.

She's my secretary, albeit temporarily. She probably fucked my father to get this position, and at this point, I wouldn't put it past him. But, I'm just a man, and maybe I won't fuck her today – I do have some standards, but that doesn't mean I won't let her put her bright red lips around my cock and show me how she can help me get…settled in.

Her eyes remained locked on my erection as she licked her lips. "Let me help you with that, Mr. Chapman." She sauntered forward slowly as I sunk back into the black leather chair that sat behind my large, glass-topped desk. Unzipping my pants, I pulled my erection from my slacks and stroked it once, twice, as she got down on her knees between my tense thighs.

"It's so big, I bet you taste so good. Here, let me." Placing my hands on my thighs, I watched as her manicured red fingernails ran up and down the length of my cock as it continued to harden under her touch.

Pre-cum dripped from the tip, and she leaned down, opening her mouth to lick it up like a good girl. This isn't her first time. Her mouth devoured me as she swirled her tongue around the head of my cock, and my hand went to her hair, wrapping her ponytail around the palm of my hand until I got a good grip. I heard her gag as she took more of me down her throat, and I leaned back into the chair and groaned as I relaxed into her warm, wet mouth.

I lifted my hips and pulled her hair tighter as I closed my eyes and continued to thrust into her mouth over and over again. Gag and moan, gag and moan, she knows she possesses a certain skillset, and she's using it to her advantage. It's rather entrepreneurial, honestly.

I felt my orgasm building in the base of my spine as she ran her manicured fingernails under my balls, and I pulled her head down further until I felt the tip of my cock touch the back of her throat. Her big blue eyes looked up at me as I opened my eyes and she smiled around my length, saliva leaking from the corners of her mouth, that was all it took. I stilled and shot stream after stream of my cum down her throat.

She waited for me to finish, eagerly swallowing down every last drop I would give her. Then without a word she stood from her spot between my legs, gently wiped the corners of her mouth and straightened her skirt as I zipped my pants back up.

"If I can ever be of assistance Mr. Chapman, don't hesitate to let me know. I'm always *willing* to go above and beyond to get my work done and completed in a timely manner. Oh, and you have a message from a security company. Something about wiring up your office here in the building. I left it in the desk drawer for you. Top left drawer. The boxes with your office supplies should be up within the hour."

"Thank you, Amanda, you're dismissed." She closed the door behind her as she walked out of the office and left me alone, looking out over the city, sitting behind a desk in an office that I swore I would never step foot in.

CHAPTER FOUR
REID

"I can't say that wasn't enjoyable for me." Alex answered the phone immediately when I dialed his number from my cell phone, as I continued to gaze out over the city.

"You've already been here, haven't you?" I grabbed my black-rimmed glasses from the desk, having to get used to wearing them again, and slid them on. As an agent, I'm usually required to wear my contacts, but for this particular assignment, I am wearing my glasses. I guess that's what happens when you go from blending in with hardened criminals to a damn insurance adjuster.

"Wired your office up last night, I was in and out. Kind of like you about five minutes ago. Really, Chapman? Your secretary, a little cliché don't you think?" I could hear him chuckling as I groaned through the line having not considered Alex beat me here and installed cameras. They're for my safety, and a requirement of the Bureau, but a heads up would have been nice.

"You are sick in the head man; I don't know what they did to you in prison. Wipe that footage, you know the drill." I clicked the computer to life on my desk and logged into my email, still not used to seeing my name associated with the Chapman Group logo.

"I got you, I will add it to my personal stash. Stay away from the secretary though, I ran a background on her, and she has a clientele list a mile long when she's not working for Chapman, if you get my drift."

"If it feels like a professional blowjob…"

"It's probably a professional blowjob." I grinned as he finished my sentence for me.

"What do you have in terms of connections between my father and Wilks?" I asked, knowing that Alex thoroughly scanned this office for potential bugs when he wired it up. There is no chance anyone is hearing this conversation, other that the higher-ups at the Bureau. Even then, they hear only what we want them to hear. Alex may take his pay from the federal government now, but he will always be one step ahead of them. It's just the way it is, and personally, I'm happy he's on my team.

"I found some easy stuff right away, mostly public records and filings. It all looks legal on the front-end. Wilks purchased some old ass haunted house, Anderson something-or-another a few months ago. Your father insured it for a hella lot of money for him. A fire was reported on the property within a week of all of the doc's being finalized. The money is moving."

"So, we see the money. Any news on the trafficking investigations? Where is he hiding them?" I asked as I rubbed my jaw and considered my reality. My father is probably going to prison, and I'm going to be the one that put him there. Dammit.

"Tunnels. There are tunnels under the Anderson property. They lead to railroad tracks that lead directly to the harbor. We don't have a solid location on any current transports, but it's a perfect storm." I could hear Alex clicking away on a keyboard in the background as he answered me.

"What about Adkins, got anything on him?"

"Not yet, but I think it's possible his daughter may be involved." Interesting. In our world, it's the men that take over the family business throughout the generations, taking over the dirty work. It's rare we see a woman step up.

"Really? A daughter?"

"Yeah, he has three. The oldest, she's a country club socialite, lives well above her means with her podiatrist husband and three kids – all signs indicate she's clean as a whistle. The middle daughter is a wild cat, she writes sex novels for a living. That genre is surprisingly popular. Anyway, she's been in Europe for the last year, I don't think she's involved, nor do I think she has any inclination that her father is who he is. The youngest, Holly Adkins, turned thirty recently. She owns a design company – LGM Décor and Renovations. Bio on her website says she specializes in historic property design and renovations. Guess what project she's working on right now?"

"You know I don't like games Alex, tell me."

"You're no fun."

"Alex."

"Midtown Bank Café." He paused as he dropped that bomb on me.

"Bill and Shelia's place? You're fucking with me. Uncle Bill is involved in this shit?" I thought back to all of my childhood memories that involved Uncle Bill and Aunt Shelia. Hell, I spent most of my teenage years hanging out in that very café. Bill was more present in my life than my own father.

"Eh, he doesn't appear to be involved. Maybe coincidence…"

"There are no coincidences in this business, you know that as well as I do." I interrupted him mid-sentence.

"Well, I haven't found anything that ties them to our current case, with one exception. There was a flood recently at the café, the city was involved. Your father wrote Bill a hefty policy on that property years ago, and now with Adkins doing the renovations…" He let his voice trail off, knowing I would make my own inferences.

"Dammit, Adkins is working with my father." I answered immediately.

"Ding, ding, ding. Holly Adkins. And guess who's doing the renovations on the old Anderson place for Wilks?"

"Adkins."

"Right again, you're on a roll tonight. Wanna fly out to Vegas? I'm feeling lucky."

-o-
HOLLY

"This is bad." I turned a slow circle around the

Midtown Bank Café as I took in the damage caused by mere minutes of flooding. According to Beth, Manager of the café and one of my best friends, the city neglected to turn off a main water line when they were performing some routine maintenance and the pressure build-up caused a pipe to burst inside the historic bank turned coffee shop and bakery. The city claims they aren't at fault because the pipes weren't up to code. I'm calling bullshit on that, doesn't much matter anyway because the insurance policy covering this place is sufficient enough to restore the damage and do some minor renovations. The only issue is, well, insurance.

Insurance adjusters are a pain in my ass. They like to take their sweet time assessing the damage, then they want to question every single decision made during the restoration process. As if those paper pushers know a damn thing about restoration or design.

What's worse, they're usually men. Men that don't think I know how to do my job all because I have a vagina instead of a dick. I don't say any of that to Beth though as I look around the café taking notes on my tablet while we wait for the adjuster that's been assigned to her case to show up. I don't want to worry her, because I know that irregardless of the fight that might ensue surrounding these renovations, I will win. I always win, and this property will be gorgeous when I've completed my work. Signed. Sealed. Delivered.

I made notes on what we could and could not salvage, sketched ideas on my digital notepad that would be sufficient until I could get back to my office and draw out the mock-ups with my ink, and I listened. I listened to the walls, felt the energy in the space and tried to imagine what this bank was like when it was originally built. I let my mind travel back in time as I imagined the shine of the fresh laid hardwood floors and the intricate details of the crown molding; little details that most people don't see, but I do. I don't just see the details, I feel them. I let my mind wander until the design begins to take shape and I can imagine the potential of the space we stand in.

Until I was abruptly jerked from my thoughts by a loud knock, I internally groaned at yet another interruption. Despite pushing out numerous social media posts and a sign on the door that we had to prop open to allow for some fresh air to flow through the damp building, regular customers of the café have been stopping in all morning. Poor Beth, the look on her face every time she has to send someone down the street, it's sheer agony for her to turn her regular customers away, as a business owner myself, I totally get it.

A sense of awareness caused my spine to tingle as I felt an odd presence at my back, and I heard a deep voice from the front of the building speaking to Beth. Something in that voice caused me to pause and listen. My heart started racing for no apparent reason, and I worried for a moment that I might be having a stroke. What the hell?

"Beth, I presume? I'm Reid Chapman, from the Chapman Group. Sometimes referred to as the entitled, pretentious…what was it?" He hesitated for only a second, and in that time, I slowly turned to see the man standing in the doorway as he rubbed his hand over his jaw, pretending to think. "Ah yes, prick." He was repeating the words I may or may not have spoken to Beth just moments before, whoops.

I squared my shoulders, preparing to face the consequences of my words as I heard Beth squeak out my name. I hate to stereotype, really – I do, but most of the insurance adjusters and claims specialists I deal with, especially on these older, historic properties, well, generally speaking, they fit a certain criterion. Meaning, they're usually progressed in their age, wear their pants belted over their large bellies, they smell like expensive cigars, and look like they spend time with my father at the country club on the weekend. What can I say, I just call em' like I see them, and I've seen my share.

But that is not the man standing in the doorway to the Midtown Bank Café. Oh hell no. This man, well, he looks like sex and smells like…hold on. I need to get closer.

I'd be lying if I said I didn't sway my hips the way my mother did on Thursday's when the pool boy followed behind her like a stray puppy as I walked towards Reid Chapman. I don't have much of an ass, Noel got the curves, but that's ok, I know how to work what I do have to my advantage. I held my head up high and portrayed an air of confidence that I didn't necessarily feel. Damn Chet for putting a kink in my self-esteem. I'm working to get it back though, and a feeling of empowerment washed over me as the tips of my stilettos touched his freshly shined, black leather loafers.

"Holly Adkins, owner of LGM Décor and Renovations. Thank you for meeting us on such short notice, Mr. Chapman." I pronounced every single syllable in his name as I rolled it over my tongue, crossing my arms in front of my chest and popping out my hip because apparently, I'm all-in committed to my cause now – no turning back.

Dammit, just as I thought, he smells like expensive cologne and safe words. I let my eyes wander over his thick biceps and the way his black dress shirt was neatly tucked into his gray slacks. Slacks that were obviously pressed just this morning and clung to his muscular thighs like they were tailored to fit his body. I let my eyes travel up his broad shoulders, over the veins in his neck and his carved, square jawline until my blue eyes met his behind black framed glasses that did nothing but enhance his sex appeal. His dark brown hair was cut short on the sides with a hard part set just off center, but the top was a little bit longer and styled to perfection. Not a single hair out of place.

He watched me as I took him in, the corner of his lip curving up. This is a man that knows he is sex in the flesh; the arrogance rolls off of him in waves.

I extended my hand to him and waited. A test.

Men are so easy, and you can usually dissect their entire personality from a single handshake.

Grab my fingers delicately, and you just showed me that you think men are the superior species. That you don't see me as an equal, but as a woman that has to be treated with kid gloves, gently.

There is nothing gentle about me.

Grip my hand like we're business partners, and I know immediately that you see me. You might not like me, but you see me for what I am – a force to be reckoned with.

Reid's large hand engulfed my small hand, firmly, as I

felt lightning shoot through the tips of my fingers and into my arm. His eyes shot to mine and his jaw firmed. He feels it too. We stood, staring at each other, neither one of us willing to relinquish the foreign sensation that linked our hands together until finally Reid dropped my hand and stepped away from me, dismissing me, and addressing Beth.

I listened as Reid explained to Beth the claims process, and that he would serve as the adjuster assigned to the claim. He mentioned something about knowing the owners of the café, and all the while I couldn't take my eyes off of him. There's something about him, and I can't put my finger on it. He's an insurance adjuster, boring with a capital B, and yet I feel something dangerous in the air, my senses are on high alert. It's bothering me that he's not what he's supposed to be, who he's supposed to be. And every few minutes, I feel his eyes on me. He's looking at me too.

When he mentioned that his timeline was six weeks I spoke up, I pushed back. I need this job done in four. I have a signed contract for the Anderson House project sitting on my desk. It's a once in a lifetime opportunity, and I will put my own money on the line before I let an insurance claim tie up my timeline.

CHAPTER FIVE
REID

"Well son, how did the meeting go down at Bill and Shelia's this morning? I know it's been a while since you've worked a claim. Like riding a bike, huh, kid? I bet you had them eating out of the palm of your hand." I internally rolled my eyes as I walked into my father's office, just one floor above my own. I've been trying to avoid him as much as possible, the less we have to work together for me to get this done, the better.

He leaned back in his chair, comfortable, he doesn't see me as the threat that I know I am. He trusts me, and that's unfortunate for the both of us. His large gut pulls dangerously at the buttons of his pressed, white button-down, tempting the seams between the black suspenders he wears every day. I'm not sure if he wears them because he thinks they look good, or if he genuinely cannot keep his pants up at the awkward position over his gut without them. My bet is on the latter. His silver/gray hair is slicked back, curling at the tips just at the base of his neck, and his jowls are clean-shaven, as they always have been. I've never seen my father with facial hair, he detests it, swears it looks lazy, which in turn makes you look incompetent.

"Actually, Bill and Shelia weren't there, they're out of the country. I spoke with Beth Holt, the manager of the café, and Holly Adkins, the designer on the restoration project." I watched my father as I said their names, waiting for a reaction. Does he know Holly? Has he worked for her before? Or does he believe that his relationship is strictly with her father?

"Huh," he grunted. "I guess ole' Bill is finally getting tired of running that damn coffee shop. That was always Shelia's thing, and Bill, well, he was pussy whipped. He's been following that woman around since we were kids." The way he spoke about a woman that I've known as my aunt the majority of my life made my gut roll. Have I been that far removed? Or was I just blind to it as a child?

Ignoring his crass statement, I pushed forward. "They think the project will be complete in four weeks, which seems a little extreme. Sounded like Adkins didn't mind fronting her own money to get the ball rolling though."

"These things take time, but it's possible we can fast-track the claim on our end. We've got some accounts set up that make the paperwork a little easier. All things I will teach you in time, boy. I'm just happy you're finally here to learn the family business."

Accounts.

Ease the paperwork.

Red flags popped up all over the place. The damn family business.

"Hey, Dad," it killed me to even call him that. "What do you know about Anderson House? I saw the file on the public network yesterday. Are you handling that account personally or will you assign someone to it?"

"Sylv Wilks is my client, a friend of mine." He confirmed my suspicions as he rolled his chin between his thumb and forefinger, something I've seen him do numerous times before when he's toying around with an idea.

"I apologize, but I'm not familiar." I baited to see what information my father might reveal to me.

"Sylvester Wilks, owns Wilks Luxury Auto. Not a guy you want to piss off, but I think this may be a good claim for you to take on. We can work together on the project, and I can show you the ins and outs of the business as my father did before me." Jesus, at least my grandfather is dead, I would hate to have to lock him away too.

The thought of working with my father on the project didn't sit well with me, but maybe this will give us the information we need to connect all three of our main players.

Not to mention, I wouldn't mind seeing Holly Adkins again. I knew exactly which woman she was of the two that stood before me when I walked into the café this morning. She's tiny, like a compact stick of dynamite. Even in her seductive, black stilettos the top of her head barely hit my chin. I could probably grip both of her hips and my fingers would connect around her center.

Her sleek blonde hair fell straight around her

shoulders, and dammit if blondes don't set my blood on fire. Standing in a solid inch of water in black pants that molded to her slender curves, a matching black blazer, and a hot pink silk top underneath, I couldn't pull my eyes away from her, even as I tried to focus on Elizabeth Holt and her claim. A claim that, if not connected to this case, I honestly don't give two shits about.

She's a powerhouse, and her attitude tells me that she very well could be involved with her father. She's confident and sensual without even trying. I should be more concerned with her connection to this case and less concerned about the slight outline of her nipples that I could just barely make out as they pressed tightly against the silk fabric of her camisole.

I've always kept my sex life separate from the cases I work, never willing to risk blowing a case up over one night of pleasure, because they're all the same. Interchangeable.

But, Holly, she's got me wondering what lengths I may be willing to go to, to get a taste.

Just one bite.

Would she bite back?

-o-
HOLLY

"Hold up! Stop it right there. Anderson House, as in creepy as hell haunted mansion just outside of Carlton? I watched a documentary on that place, and I swear that I didn't sleep for a week straight." Olivia's face looked horrified as she spoke up and I sipped on my mimosa, unaffected, telling the girls about my upcoming project over our semi-regular Sunday brunch.

For nearly a year now, I've been getting together with a small group of my closest girlfriends for brunch once or twice a month on Sunday. We always try to pick somewhere new and different, and yet even though the scenery changes, we order the same things – bottomless mimosas, an extra-large charcuterie board, and when we're feeling extra fancy, the assortment of mini muffins - those are Olivia's favorite. We love our spontaneity, you know – as long as it's properly planned.

It's becoming increasingly more difficult for us to get together as our lives continue to get busier. Megan and Ali, the twins, are both at different stages of their pregnancies. Olivia and her new husband, Jason, recently adopted a teenage boy – yeah, you can only imagine how full their hands are. And Beth, well she's dealing with the café, and I have sneaking suspicion that she and Asher Cohen, the hottest local chef in the Carlton area, are cooking up something else on the sly. Sometimes it's just nice to sit around a table together and stuff our faces with miniature calories and fancy alcohol – disguised as a breakfast beverage.

"One and the same. I got a call about the project last week. I know it sounds crazy, but I couldn't let the opportunity pass. I specialize in historical renovation and design, but honestly – those projects are few and far between. The revitalization efforts here in Carlton have kept me busy, but when do those run out? At some point I'm going to be back to designing closet spaces and nurseries for babies. No offense, I love helping you guys, you're my family. But my heart, my heart is in the century's old bones of older properties. The stories they tell, they speak to me."

"Tell us how you really feel, why don't you?" Ali teased as she rubbed her almost non-existent belly. She and Megan both are tiny, but Megan is a little further along in her pregnancy.

"Watch it, you know I designed your entire mansion of a house, and you better let me in that nursery when it's closer to time. It's only fair!" Ali is an artist that runs a non-profit for women that have faced abuse or are currently in abusive relationships, *Hope for Magnolia*. She was one of the first people that knew about my destructive relationship with Chet, and she, along with Olivia, who is employed as her personal assistant and business manager, helped to get me on the right track to recovery. They saved me, and I will forever be indebted to them for that.

Ali married multi-millionaire Ryan Walsh, and they live in one of the most beautiful historical properties in Carlton, Magnolia Mansion. My design firm helped Ryan restore the mansion when he originally purchased it, and then again assisted Ali when they added the gallery for her artwork and non-profit organization. I'm heavily invested in that property, and she knows I would be hurt if I didn't get to at least put a tiny touch on the nursery designs for their baby.

"You know I'm teasing, if you live through Anderson House, I've got a room picked out and an empty slate for you to work from. My artwork is limited to canvas; it does not extend to room layouts and design." She brushed a piece of her dark brown hair out of her face that had somehow escaped the confines of the loose braid that wrapped over her shoulder.

"If I live?! You guys! Go ahead and publish my obituary, won't you." I threw a grape across the table, and it landed directly in Ali's glass of water. Bullseye.

"The documentary I watched said that house has been abandoned for over a century. The gates locked up tight and rusted shut with age. But at night, screams of the women and children that were tortured and died there can be heard through the woods that surround the plantation." Olivia whispered like we were sitting around a campfire telling ghost stories, her violet eyes narrowing as she weaved her elaborate tale.

"Get outta here, I thought that place burnt to the ground a few months back. I could have sworn I read something in the papers about that." Beth asked as the waiter re-filled her champagne flute.

"I'm going to be honest, when I got the call, I was a little confused as well. I had the same understanding, but apparently, while there is some fire damage, the majority of the house is still very well intact. According to the woman I spoke with, insurance is going to cover the damages, and that's part of where I come in. I'm going to be working with the adjuster on the damage claims as well as completing the restoration of the plantation house."

"Speaking of insurance adjuster. Can we talk about Mr. Reid Chapman? Holl's over here has the hots for the agent on our claim at the café. Admit it, woman!" Beth called me out in front of our friends, never wanting to talk about her own personal love life but quick to call attention to anyone else's. I get it, it's her diversion tactic, but dammit man, pick on someone else.

"Wait, what? Holly are you holding out on us? I never saw you with an insurance agent, to be honest. Real estate mogul, sure. Brain surgeon, ok. But, insurance claims?" Megan raised an eyebrow.

"Says the woman that is married to an accountant?" I shot back, Megan is also an accountant, but not like the boring kind that sits around and does tax returns all day. Megan is a boss babe with a calculator that's well on her way to partner of one of the largest accounting and auditing firms in the country.

"First of all, you know as well as I do that, he left his career in accounting to run the Harbor venue and perform the business side of Retherford Farms full-time, which I might add has been phenomenally successful. Second, have you met my husband? I mean really, the man's so hot his suit practically melts off of him." You could see the moment her green eyes shifted from defending her man to imagining him with his clothes off; the transition not even a little bit subtle as she pulled her plump bottom lip between her teeth.

"Oh God, don't get her started on the man pants. We'll be on that topic of conversation for a solid thirty minutes." Ali jumped in, cutting her sister off.

"And yet, most of the women here have benefitted from the man pants enlightenment theory. You're welcome." Megan crossed her arms over her baby belly with a satisfied smirk.

"She's not lying. A good pair of man pants is almost

as sexy as a good pair of sweatpants…almost." Olivia twirled one of her bright red curls between her fingers as she spoke. Most days, her red curls fall in smooth, shiny loose waves down her back, but today – well today, they look like she's been at the beach for weeks without a hairbrush. Her red curls are all over the place, and yet according to the conversations I've overheard about her new hubby Jason, that's the way he prefers them. Wild and free. Honestly, she's stunning, and can pull off either look.

Olivia has this unique vibe about her that can't be duplicated. She's covered in freckles, and her eyes are the strangest mixture of colors I've ever seen. She's one of those women that are effortlessly beautiful, and I can't say that I don't envy that about her.

"So, spill, when do you start the project? Ya know, in case we need to start planning a funeral." Ali spoke as Beth's snorted laughter rang out behind me, and I chose to ignore her.

"Four weeks. As soon as we close on the café project for Beth. I'm moving in as soon as possible so that I can get the ball rolling. Fire damage, like flood damage, is sometimes tricky with insurance claims. It's time sensitive, and I'm not going to lie - I'm a smidge excited, and ok, a little nervous." We won't mention the rosary I purchased on Amazon last night while I was scrolling aimlessly on my phone before bed.

"All I heard was…blah blah blah…you're moving into the damn haunted house?!" Olivia's eyes widened, and I'll give it to her, she looks genuinely scared for me. Huh.

"Uh, yeah, so not exactly in the house, per se. But there was a requirement that in order to get the project, I had to agree to stay on the property. There is another fully functional guest's quarters of some sort that wasn't damaged by the fire. For the duration of the project, I will stay on-site in the guest house." I shrugged and beat down the nerves that began to mix with the champagne and orange juice concoction swirling in my gut as my friends all stared at me in utter disbelief.

"So, when you die, can I have your shoe collection? I mean, I know you have sisters and all, but we're the same shoe size, and honestly, I promise to love them like they were my own children." Beth was the first to break the silence.

"We could display some artwork at your funeral, how do you feel about that? Oh, I know! What if I paint your casket? We could start a new trend, open an entirely new market for custom painted caskets." Ali tried to remain serious as a smile threatened to escape from the corner of her lips.

"Sounds like a profitable business venture to me, I'm in." Megan chimed in.

"So dramatic, I swear. I'm going to be fine. I don't believe in ghosts; you are all ridiculous. I'm in it for the history, and you know as well as I do that place has it in spades."

Repeat. I'm in it for the history. I'm in it for the history.

"Yeah, right, we'll be sure to add that to your obituary. *She always put the history first, and ultimately it led to her untimely demise.* I love you, Holly, but you are insane. Legit certifiable. Wouldn't you rather stay here and play with the nice boring insurance adjuster?" Olivia suggested.

"The only men that won't break my heart are the dead ones. I want to hear this plantation speak, and I want to give it new life. A life free of its dark past. What does it say about me if I let that kind of history die?"

I spoke the words, only half paying attention because my mind got stuck somewhere back on envisioning playing with the boring insurance adjuster that I still can't shake the feeling isn't as boring as he seems.

What's your deal Reid Chapman, and why do you look so damn good in the man pants?

CHAPTER SIX
REID

"And you have absolutely nothing on her?" I leaned forward and placed my elbows onto my knees as I pulled my glasses off to rub the tension headache building in my forehead.

"I just don't think she's involved, Reid. The woman is never late on a single bill, she files her taxes on time every year. Hell, she's never even had a speeding ticket." Alex repeated the same thing back to me that he's told me three times already, he can't find a single thing that ties Holly Adkins to her father's illegal business dealings.

"Dammit, Alex. So, tell me, why is she working on both the Midtown Bank Café and the Anderson House project? Why the coincidences? She shouldn't be tied to all three of our main suspects if she isn't herself a damn suspect." We're less than two weeks out from the Anderson House claim. We've been tiptoeing around this Midtown Bank shit that has led to absolutely nowhere for weeks. We're tracking the money, but we have no indication of incoming or outgoing shipments that would tie Wilks or Adkins to the human trafficking allegations we have against them. I'm floundering here and the loss of control is driving me insane.

"I don't know what to tell you, man. I've scanned her file so many times I feel like she's my new BFF. I know what she eats for breakfast in the morning, and that she doesn't wear pajamas to sleep at night. I've been watching her for weeks, and we have nothing. Zilch. Let's re-group and try a different avenue because this one sure as hell isn't getting us anywhere."

My mind stopped thinking, temporarily short-circuiting. An unfamiliar rage boiled just below my skin, and I felt the blood rushing in my veins, my testosterone feeding my adrenalin like I was going into an undercover op and we were about to blow the lid off of that shit.

Reasonably, I know Alex is married. I know he loves his wife, and he's always the first to admit how damn lucky he is, but…the thought of another man watching Holly, of someone else seeing her as she climbs into her bed at night, it's fucking with my head.

But why? It's not like I've seen her before bed. Up until a few minutes ago, I was sure she was a suspect in my case. Now I'm wondering if she leaves her panties on or not before she slides between her sheets.

"Reid, you there?" Alex's words coming through my speaker phone broke through the runaway train my thoughts had become.

"Yeah, I'm here. Alex, send me that file."

"Holly's file? I'm not really…"

"Send me the damn file, Alex." I interrupted him mid-sentence, the demand in my own voice surprising me.

"I'm going to ask you a question, Reid. This is completely off the record, as your best friend. Do you need to step aside from this case? I know tensions are high with your father involved. Usually, you wouldn't even be on this case for that very reason, but this was a special set of circumstances that we all agreed to."

"Fuck no, I'm not stepping aside from this case. I have never stepped down from a case, and I don't plan to start now." That anger that I felt earlier continued to boil just below surface level as I argued with my best friend about something I didn't even fully understand myself.

"And this file. Holly. Because we have deemed her non-suspect there is no reason for you to have her file. But you want it? Is that what I'm hearing?" He edged, as he began to put pieces of a puzzle together that he has no business assembling.

"Alex, watch it. Don't insinuate something that isn't there. I want to review the file to see if something was missed."

"And yet, you want to insinuate that I can't do my damn job properly? Just go ahead and admit you're attracted to her, Reid. Blonde hair, blue eyes. You have a type, and it's staring me in the face as we speak. You know she wears the boy shorts to bed, right? The tight ones that hug their ass and their cheeks peek out of the bottom, teasing you to touch." He's baiting me and dammit if it isn't working.

"Fuck you, asshole. Email the file over. Good night,

Alex. Tell the wife and the babies I love them." I hung up the phone and leaned back into my office chair, closing my eyes in an attempt to ease the throbbing from my temples.

I tried to imagine the calming waves of the ocean, some bullshit method of tranquility and calming one of the bureau's many therapists suggested to me once. Instead, all I ended up imagining was Holly climbing into bed, ass swaying in the air taunting me in a pair of hot pink boy shorts, the same color as the camisole she wore the other day at the café, and nothing else.

-o-

It's nearing midnight and the building that houses the Chapman Group is silent. I sent Amanda home hours ago. She wasn't discreet in the least when she offered to stay and *work late*. But after talking to Alex, I just wanted her to leave – that in and of itself is concerning on more than one level.

I enjoy sex, I always have, ever since Julie Campbell touched my dick when we were fourteen. I remember it like it was yesterday, we were in the boy's locker room of the gym at our high school after Winter Formal. I pulled my cock from my khaki slacks as she stared on in a mixture of curiosity and amazement. It was like her hand held magical properties as she licked her pretty pink lips and reached out to touch me. She stroked the head of my cock with her delicate, manicured fingers, and I came all over her sequined blue dress within seconds. The next day I made sure to thank Alex for not taking her to that dance; sometimes you win and sometimes you lose.

Unless you're me, and fuck if I'm not always a winner.

I probably should have been embarrassed by my lack of performance and quick...response, but I wasn't – I got mine, and God, it felt good. My life was changed forever with that one touch. Not to mention, I made up for it a year later when I took her virginity with a practiced skill well beyond my young age.

I'm not picky, although Alex is right, I tend to lean towards a certain type. What is the saying, blondes have more fun? Well, I may not be blonde, but I've done enough *research* to determine that blondes are my favorite kind of bombshells in the bedroom...or the shower...or the penthouse suite of the nearest hotel. Something about that light, golden hair fanned over my olive skin, wrapped around my calloused hands, it's my kryptonite.

My fingers itched as I waited for my email to alert with the file Alex was sending over.

How is it possible that Holly Adkins is the direct bloodline of an elite mafia family and has no idea? That somehow the company she owns is working on projects for both the Midtown Bank Café and the Anderson House, which are both insured by my father. That Anderson House is none other than a historic plantation home owned by Sylvester Wilks, one of the most elusive and filthiest ring leaders in the trafficking of young women and children in the world. Something is tying them all together, but I can't find my missing link.

Alex and I make a good team. Alex is data oriented, he's very black and white. He's one of the most brilliant minds in the country when it comes to coding, hacking, and the dark web. His one weakness is his inability to see the grey area. Alex is so precise that he alienates the feeling from our engagements, where I act on my gut. I rely on my senses and years of experience to make split second decisions that often mean the difference between life and death. Not just my life, but the lives of other agents and the innocents that we fight daily to protect from the evil of this world. Apart we are both good agents, great agents even, but put us together and we are unstoppable. It's one of the reasons the bureau doesn't even consider separating us, even though our history extends back our entire lifetimes. We're worth more to them together than we are apart.

Alex is quick to dismiss Holly because his data says she isn't a threat to us, so why waste our time?

My gut is telling me that there is a reason for all of the coincidences we see with Holly, there has to be, but I can't isolate what exactly it is.

Why am I so drawn to this woman, when no woman before has ever even made me take a second look?

After hours of waiting for Alex to send over the file, my computer finally came to life with an incoming encrypted email. Knowing Alex, this email is set to self-destruct within a matter of hours, if I'm lucky. If he was feeling particularly prickly this evening, I may only have minutes before the file merely evaporates, like its existence was only a figment of my imagination. It's amazing what that man can do with a monitor and a keyboard.

Holly Guinevere Adkins. Guinevere, I chuckled to myself as I said the name out loud.

Age thirty.

Blonde hair.

Blue eyes.

Five feet, four inches. – Yeah right, in heels.

I flipped through Holly's file, memorizing every detail, knowing that my time was limited to how generous Alex was feeling when he hit that send button.

She attended an all-girls, private school up until she was accepted into an Ivy League school for design. No real surprise there. What is surprising is the fact that it appears as though her education was paid for with scholarships and grant awards, not dirty money.

Scrolling further, I noticed the coveted internship she received with a world-renowned designer in New York City, where she went on to study some sort of advanced historical architecture. She graduated with honors and moved back to Carlton during the beginning of the city's revitalization efforts and founded LGM Décor and Renovations.

Bank statements and loan documents showed the opposite of my initial assumption. Her business was funded with a legitimate business loan that she paid off after completing the renovation for the historical Magnolia Mansion for Chief Executive Officer of Walsh, Inc., Ryan Walsh. There is no indication in any of her financial records that she receives any type of funding from her father or his estate. Interesting.

Sitting in a nice and secure account just off the coast is a hefty trust fund in her name that remains untouched. According to these documents, she could have accessed the funds years ago, and yet it sits stagnant.

I noted documents that confirmed many of the things

Alex had previously mentioned, two sisters – one married with children living a similar lifestyle in which it appears they grew up, as well as a second sister that is currently living abroad. Her sister's names are Noel and Mistletoe? I'm definitely filing that away to be addressed at a later time.

Holly lives alone, in a conservative apartment in a hipster, artsy area of Carlton.

She's single, but recently was involved with a man named Chet Atwell, owner of Atwell Commercial Construction. Similar industries, but while her business has soared over the last year, it appears as though his is plummeting.

My hand paused as my eyes scanned over the restraining order filed a little less than a year ago on Holly's behalf. My knuckles whitened and my grip hardened around the computer mouse as my heart rate escalated. And just like that, Chet is on my list. It looks like he could use a visit. Ya know…just to say hello.

Records indicate that he may have roughed her up a bit, broken into her apartment, and caused enough damage to Holly that she had to contact a non-profit organization for women in abusive relationships.

Maybe she's not quite as tough as her exterior portrays. There's a name for men like Chet, men that get their kicks from feeding on powerful women. Women that are powerhouses in their own rights. These are the women that have their shit together, that stand at the top of the mountain. It's men like Chet that make it their goal to bring them down, because they feel threatened by a successful woman. Instead of seeing that woman for what she is, a rarity – the diamond among so many basic gemstones - instead of appreciating that they are holding something rare, they want to conquer it. They want to steal the diamond and dull its shine because they're insecure and that makes them feel powerful.

I commend Holly for getting out of that relationship, because the woman I met at the café by no appearances was insecure. She was fire, she stood at the top of her mountain, and dammit if that's not where she deserves to be. As long as she's not at the top of a mountain of mafia sex and drug lords, that is.

-o-

Thirty minutes. I've been in the file for thirty minutes, and I still have access. I have yet to find a single piece of incriminating evidence, just as Alex assured me I wouldn't. I should wrap it up and go home, knowing that the email is probably set to destruct any minute. But that's not what I do, because I'm an asshole that can't stop thinking about Holly Adkins and her shiny blonde hair that hangs just over shoulders, and her red bottom high heels that I know cost as much as one of my custom-tailored suits. What I wouldn't give to have those toned thighs wrapped around my waist, her pretty little feet in her expensive high heels digging into my bare back.

I sent Amanda home tonight, a sure thing, because I just can't get the damn woman out of my head. Sure, I could have closed my eyes and pretended. It wouldn't have been the first time. Hell, Amanda would have even let me call her Holly, but it wouldn't have been the same.

I can't stop this overwhelming need for the real thing. I want to touch, I want to taste, I want to hear her say my name over and over again as she begs me to let her come. And she will beg, God will she beg. It's pissing me the fuck off. Why am I so strung out for this woman? A woman that I don't even know.

I scrolled forward, past more documentation on her therapy sessions after Chet and the renovations she's been working on recently. More financial documentation, and even some shit about brunch with her girlfriends. I scrolled until I stopped on the video files that Alex mentioned earlier. I clicked them open one at a time until I found what I was looking for. There is no volume on these videos, but I don't need it. The visual is more than enough for me. I leaned back in my high-back black leather office chair and like the asshole that I know I am, I unzipped my pants.

Too bad, so sad if Alex is watching right now. Hell, he's probably watching with his wife before bed. They're both dirty perverts like that, they like to keep it fresh in the bedroom, and who am I to judge their perfectly healthy marriage.

I hit play on the video and watched Holly walk out of her bathroom in nothing but a pair of black boy shorts as I gripped my cock in my hand. She's petite, her hips are narrow, but her ass is thick enough to fill both of my hands. My eyes are immediately drawn to her perfect pink nipples as her breasts bounce in step with her movements as she walks toward her bed with a glass of water. I imagine gripping her full breasts in my hands, they aren't overly large, but they're enough that they would easily fill my mouth.

I spit in my hand to lubricate it and begin to stroke my cock. I watch Holly and imagine pulling her nipple into my mouth, sucking it to a peak as I grip her opposite breast with my free hand and pinch her nipple. Hard. Would she like the pain? She would grow to like it; I can teach her how the pain leads to more immense pleasure. How I can make it hurt so good for her. For both of us.

I watched as she bent over slightly to sit her glass of water down on her nightstand and the cheeks of her ass peaked out from the fabric of her boy shirts. I bet if I look closely enough, I can see the outline of her pussy against the thin fabric between her legs.

Pre-cum dripped from my cock as I stroked myself harder, wanting her, wanting to slip my cock into her wet pussy. Would she put up a fight or would she be submissive? She looks like a fighter. My cock thickened in my hand, the veins angry and hot as I imagined sliding my length into her tight pussy, as I imagined her bucking against me – fighting me for control.

I might ease up, just enough to let her think she's winning, and when the sweet sound of satisfaction graces her lips, I will fuck her harder to remind her who's really in charge.

My grip tightened as I pumped faster, watching her as she flipped the lights off and the video turned to night vision, her ass swaying just as I thought it would as she climbed into bed. What would she do if I cuffed her? If I took away her ability to fight, and instead, she was at my mercy as I fucked her sweet, tight pussy. God, this woman, what is she doing to me?

I'm so close.

Forgetting the video altogether, I close my eyes and let my imagination take over. I envision her naked in my bed, golden hair fanned out over my black sheets. Arms tied securely behind her head as I pull her to me again and again, listening to her scream my name.

"Take it Holly, take all of it." My rough voice shouted out into the empty office as my hand became her slick pussy and my senses were overtaken by need. Endorphins flooded my system as my orgasm overtook my body, and I roared out her name over and over again.

My cock jerked in my hand as I squeezed harder and stream after stream of my cum hit my pants, the desk, the chair, and hell the floor. I was flying without a parachute, falling, chasing an orgasm that seemed to go on forever. I tumbled through the clouds riding my high until I was spent.

Slowly, so slowly, I landed from what has to be the most intense orgasm of my life as the flicker of my computer grabbed my attention, and it was at that very moment that I watched as every file I had pulled up vanished, leaving a blank home screen.

I couldn't help it, as a small smile lifted at the corner of my lips. I was satisfied, even if only for a moment. I should be pissed at this woman's ability to control me. What's worse, she doesn't even realize she's doing it. But instead, right this minute, I feel damn good, and I don't care who knows it.

"Fuck you, Alex." I spoke into the office. Knowing that his impeccable timing wasn't by accident. He's a sick S.O.B., but I love the man.

CHAPTER SEVEN
HOLLY

I stepped out of the shower in the bathroom of my conservative, yet chic, loft-style apartment. Quickly grabbing the cheetah print wrap that hangs near the shower door, I wrapped up my soaking wet hair and then grabbed a towel to wrap around my body.

Why can't historic old buildings have decent heating?

I swear, I chose this particular loft in this exact building because of the primo location and the history attached to it, but the heating in this place leaves a bit to be desired. I lost feeling in two of my toes last winter, and it took almost three months to get it back. I thought for sure they were going to turn black and fall off, and what would I do then? None of my shoes would fit anymore, and that would be a damn travesty.

I live in the art district of Carlton. When I moved back from New York, my mother offered up their pool house as an option for possible living accommodations. I considered sleeping in the same bed my mother screwed the pool boy in for all of, um, yeah zero seconds before I rented a hotel room and went in search of the perfect apartment. I mean, I'm sure the sheets and mattress were replaced at some point, but still, the argument remains valid – that's just nasty.

My internship in New York was paid and included a small studio apartment. Capital P.A.I.D, a rarity in my field of study. Most design internships are experience only - resume builders. Having that extra source of income allowed me to put any additional money I made back into my savings account.

I worked my ass off to score an internship with none other than Ritchi Cavali, world renowned architect and designer. His studio headquarters was located in New York City, a place where, up until that point, I had only dreamt of living.

I knew if I played my cards right, I could complete my internship and apply for the program of studies I was drooling over at the New York Institute of Design. I know at that time, my particular field of study was far more popular and easily accessible overseas, mostly Europe. The New York Institute of Design was the only college in the United States that was offering the course studies I needed to complete my degree.

I had to apply for the program over twenty times before a slot opened and the stars miraculously aligned, allowing me to complete my degree simultaneously with my internship. Don't get me wrong, it was hell. I survived solely on five-hour energy shots and cheap coffee, but I survived. Now, I'm one of the only females in this part of the country that's qualified to complete the type of work I specialize in.

I look cute, I'm tiny and petite. My mother loved showing me off as her little Barbie doll when I was a little girl, but I'm no princess. The Adkins, my parents, they have money. They're pretentious and haughty. Their noses are so far stuck up in the damn air it's miraculous they can even see to walk. I thank the good Lord above that I was the last born; the forgotten, mostly.

I was able to slip by with the occasional comment here or there and a couple of forced etiquette courses, but my life wasn't controlled. Not the way they controlled Tilly and tried – and failed – to control Noel. Maybe that's why they just gave the hell up when they finally got to me.

All of my accomplishments are my own, and I dare someone to say otherwise. I'm a fighter, and I'm sneaky because I'm so damn adorable. You don't even know I've got you until it's too late, and I've already kicked your ass – hypothetically speaking, of course. I'm not really one for violence…unless it's in the bedroom.

Now that, well, that's another story entirely.

I dropped my towel at the foot of my queen-sized bed and picked up a pair of hot pink silk boy shorts. It may be freezing ass cold in here, but I just can't sleep with clothes touching my body.

Picking the towel back up, I walked back to the bathroom to brush out my hair and blow it out before bed, because kinky hair isn't as sexy as it sounds like it should be. I will flatten it out in the morning to bring the shine out.

I filled up my glass with water and walked it back out

to the nightstand, now sufficiently warmed from the heat of my hair dryer. I glanced down to make sure my cell phone was already plugged up and walked over to the light switch to flip it off for the night.

I'm a night owl, sometimes I work well into the early morning hours. It's nearly two a.m., and I'm just now sliding into my sheets and cocooning myself under the fifteen blankets I keep on top of my duvet to keep me warm through the night.

Snuggling in as far under the sheets as I could possibly go, I was just closing my eyes when my phone rang and a string of curse words left my mouth, sure it was Noel calling again without checking the time difference. Noel is notorious for calling whenever she damn well pleases, who cares if it's the middle of the night and my brain was finally going to let me rest. In Noel's mind, this is her world, and we're just living in it. She came here like that, but it still doesn't make me want to whisper sweet nothings to her over the phone when I answer.

I didn't even bother to duck my head out from under the covers as I reached my hand blindly over to the nightstand and felt around for my cell phone praying, I didn't accidentally knock my glass of water over in the process.

Success!

Locating my phone, I slid my finger over the screen to answer as I pulled it into my warm igloo.

"Two in the morning. Noel, it is fucking two in the morning. Where are you? Australia? The other side of planet Earth? A time zone so far away that you obviously think it's mid-day and not the middle of the night? This better be good. If you're calling to tell me about your newfound love for threesomes or how much Pablo's abilities in the bedroom have inspired your new novel, well...proceed. I mean, I could totally use a bedtime story now that I think about it. What is it, Noel? And make it good, woman. Good, not weird, turn on your audible voice and let me forget we're related. Remember that." I finished my rant, the warm air from my breath only warming my little cocoon even more as I spoke.

"I'm not sure how audible worthy my voice is, but fuck woman, I'll talk dirty to you while you touch yourself. Are you sleeping naked? Let me guess...boy shorts? I don't know why but you just seem like the type that sleeps in boy shorts." I froze as a deep gravelly voice slid through my phone, not at all the voice I was anticipating.

Slowly, without saying a word, I turned my phone around so that I could see the screen. Squinting my eyes to focus as the space in my tiny bubble lit up, I read off a series of numbers that were unfamiliar to me.

I gave myself two deep breaths to consider my current options and then pulled the phone to my ear again.

"Wrong number?" My voice cracked with embarrassment as I squeaked out the words, not at all the witty response I played out in my mind just two seconds before during my two breath deep breathing exercise that apparently failed.

"On the contrary, you're the exact person I was calling to speak with, but I was expecting a sleepy hello. Maybe a fuck off. But threesomes and sexy bedtime stories? I can't believe I'm saying this, but you took me by surprise,

Holly."

Holly. Oh God, he knows my name?

Client. Client. Client.

Who is this?

Voice like sex.

Middle of the night phone call?

"Reid fuck-off Chapman." My heart did that weird racing thing it's been doing lately and all of a sudden there is a fire blazing under these blankets. Hot flashes. Really? I'm not that old. I need to get the doctor to check me out stat. I kicked out from under my tent and sucked the cold air into my lungs trying to calm my heart and reduce my body temperature from the inside out.

"There she is. Say fuck a couple more times babe while I touch myself. At least one of us can get off tonight." Who says things like that to a stranger? Who?!

"Reid. I'm going to use my calm voice because apparently you get your kicks from my pissed voice. Why are you calling me in the middle of the night? Where did you even get this number?" I don't remember giving him my cell phone number. I explicitly remember leaving my office line on all of the paperwork with his company, not even my direct line, nope – I gave him the line to my assistant – a lot of good that did me.

"Oh baby, you could suck the helium from a balloon down your sexy throat, and I'd probably get off on that too. I had a question about your claim."

"At two in the morning?"

"Some of us have work to do, princess." Is he serious right now? Princess?

"Do not call me that, Reid. I literally just laid down.

What is it that you need specifically?" Exasperating, he is totally and completely exasperating.

"Why are you fronting the money on this project? Why the rush?" His direct questions momentarily surprised me. Somehow that's not at all what I was expecting him to ask.

"Why is that any of your business?" Something about the way he asked bothered me. I'm not hiding anything, but why is Reid calling me in the middle of the night to ask me about something that doesn't even pertain to him.

"It's not. Actually, I was just calling to let you know that our payment on the claim will be processed this week. The deadline is now in your lap." He brushed off his earlier questions and accepted my indirect question as an answer, as if it wasn't important enough that he would call and interrupt my sleep. Even if I wasn't truly asleep yet.

"That was quick, and a little too easy. What's the catch? I've worked with enough of your type to know there has to be a catch for it to be this easy. It is never this easy." I asked, curious.

"My type? Now we're stereotyping. Really, Holly? I thought you were above that."

"You overestimate your overwhelmingly annoying ability to bring me down to your level."

"Have dinner with me." Wait, what? This man is giving me whiplash.

"Are you bribing me, Chapman?"

"Bribery per its legal definition is to offer, give, or solicit an item of value as a means of influencing the actions of an individual holding a public or legal duty.

Technically, I am offering myself to you, but I am not doing so in order to influence a specific action or result. Unless that result ends with your wrists tied to the bedposts of my kind-size bed, in which, case maybe you have a point."

He's arrogant. God, is this man ever arrogant. I'm exhausted, and I'm annoyed that he thinks he can speak to me like I should just fall at his feet because he's handsome and his voice sounds like the damn men Noel hires for her dirty books on audible. Yes, I listen to my sister's books. I spend a good bit of time in the car driving to and from client locations. Go ahead, judge me.

"I'm hanging up and going to bed. Mail the check and go do whatever it is insurance adjusters do at night. Drink warm tea and snuggle your cat or something. Or, I don't know, maybe try sleeping like a normal person." I rolled my eyes knowing he couldn't see me, but the audacity of this man, I swear.

"Holly. Dinner." His voice went from playful to demanding. Not demanding angry, more demanding dominant. Trust me, I've spent enough time with my therapist to know that there is a very clear difference between abuse and dominance. That is a line I will never again allow myself to cross.

And maybe that's why I hesitated, if only for a moment. I'm a dominant. I'm a smidge of a control freak. I don't want a man that backs down when I push. I need a man that's going to push back, and this is where the line lies. I need a man that will push me to my limits, without pushing over. I need an equal, someone that feeds off of my success, and in return I feed off of his. So maybe that's why I considered, if only for a second, Reid's demands. Until I remembered that he's conceited and tactless and has no respect for business hours or personal boundaries.

"Goodnight, Chapman." I hit end on the call without allowing him to respond, powering down my phone for the night and laying on top of the multiple layers of blankets on my bed to cool down from the inferno that was currently burning me from the inside out.

I should be pissed at the intrusion of my privacy. I mean, what did he say about the boy shorts? It's creepy that he guessed what I sleep in, like dead on guessed it. I should be annoyed at his inability to take a hint and his massive ego. Given my track record with men, my brain is telling me that I should stay far, far away from this one.

So why is my heart still racing and every nerve ending in my body tingling?

Why am I sweating when I know it can't be over sixty degrees in this room?

And most importantly, why the hell are said boy shorts now soaked through, and I have an overwhelming need to relieve the tension myself that Reid somehow managed to build inside of me with his crass words and arrogant demands?

CHAPTER EIGHT
REID

"You did good work on the claim down at the Café, son." My father complimented me out-right for probably the first time in my entire life as I pulled the chair out for my mother to sit at the dining table in my childhood home.

I've been home for a few weeks and have been avoiding my mother. A mother has a way of seeing things when no one else can, and I was afraid to take the risk that she might see straight through me, that I could compromise this mission just by merely existing in her presence. So, I've stayed away, until she called me personally and invited me to dinner. I didn't have the heart to turn her down, especially when I'm here, in the same town as she is, for the first time in years.

"Should have the check to them next week. I'm still learning the ropes, but I'm learning quickly." Brief and to the point.

I got exactly what I needed from processing the claim on the Café. Access. My father was more than willing to show me what he meant by easing the paperwork and expediting the claims process.

A few clicks of a mouse that I never even saw from the back end and Alex was able to pull every single account my father held. He pulled financial information, personal files, and email correspondence. Enough information to put my father away for a long, long time as well as tie him to Victor Adkins and Sylvester Wilks.

However, my father isn't our main target. Sure, the work he does is fraudulent and highly illegal, but we've been after Adkins and Wilks for years. For now, we're filing away information and using the information we do have to further our investigation. We get to Wilks and Adkins we stop a seemingly never-ending cycle of death and destruction and in the process save countless lives.

"That's my boy. I told your mother that you would give up that nonsense vigilante shit eventually. Once you got a taste of the real world and realized that true heroes don't exist. Your mother fed into that garbage for far too long when you were a boy. It's about time you realize the truth. Money is the fuel that makes the world go round, it's what breeds success. You were born to run this dynasty, not chase after false dreams that lead to a pitiful government pension, or better yet, an early grave." Spittle flew from my father's mouth as he spewed his poison. I could feel my blood pulsing in my veins as I kept my face stoic, not giving anything away, a skill I've spent years honing in my line of work.

I slid into the high-back, custom cloth dining chair

seated directly across from my mother, and I watched her. I really observed her for the first time since coming home. Her dark hair was swept up in an up-do off her face, the gray strands of her honey brown hair slowly outnumbering the brown. My mother has always been a beautiful woman, and the changes in her appearance over the years have been subtle, almost unnoticeable. Her long eyelashes fluttered against her cheekbones as she looked down at her plate while my father spoke.

She wore a pale pink dress with a floral pattern that wrapped around her trim waist. She looks slightly more frail than the last time I saw her, more delicate. I have to wonder if that is attributable to her age or if it has more to do with the man that sits at the head of the table and demands her attention just by being present. My parents were raised in a different time, they hold beliefs of a different era. My mother has always been adamant that divorce is never an option, under any circumstances.

Growing up, my mother was the primary parent in our household. My father spent many nights at the office, working late. He attended conferences and meetings that required him to travel, all things that I had come to consider were just a part of his trade. It was normal life for me, but looking back, knowing what I know now, I have to wonder how in the dark my mother truly is.

Eloise Chapman is an intelligent woman. I always considered my mother to be one of the strongest women I knew. Looking at her now, I can't help but think that after all these years her appearance remains so similar and yet her fire is gone. She's resigned herself to this life. I just hope that after the fallout she's able to regain some of what was lost. She doesn't deserve this life, the woman who raised me deserves so much more.

Her sharp words cut through the thick air that seemed to surround the dining room. "George, enough. We've always entrusted Reid to make his own decisions about his future. You got what you wanted after all; he's here isn't he?" My mother's blue eyes, an identical match to my own, lifted and locked onto mine. She stared at me with an intensity that I didn't realize she still had in her.

She's studying me as much as I'm studying her. Her strong words are meant for my father, but she looks at me with questions and knowledge of things that my father is oblivious to. That one look and I know, I don't have to be afraid for her. She might have subdued the fire but it's still there, simmering just beneath the surface. Eloise Chapman is a fighter, and she's looking at me like she sees our war and hopes we're both fighting on the same team.

-o-

After a tense dinner with my parents, I excused myself and went back to my apartment early. I tossed back two fingers of Jameson as soon as I walked in the door and crashed onto my king-size bed hours before I normally even consider falling asleep. Sleep doesn't come easy when you've seen the things I've seen. Sometimes you just have to knock yourself the fuck out to get some decent rest, and after enduring the torture that was dinner with my parents, I couldn't afford to let my mind wander into itself tonight. I needed to not think.

I woke with the sun, having forgotten to close the

blackout shades when I got home last night, my eyes burning and my head screaming at me for all the hell I put it through the night before. I ran my hand over the thick stubble that lined my jaw and reached for my glasses on the nightstand so that I could see well enough to check the actual time.

At just after six, I have plenty of time to go for a quick run, shower, and grab some coffee before heading into the office. I need to finalize the details on the Anderson House project from Chapman's side so that we're prepared to give the impression at least that we are processing and handling a legitimate claim.

I extricated my body from the bed and walked to the closet in search of clothing. After I wake up and my mind officially turns on for the day there is no turning that shit off.

Holly, sweet Holly. She's not the only one that doesn't like to sleep with clothes on. Except where Holly wears those cute little boy shorts, I wear nothing at all.

Opening one of my drawers, I pulled out a pair of black briefs and slipped them on over my semi-hard length. Damn thoughts of blonde hair and blue eyes.

I grabbed running shorts and a white t-shirt and threw those on too, using my frustration with the train of my thoughts to fuel my need for a run. I slipped on my running shoes and grabbed up my earbuds and cell phone before heading out the door. Everything else can wait until I get back and have hopefully run off some of my pent-up aggression. Aggression from dinner last night, aggression from the walls we keep running into on this case, and Holly.

Waving to the doorman, Ralph, on my way out, I relished in the crisp fresh air as I took off through downtown Carlton in the early morning. The sun is up, and people are just starting to stir. Shops are preparing to open, and the dew is starting to evaporate from the benches that line the sidewalks. Normal people, living their everyday lives, completely oblivious to the constant evil that surrounds them as they prepare to begin a new day.

I had no predetermined path when I set out on my run this morning, I haven't lived in this part of town long enough to have an established running trail yet. I turned down one street and then the next until two blocks over I looked out across the street and felt my breathing become labored. I'm not in my twenties anymore, but I train with men that are. I'm in the best physical condition of my life because I don't have the option not to be. When the time comes and I find myself in a difficult situation, I have to be able to count on my body to do what I've trained it to do.

But right this minute, as my eyes catch on that same blonde hair, I was daydreaming about this morning in a pair of skintight black leggings my lungs stop working, my heart races, and I start to question every hour I've spent training for the last fifteen years.

Somehow, I've made my way back to the café, and I can't say that I'm disappointed, as I watch Beth unlock the door to let Holly in. She's dressed more casual today than I've ever seen her, and yet she still somehow manages an air of elegance. She's wearing leggings that leave no curve to the imagination, a lime green tank top that exposes the creamy white skin of her shoulders and matching green sneakers that I'm sure if I got close enough, would not have a single scuff on them.

On a whim, I called her in the middle of the night a couple of nights ago. I don't know what came over me. I was working from my laptop in bed, and I had my father's case file opened up. I was scrolling through the information we had on the café and trying to map connections to Adkins, and it was like my fingers had a mind of their own. I memorized her cell phone number the night Alex gave me access to her file; it was one of the first things I did, not knowing how long I would have access to her information.

I honestly didn't expect her to answer the phone, and I most definitely did not expect for her sultry voice to come across the line and speak of threesomes and fucking. It was obvious she thought I was her sister Noel, but it was entertaining all the same.

The more she spoke the more I wanted to keep her on the line. For the first time in my life, I wasn't searching for a reason to get away from a woman. No, instead I was racking my brain looking for a reason to keep her talking.

Am I so invested in this case that my mind is subconsciously using Holly to get more information? Or, do I genuinely want to know this woman? I'm conflicted. My gut is still telling me that there is something that I can't see, something that I'm all over, and yet I can't seem to find it. I've been conditioned and trained to believe that there are never any coincidences and yet, Holly is swimming in a sea of them.

Is that why I asked her to dinner? Is that why I

demanded that she have a meal with me?

Am I trying to prove something to myself?

To Alex, who believes that she is in no way associated with our case?

I allowed my thoughts to distract me as I finished my run and arrived back at my apartment.

Grabbing a quick shower, I pulled on a pair of jeans and a polo shirt, a little more laid back than my usual business attire for Chapman, but I don't have any meetings scheduled for the day, and I walked back out of my apartment just thirty minutes later.

Deciding to walk instead of drive, I took the same path my run took me on earlier, but at a more leisurely pace. I retraced my steps until I arrived at my intended destination, finding the door already propped open, almost like they were waiting for my arrival.

"Looks much better in here ladies without the river flowing through, although I will say the water feature did add a certain level of ambiance to the place." I walked right into the café without waiting for an invitation, as if I've ever needed one, and leaned up against the empty display case.

My eyes studied Holly as she sat with her legs crossed on top of one of the only round top tables still sitting in the dining area of the partially renovated café with a tablet in her hands and a pencil stuck behind her left ear.

With her hair pulled up today, her eyes look a little bit bigger, the blue a little brighter. I observed her pupils as they dilated just slightly as she ate me up with her eyes. She can't help it; she tries to ignore me. She puts on a front, but her eyes, they tell her truths.

I watched as she ran her manicured hand through part of her hair that escaped from the confines of her hair tie, adorably frustrated with my interruption. "I will repeat, since it is evident that you are hard of hearing, why are you here Reid?" Oh, did she speak earlier? I must have missed it, too busy studying her.

So much anger, so much fire. If only she would give me the opportunity to help her harness her anger for good instead of evil.

"Well, aren't you warm and cuddly this morning, Ms. Adkins." I pushed off the display case, sauntering slowly toward Holly's perch in the center of the room, needing to get closer to her, to feel her presence. Maybe, if I can get closer, I can get a better handle on my emotions and the strange thoughts that surround my curiosity with this woman.

She let out an audible sigh as I approached her spot on the tabletop and the mint of her breath bathed my skin. "What is it, Reid? What do you need from us?" She sat her tablet down gently in her lap and placed her hands behind her. I didn't stop, I continued my approach until I was so close that she had to crane her neck back to meet my eyes with hers.

I nearly groaned out loud as the action caused her full breasts to push upward and overfill the tank she wore. I let my eyes follow the slim line of her neck, pausing over her breasts for an indecent amount of time. But really, it's quickly becoming apparent that no amount of time will be enough to get my fill of looking at this woman. Eventually, I drug my gaze back to meet hers. I don't even have it in me to look guilty.

"Just checking in. I was walking by on my way to grab a quick cup of coffee from…Carl's, when I noticed the lights on. I thought my two new favorite ladies might be in, so I wanted to say hello. But…now that I see you're busy, I'll leave." I shrugged one shoulder and stepped back away from the table, putting some distance between the heat that sparked off of the two of us like an electric current.

"Good to see you too, Beth. Payment on your insurance settlement should be in next week." I smiled kindly at Beth, acknowledging her for the first time since walking into the café, before heading toward the door.

I paused just as I passed through the entrance to the café and spoke without turning, ignoring the overwhelming urge I felt to turn and watch Holly's response to what I was about to say. "Oh, and Holly, that thing I called you about the other night. I get what I want. Always."

And with that I turned and walked back down the street to grab my morning coffee from Carl's before heading into the office.

CHAPTER NINE
HOLLY

Do not turn and look.

Do not turn and look.

I repeated the words in my head over and over again like they were the chant to a sacred ritual, and I was trying to summon rain in the desert as I felt Reid walk out of the café and down the street.

My eyes bore a hole in the tablet that still sat in my lap, a useless weapon against the force that is this utterly infuriating man and inhaled a deep breath in the hopes that it would slow my racing heart. I haven't been able to stop thinking about Reid Chapman since that night he called me and asked me to dinner.

The night that I answered my cell phone and unknowingly asked him to tell me about threesomes and fucking. That's a mortifying conversation that will forever be burned into my brain. I could feel the blush creep up my neck as the memory of his rough voice sliding through the phone and into my bed began to awaken the unyielding need I seem to have for this man.

"Don't." I held up my hand before Beth could even ask the questions that I know sit on the very tip of her tongue, hoping that if I said it firmly enough, she would save me from the embarrassment. It's bad enough that the girls already think I'm crushing on Reid. I can't have a full-on conversation about it. I'm not ready to dissect whatever these weird feelings are. I'm not prepared to speak them into existence and give them life. I would rather just avoid them like the bubonic plague I know they are.

Nothing good can come from a man that looks like that in a pair of jeans and makes my hands sweat and my heart race every time we're in the same room. He's given me the damn sex flu, is there a vaccine for that? Maybe I should have gone to medical school instead of design school. I'm sure all of womankind would benefit from a vaccine that made you immune to men like Reid Chapman, men that think they are God's gift to women. What's worse? The arrogance makes them even sexier. It's a nasty, unending cycle.

Three deep breaths, a short prayer to the good Lord above, and one quick visit down memory lane, as a reminder of Chet the asshole, and my heart rate slowed back to its normal rhythm.

I have a job to do, and any distraction has the possibility of derailing my timeline. Normally, I'm a bit more flexible, but the signed contract for Anderson

House that still sits on my desk at home is ironclad. If I don't complete this project within the next two weeks, I can kiss putting my stamp on one of the most unique pieces of history in the Carlton area goodbye.

Tapping the screen on my tablet, I brought my design program back to life and pushed out the external factors that threatened to block my ability to really feel the space, mainly Reid and his stupid, sexy glasses.

I felt the warmth from the solid oak wood flooring beneath me. I had to beg and plead, and maybe I offered my first-born child, but I finally found a contractor willing to agree to help me restore and refinish the water damaged floors of the café. These floors hold so much character, they tell much of the story of the bank that once was. It was important to Beth as well as the owners of the café that we attempt to save them. More than that, it was important to me that we protect this vital piece of historical significance.

The sun filtered through the windows and lit the room, allowing me to see a vision of what would be, of the whites and light grays we could use to brighten the space. How the light contrasted with the natural woods and the dark steel of the vault door that once functioned as the heart of this bank played off of each other in a perfect symphony of clean lines and modern details while maintaining the historical properties that make this café so special.

At one time, this bank was the only bank in the city; it was a central meeting point for the business men and women of Carlton. A constant stream of activity flowed through these doors just as it does today. This café represents everything I love about history, breathing life into something that once was the lifeblood of each and every business in this city, the culmination of a structure that built the very foundations of the economy this thriving city is built on.

History lives on in our ability to maintain it, nourish it, and allow it to grow and change with a new generation.

Beth and I spent hours finishing up the design process, taking measurements, and certifying the finalized images before locking down the café for the night. I will go home and draft the designs on paper with ink before I send them off to my team to set all the wheels in motion. We've done the legwork, now we just need to see it through to the finish line.

Rush or no rush, I don't do anything halfway. I put everything I have into each and every property that I touch. I've built this business from the ground up, and building my own reputation, a reputation not associated with the Adkins family name, means everything to me.

-o-

"I don't have words, Holly. It's magnificent." Beth held back tears and crinkled her nose as her eyes darted around the dining space of the café unable to focus on just one of the many changes we made during the remodel and renovation. In just a few short minutes the ribbon will be cut, and the celebration will begin for the official soft re-opening of the café. Ironic that the mayor is here on behalf of the city for the ribbon cutting. It's a good thing Beth is all up in her feelings, or she might get extra ragey with those giant scissors after the hell they put her through to get to this point. I don't know, now that I think about it, it's probably better that they don't give her over-sized sharp objects.

"I don't need your words; I just need a check and your stamp of approval. We did a damn good job didn't we?" Pride swelled inside of me as I stood in a pair of trim, black editor pants and a white silk blouse, tucked in. These pants tie at the waist with a bow, giving what would normally be a masculine pant a more feminine touch. I came straight from the office, but I stripped my jacket off in the car, not needing to be quite as formal, especially since I don't plan to stay for all of the festivities planned for tonight.

"We? No, this is all you, girl. You killed it. I mean sure, I unlocked the door for you to come in and do your thing, but this was all you." I looked to Asher as she spoke and he stood behind her gripping her hip possessively, the man hasn't been able to take his eyes, or his hands for that matter, off of her since we got here. That inkling I had at brunch about the two of them, yeah, I was so obviously right.

"Just let her tell you how wonderful you are. I've been trying to sprinkle my praises over her all night, but she isn't having any of it." He squeezed her hip and the sly smile in his brown eyes tells me that he's going to shower Beth with *all* of his praises later tonight.

Watching the two of them together set off flurries in the base of my stomach. My entire life I watched my parents train wreck of a marriage. Their marriage was purely a facade, for what I don't even know. Other than the fact that my mother would die before losing the Adkins name and ruining her luxurious lifestyle. God forbid she couldn't host a damn dinner party for her friends. Then again, without that name she wouldn't have any friends.

I watched my oldest sister follow in the family footsteps and marry into the land of the elite, followed by Noel who, well, we all know what she does. I hate to say it, but I've just never allowed myself to give in to the hype.

True love? The stuff in the fairytales? I never believed in that stuff. Or at least I didn't until I watched my girlfriends, one by one get picked off. I watched them find true love. What is it Olivia says? *The always and forever kind of love.* And it's staring me right in the face as I watch on like a voyeur at the way Asher watches Beth, at his soft touches and protective stance.

It's kind of like the rare pair of one-off Louboutins I saw on the runway once during fashion week when I was living in New York. I know they exist; I've seen them with my own eyes. But those shoes, they aren't meant for me, never will be. So, I can stare on longingly and dream about them, I might even find a similar pair, but they won't ever live up to my hopes and dreams because they can't. You can't be something you aren't, no matter how soft your black leather is and how similar your red bottoms look. And, that pair? The one-of-a-kind pair, I can never have them.

Maybe that's why I finally agreed to let Tilly set me up on a date with one of Kris's friends. Or maybe it's because I'm willing to do literally anything at this point to get my mind off of freaking Reid Chapman.

It was a low point for me, really. I was lying in bed earlier in the week and every single time I shut my eyes, he was there. And he couldn't just be there, sitting at a desk in a suit or something equally boring like a normal insurance adjuster might be doing. Oh no, each and every time I closed my eyes, I saw him in those jeans that fit his lean thighs like the denim was made to mold to his legs. I saw the broad expanse of his shoulders stretch the confines of his polo shirt, and I wondered what his chest might look like underneath. Does he shave his chest or is there hair there? I'm not opposed to either, but dammit if I don't want to know.

How much time do you have to spend in a gym to get muscles like that? Does he have back dimples? The ones just at the base of his spine, right above his delectable ass that beg to be licked.

It was at this moment, as my thoughts continued their downward spiral, that I reached for my cell phone and dialed up Tilly.

The excitement in her voice was palpable, and she swore that she would make sure that tonight would be a lovely evening, in her words, and that my potential date would not live in his parents' basement or penthouse or pool home. I also made her promise that I would not end up at dinner at our parents' country club, just as precaution because Kris's friends are totally the type that would take me to dinner at the country club and that is a sure-fire way to make sure this night is miserable.

I felt my cell phone alert in my pocket and knew that was my cue to leave. I'm meeting my date at a restaurant downtown, Fifth Park Place. It's one of Ryan's so, in a way, it feels like we're meeting on my turf.

"I hate that I can't stay for the celebration, but I am so, so proud of you Beth, and I appreciate being given the opportunity to work on this project with you." I squeezed Beth's hand as the café began filling up with our friends and the friends and patrons of the owners of the café, milling about just before the big event was set to begin.

"You know there was never another option, you were the first person I called when I hit the panic button. And you? I'm glad to see that you're finally putting yourself back out there, even if it isn't with the sexy insurance adjuster. One step at the time, I guess." She winked at me but quickly got distracted as something caught her eye over my shoulder.

"Bye, Asher. Keep an eye on this one tonight, don't let her get too close to those giant scissors the city brought over. I work with design, but if she needs a lawyer, she's going to have to get Ryan for that shit." I smiled, genuinely content, and turned to slip out unnoticed, the remainder of our normal crew is filing in, and I don't need a scene as I leave, and believe me, they are all about making a scene.

My black strappy stilettos crossed over the threshold from hardwood floor to the concrete of the sidewalk and I filled my lungs with a deep relaxing breath, but instead of the fresh air, I expected my lungs filled with the scent of leather and something a little woodsy.

My chest tightened instantly, and awareness tingled at the base of my spine. My eyes immediately shot upward, and to the left in search of the cause of my body's reaction, but I didn't see him. I didn't see anyone. I'm losing it, this is exactly why I need this date tonight. I have to clear my mind of everything that is Reid Chapman before I walk into the Anderson House project in just a few short days.

CHAPTER TEN
REID

Should have looked right, princess.

I stood next to Alex in the shadows of the alleyway that adjoined the Midtown Bank Café as we put off making our separate entrances into the event until the last possible minute.

Color me surprised when I heard the *click, click, click* of high heels and then caught sight of my favorite petite blonde puzzle that I just can't seem to figure out - my walking, talking coincidence in stilettos.

Mine.

She looked around like maybe she was searching for someone before crossing the intersection over to her sleek, black sports car with tinted windows and custom fitted black rims. Fitting…for a mafia princess.

"She's hot as fuck, right? She's like a tiny stick of dynamite just waiting to explode. She's fun sized…" Whatever Alex was planning to say next was cut off with one swift elbow from his wife knocking the breath from his lungs and quite possibly cracking a rib.

He's messing with me. It's a good thing I know his game because if I didn't, he wouldn't still be standing. He's not wrong about anything he said, but the fact that the words left his mouth and not mine pisses me the fuck off. And the fact that, that pisses me off only makes me that much angrier at the entire situation.

"She's not staying." The realization that she was leaving before the event even began hit me as she pulled out of her parking spot and down the adjacent street.

"Appears that way, but what does it matter?" He shrugged nonchalantly. "I sent the files up the chain of command; they also agreed that we have nothing tying her to this case. I'm here tonight for personal reasons, and to make sure you don't do anything stupid – lucky for me, it looks like your stupid decisions just left in a sweet little sports car, so I'm off the hook. In case you needed a reminder, you're here to verify that Bill and Shelia have nothing to do with our current case now that they're back on U.S. soil. As far as everyone in that building knows, we are in no way connected. Are you ready?"

"Jesus, guys, I've been ready. They put the tiny cakes out ten minutes ago and the demon that lives in my stomach is about fifteen seconds away from clawing its way out and destroying everything in its path." Emily pushed off of the wall we were leaned against with a grunt that sounded more male than female, she is just one of the boys after all.

"That was a lovely visual, Straton. Why don't the two

of you go on in, and I will follow in a few minutes." I pulled the heel of my leather loafer up behind me as I crossed my arms over my chest and continued to hold the wall up with my body in the dark recesses of the alley wishing more than anything that I was in my combat boots and not these damn frat boy shoes.

I received an invitation tonight to appear on behalf of the Chapman Group. Obviously, my father was above making an appearance, and since I worked this claim, that responsibility landed on me. I couldn't have planned it better because I haven't seen Bill and Shelia in over a decade. I need to speak with them, if only for a minute, to confirm my suspicions that they aren't involved in any of the illegal shit my father has his hands in.

I stood against the wall counting down the minutes, unable to keep my thoughts from wondering what Holly needed to do that was so important she would miss this event. She's been working on this project for weeks, and tonight will be the first night the finished product is revealed to the city and its patrons, and yet she left before it even began.

It's not any of your business.

One of the things that makes me such a good agent is my ability to control my emotions in any given situation. I'm a chameleon of sorts, I adapt to any situation I'm thrown into with ease and precision. I'm constantly in the zone, but Holly is doing something to me. She's messing with my ability to maintain that control, and I can't figure out how she's doing it. So, sure, maybe Alex cleared her as a suspect from this case, but I can't clear her from my fucking mind as easily.

-o-

"Would you look at that, Reid Chapman, so nice to see you could make it tonight." I recognized Beth's voice speaking from behind me before I even turned, the distinct slow southern drawl of her words giving her away.

I spoke with Bill and Shelia when I arrived, and they were exactly how I remember them from decades ago. They've always been like family to me. Hell, more so given the current circumstances. It was apparent within just a few moments of our conversation that they were merely nearing retirement age, and ready to travel instead of run a full-time business. There was no evident malicious intent, nor was there any indication of illegal activity involvement with my father or his colleagues.

I watched on earlier as the ribbon for the café was cut and from my corner in the back of the crowded establishment, it appeared as though they named Beth their new partner and future owner of the café. Beth preened under their praise, as if maybe in some way they are her family too.

If working this case has taught me anything it's that blood doesn't make you family. I live out the majority of my life in a lie, if you want to look at it that way. Ninety percent of the time I'm not who I say I am. Hell, half the time I forget myself. Even then, if I truly am who I say I am – like right now – I'm really not who I appear to be. My inner circle is small because it has to be, and the people inside of that circle are the people that I consider my family.

I turned slowly, expecting to meet Beth's blue eyes, but instead I was first met with a pair of dark brown eyes. Asher Cohen, world renowned chef, and widow. Doesn't look like he's so lonely anymore. I make it a point to know all of the players in each and every case I walk into, even the ones that initially appear to be of no significance, like Mr. Cohen here.

What's more interesting? Asher Cohen purchased my penthouse in the Shaeffer building. He's living in the home I had custom built for myself, which means that through technology we installed years ago, Alex has had a front row seat to watching the Beth and Asher show evolve over the last few weeks.

I know him, but he has no idea who I am.

My identity wasn't released during the purchasing process of the penthouse other than some information that indicated that I was involved with the Chapman Group, which by technicality, I actually was not.

His eyes watch me, he's hesitant. He's determining if I'm a threat to him or, more importantly, to Beth, who he holds by the hip with a grip that's tight enough to let her know he's there, but not so tight she'll be bruised in the morning.

He's possessive, a man who clearly recognizes how quickly something precious can be lost. What's even more interesting is the way his eye contact shifts from mine and darts to a younger brunette standing over in the corner. Wild curly brown hair, similar to that of the blonde that stands in front of me, blue eyes – also similar. She's talking to Samuel Sanders, goes by the name of

Sam, recently adopted by Jason and Olivia Sanders.

I see what Asher sees as I watch their eyes dance as they stare at each other and the young girl licks her bottom lip, running her finger down the front of the boys' flannel button down shirt playfully. Cutting my eyes back to Asher, his jaw ticks once and his hand flexes on Beth's hip, maybe she will have a bruise in the morning.

"Reid Chapman, this is Asher Cohen – Asher, Reid. Reid was the claims specialist assigned to our insurance claim from the Chapman Group, remember? I told you about him." Beth spoke softly, looking over her shoulder to meet Asher's eyes, calming him.

"Asher Cohen, nice to meet you." Using his free hand, he reached out to shake mine, firm.

"Reid Chapman, it's been a pleasure. We appreciate the opportunity to fulfill our obligations. Bill and Shelia have been clients of ours for years as well as friends of the family. We hope to continue this partnership for years to come." I pasted on a fake smile and maintained my cover.

"Of course, we were satisfied with the level of service we received on the claim, especially after the disaster that was the city's denial of liability." Beth rolled her eyes and let out a frustrated breath, surely glad that the entire process is over.

"We do what we can. I will let you get back to the party, I just wanted to stop in and say congratulations." I rocked back on my heels as I began to excuse myself from the conversation. I got what I came here for tonight, and if Adkins isn't here, there isn't a reason for me to stay any longer.

"Plans tonight?" Beth raised an eyebrow and gave me a look that had trouble written all over it.

"No, not this evening." I answered honestly as I searched her eyes for a hint as to what she was fishing for.

"Ah, just trying to make sure Holly wasn't lying to me." She lifted her shoulder and shrugged, dismissing the topic.

"About?" I questioned, stepping back into the conversation, my curiosity piqued.

"Well, she ducked out early because she said she had a date tonight. I was so sure there was something between the two of you, especially after the other day in the café. So, when you excused yourself so quickly, I thought maybe she was lying about who exactly her date was with so the girls and I would stop giving her a hard time. Sorry, I guess I was wrong." The more she spoke the stronger her accent became.

She lifted her manicured finger up to tap her chin as her eyes twinkled with something I couldn't quite decipher, especially not as the blood in my body began roaring in my ears and the hard line of my jaw locked as my teeth ground down together.

"Ok Beth, no more champagne for you tonight. Let's go check in on your girl over there in the corner – her face looks like bad decisions. Thanks for everything, Reid." Asher ushered Beth over to the corner of the building where the young girl and boy were standing so close together their bodies were almost flush, but I couldn't care. I was too busy slipping my phone from my pocket and heading back outside into the night sky to locate my vehicle.

The fuck she is going on a date after she turned down my offer for dinner, multiple times.

CHAPTER ELEVEN
HOLLY

I unfolded myself from Ursula, my prized possession, in the parking lot of Fifth Park Place. Yes, I named my car after the villain in a princess movie. I might not believe in fairytale endings, and maybe it pisses me off when Reid calls me princess, but I've always felt a connection to the mermaid trapped in a life of royalty that spent her time collecting unique and lost things, restoring them into something useful.

This car was the first big purchase I made that was all mine after paying off my business loans, and she's a beauty. She makes me feel sexy, and maybe a little bit badass – sue me.

I didn't go home to change; I just didn't have the time. My office look became my event look that has now become my date night look. Wearing slacks to a first date gives off a certain message anyway, right? It says I'm not willing to part my legs wide enough for you to slip your hand up my thigh under the table. That's not necessarily something I'm opposed to, but I'm not whoring it out on the first date, especially not with the spoiled, rich country club brat that's no doubt waiting inside for me.

Remind me again why I agreed to this? Oh yeah, I need to stop thinking about Reid Chapman slipping his hands up my thighs, that's why.

I checked my phone to verify that I'm only fifteen minutes late and made my way into the lobby of the restaurant.

"Holly Adkins, meeting..." I hesitated as I spoke, having already forgotten the name that Til sent me on the drive over.

"Oh, Ms. Adkins, I have you down right here. I've just seated Mr. Karrington." Karrington, of course. I rolled the pretentious name around on my tongue in distaste. He's probably a III, no doubt.

I followed the perky waitress into the dimly lit restaurant, watching the sway of her hips as they filled out the black dress she wore that fit her like a second skin. Her dark brown hair flowed down her back in big, loose curls, and I just could make out a little ink that slipped from underneath the strap of her dress. If Karrington doesn't work out tonight, maybe I could pick up a little untethered distraction from somewhere else, it's been a while...

"Here we are, Ms. Adkins, I hope you enjoy your evening." My train of thought was interrupted as I was halted abruptly in front of a small round table hidden in the back corner of the restaurant.

Oh my damn. Thank you, Tilly, thank you so very

much.

My attention was diverted again as the man, already seated at the candlelit table, pushed back and stood to his full height, which towered a full foot over my petite frame. His brown eyes sparkled dark, almost black, with just a hint of danger as he took me in, and all of a sudden, I was beginning to wish I'd just worn the damn dress. He wore a custom-tailored navy suit with a price tag that undoubtedly rivaled what I paid for Ursula. That part was not surprising, but the way it fit over his sculpted body – well, he got his money's worth out of it.

"The elusive Holly Adkins, I'm Duke Karrington III, it's so nice to finally meet you in person." I internally groaned as my vagina threatened to shrivel up and blow away in a cloud of dust. Ignore the III. Ignore the III. Why did he have to be a III?

He walked around the table, barely brushing my arm as he passed, and pulled my chair out for me to sit. No sparks, no butterflies gently fluttering in the pit of my stomach, nothing. Dammit.

This man is gorgeous, he has better hair than I do, with his chocolate brown locks meticulously styled and his facial hair trimmed to perfection. He is exactly my type, except he's not. Something is missing.

Do. Not. Think. It.

No, Holly.

"Duke, nice to meet you as well. I'm sorry, but I have absolutely no idea who you are, other than the fact that you obviously must know my sister Tilly and her husband Kris." I spoke bluntly, ignoring every etiquette lesson I've ever attended. My mother would be mortified, but my mind is too busy trying to work out its own issues, leaving no brain capacity to focus on formalities.

He smiled as he sat back down across the table and summoned a waiter who seemingly appeared out of thin air to fill our glasses with wine, his teeth were sparkling white, clearly bought and paid for. Typical.

"You know, you're funny. It's rare I meet a woman in our circle that actually has a personality. Most of the women I meet are so self-absorbed they can barely string a sentence together, let alone infuse a little humor into a conversation." Well, at least we can agree on something.

"Thank you…I think." I lifted my glass of wine and was pleasantly surprised when the red he pre-selected was more sweet than bitter. Perfect choice.

"I'm a doctor. Kris and I perform procedures at the same surgery center. I met Mistletoe a few months ago, and she hasn't stopped talking about you since."

The wine I was sipping shot straight up my nose, and burned like a thousand suns, as I snorted at his use of Til's full name. My mother is the only person on the planet that calls her Mistletoe.

"Are you okay?" He asked, raising his eyebrow in question, the action making his perfectly carved face look even more handsome. It's a shame I can't get my tingles on board with this man.

"I'm sorry, I'm fine. It's just, I rarely hear people refer to Tilly as Mistletoe. It's kind of a joke between us. I apologize, what kind of doctor are you? If you don't mind me asking." I collected myself, and tried to regain a bit of my composure. I don't want to come off as a total flake, even if I'm not particularly interested in this man. It's unfortunate really, because he is beautiful to look at.

"Oh, I didn't realize. It's funny, no one ever corrected me. I guess the joke was on me." He laughed, the sound genuine, suffice to say I didn't hate it.

"To answer your question, I specialize in orthopedics, I know it's not feet but..." He trailed off the corner of his mouth tipping up into an adorable grin.

"Thank God, it's not feet. No offense to Kris or anything, but I just can't imagine investigating toe jam all day." I cringed, and yet I felt myself relaxing into our easy conversation. Maybe I'm not going to go to bed with this man, but he's easy to talk to and a welcomed distraction from the constant push and pull of every interaction I've had with Reid over the past few weeks.

Normalcy, maybe that's exactly what I need tonight.

-o-

REID

I gripped my phone in my hand so tightly that I threatened breaking the screen as I texted Alex from the driver's seat of my black government-issued SUV, still parked on the street outside of the Midtown Bank Café.

Reid: Where did she go, Alex?

Alex: Who? Where did you go?

Reid: Dammit Alex, where is she? I know you well enough to know that you are sitting on the answer to that question.

Alex: We're partners. It's my job to make sure you don't make stupid decisions while on a case. Let me point out that it is of my professional opinion as a sworn in agent of the law that this is a stupid ass decision.

Reid: We're best friends, and I already know she is on a date. Where is she?

Alex: Really? You're going to pull out the best friend card? How old are we, Reid?

Reid: Remember that time Jackson Rogers was picking on you in elementary school out behind the playground after school? He was bigger than you, and he had you pinned down in the dirt.

Alex: You had your cape on, the homemade one that your mom made with the letter R on the back. You ran over screaming at the top of your lungs that you were coming to save the day.

Reid: And we both got our asses kicked, but we did it together. You're my best friend, Alex. I'm asking you, as my best friend, to tell me where the fuck she went.

Alex: Fifth Park Place

Reid: I love you.

Alex: Don't make me send my wife to rescue your stupid ass.

I rolled my eyes as I sat my phone down and shifted the SUV into drive. Fifth Park Place, owned by Walsh, Inc. I'm familiar with the place, and luckily, it's not too far from here.

I handed my keys off to the valet outside of the entrance to the restaurant, not wanting to waste time looking for a parking space. It's been over an hour since I watched her walk out of the café. It's possible they've already left, and the thought of someone else touching Holly only caused the testosterone to pump through my system that much faster.

I don't want to take time to pause and evaluate why I feel this way, nor do I want to know the answers to the questions that are repeatedly running through my mind right now.

She could have accepted my dinner invitation. We could have done this nicely, but no – she had to be difficult about it – she took away the choice, and now she hasn't left me with many other options.

I approached the hostess stand and scanned the dining area, unable to spot the golden blonde locks I was so desperate to find.

"Can I help you, sir?" A beautiful young woman with dark hair, wearing a black dress looked up at me with big green eyes as she approached her post with a tablet in her hand.

"Yes, I'm a friend of Ryan Walsh, reservation for Chapman." I slipped my hands into the pockets of my slacks as I waited.

"I'm sorry sir, we don't have a Chapman reservation this evening, we're all booked up." She spoke without so much as a glance at her tablet.

"Please, if you wouldn't mind checking again. It was a last-minute reservation. I apologize." I smiled the smile that has been melting panties off of the female population since I hit puberty, and I watched as her cheeks blushed. She tapped her manicured nails on her screen until she found what I already knew was there. Thank you, Alex Straton.

"I see. Right this way, Mr. Chapman." I followed as she led me through the restaurant, full of men in overpriced suits and women dressed for a night out. Fifth Park Place is a five-star dining establishment and has a waiting list that spans months. The man that brought Holly here tonight either pulled some strings to impress her, or he had this table booked well in advance, I don't particularly like either option.

She stopped at an empty table set for two near a window that overlooked the sparkling lights of the city of Carlton. "Your waiter will be with you in a moment, thank you."

I skimmed over the menu, not particularly hungry, and waited to order a drink. I don't plan on staying long enough for dinner.

My phone buzzed in my pocket as my eyes took in my surroundings and I made mental notes, counting people – watching body language – anything to distract myself for a moment.

Alex: All the way at the back, around the secluded partition, private table. Keep walking, there is a hallway that leads to a private bank of elevators. Rear exit to the right of the elevator bank.

I smiled as I read his text. He gives me a hard time, but the man loves me.

I have no idea what I'm doing here, why I'm being pulled to this woman, and why I can't seem to stay away when every indicator I have is pointing me in the opposite direction. I've always made calculated decisions; sure, I base those on my gut instincts, but I also take into consideration known factors affecting our case and weigh the risks associated with those with the unknowns.

But right now? I'm going against decades of training,

making decisions on instinct alone, and hoping that my case doesn't implode as a result.

CHAPTER TWELVE
HOLLY

"Wait, so you're telling me that you are planning to move into a known haunted house, of your own accord, for the sole purpose of having the opportunity to work on the restoration process?" Duke stared at me as if I'd grown an additional head, thoroughly engrossed in our conversation.

Til did good. Duke checks off all the boxes, he is perfect on paper. If we'd met even two months ago, I might have been more willing to overlook the lack of butterflies. Hell, I may not have even noticed what was lacking. But now that I've been close enough to the fire to feel the heat, there's something inside of me that's just not willing to settle for lukewarm.

"I won't be merely working on the restoration process, it's mine. The entire project is mine to oversee and will be added to the LGM Décor and Renovations portfolio as a centerpiece for years to come. The only stipulation was that I move into the guest house that is located on the property next week for the duration of the renovations." Duke leaned back in his chair, having finished his filet and crossed his arms over his chest as he continued to stare at me, not believing my willingness to move into Anderson House, and obviously not understanding the extent of this opportunity.

"What, like you really believe in ghosts? Sure, the story is a little creepy, but come on, I don't believe for a second that there are legitimate spirits haunting that place. Nor do I believe they are a danger to my well-being." Or at least that is what I'm going to continue to tell myself, because if I choose to dwell on the morbid portion of the past of the plantation house, I might talk myself out of one of the biggest opportunities of my career.

"Next week. Wow, that's soon. I guess if I'm going to ask you out again, I need to act fast, assuming you survive your encounters with the ghostly spirits of the plantation." His voice took on a spooky tenor as he did his best to imitate a ghost. His smile kicked up into a boyish grin as he watched me expectantly, and for a brief moment I considered what it might be like to date someone like Duke. He's genuine, kind, and he seems to be very interested in me.

But those thoughts were short lived as I felt my spine snap straight in the chair on its own accord, and for the first time tonight, I felt goosebumps as they rose up my neck and spread down my arms. I broke eye contact with Duke as my eyes searched the aisle to my left, unsure of what I was even looking for.

I knew the moment his long, muscular legs strode past

our table, my eyes tracked dark brown leather loafers, up a fitted pair of gray slacks that sat low on his hips, and over a black button down that fit snugly over broad shoulders. He didn't even so much as glance at me as he walked directly by our table and into an open doorway to the rear of the restaurant.

"Everything alright?" Duke questioned as he recognized my sudden change in demeanor, and I couldn't blame him, my infatuation with the stranger that passed our table was completely noticeable. I felt as though all of the oxygen had suddenly been sucked from the dining room. Heat flamed my face, and a swarm of butterflies took flight in the pit of my stomach.

"Yes. Actually, if you'll excuse me for just a moment, I need to locate the ummm…powder room." I racked my brain for terminology that I'm sure my mother would be proud of as I came up with an excuse to escape for a moment and find out what kind of game Reid was playing.

Why is he here? How did he find me?

Scooting my chair back, I stepped away from the table and followed the scent of leather and fresh cut cedar through the same doorway at the back of the restaurant I watched Reid disappear behind moments ago.

As soon as I crossed the threshold I was yanked from my feet. A large, calloused hand folded over my lips to cover the screams that should be ripping from my chest, but they never came. A strong arm wrapped tightly around my waist, carrying me as if I weighed nothing so that my feet didn't even touch the floor.

I should be scared, terrified even. But as I kicked my

legs out and threw my elbow backwards to fight against my captor, I wasn't afraid. I clawed at the skin on his wrist and bit the inside of his palm as he carried me around a corner and to a private bank of elevators where he pressed a button and the doors slid open until he pulled us both inside. I watched the doors shut behind us as I took in my wild expression in the reflection in the mirrored wall. He didn't give the elevator a second to move before he pulled the emergency stop switch, essentially trapping us inside.

Leaning into my ear, he didn't release me, as he spoke in a low growl. "I asked you princess. I asked nicely, but I guess you don't want to play nice." He slid his hand from my mouth and used it to grab my wrists and pull them behind my back as he pushed my breasts against the mirrored wall of the elevator. I watched his eyes, they held no evil, no malice, only hunger. This is his game, and heat pooled low in my belly as I made the decision to get on board and play along, even if just for a moment.

"Dammit, Reid, I'm on a date. What are you doing here? I told you to fuck off, now let me go so I can get back to my dinner." I bucked my hips backward as he pressed his body flush to mine, and I could feel his hard length like steel pressed up against my spine.

"That man? I can assure you, he's not the man you think he is. He can't give you what you want, princess. What we both know that you're craving. You see, you've been a bad girl, and bad girls don't get fairytales and white knights in shining armor. You don't want that shit anyway, do you Holly?" His voice was like rough sandpaper, and his words only threw fuel on the fire that burned inside of me.

"I can't stay. Contrary to what you so obviously believe, I was actually having a good time out there tonight, and I have no intentions of abandoning Duke." The words I spoke were true, even if they weren't the words Reid was looking for. Now is not the time for this, even if my body seems to think otherwise as my hips continue to grind backwards into Reid without my consent.

My eyes locked onto his in the mirror as he bent down toward my neck and his lips skimmed my ear. I could smell the faint hint of whiskey on his breath as it feathered over my neck. "Do not ever speak another man's name when we're together." He spoke just before his lips descended on the sensitive skin behind my ear, his tongue searing my skin as my knees threatened to give way beneath me.

-o-
REID

I left every rational thought I had back in that dining room the moment my eyes locked on to Special Agent fucking Bennett as he sipped a glass of wine and smiled at Holly from across the table.

This is my case. *Mine.*

The Director will hear about this tomorrow morning. Bennett should be nowhere near Holly Adkins, let alone sharing a meal with her over candlelight at a five-star restaurant.

My hand wrapped around Holly's delicate wrists at her back as I pressed her breasts up against the mirror of the elevator wall and watched as they spilled over the top of her white blouse. I marked her neck and collarbone with my lips, my tongue, and my teeth as I tasted her for the first time. Sweet, so sweet. She tastes like vanilla with a hint of strawberries. She's such a contradiction.

Her skin is on fire, and maybe she's a little pissed at the lack of finesse in my approach, but her hips continue to rock back into my hard length as it threatens the confines of my slacks, at a steady rhythm that tells me she's not opposed to the struggle.

And I shouldn't.

We shouldn't.

What we are doing right this moment goes against everything I've been taught and trained to do, but fuck Bennett. He can sit his ass right on down at that table and wait because he's not touching what's mine.

Using my right foot, I kicked Holly's legs apart just enough, and cursed her for not wearing a dress on a date like any other woman would. Of course, she would have on a pair of slacks, we have to do every damn thing the hard way. Slowly, I reached my free hand around to the front of her pants and pulled the fabric of the bow tied at her waist.

I watched her eyes in the mirror and felt her rushed breathing against my chest as I used my free hand to skim the skin just under her blouse at the waistline of her black editor pants.

"This, this is your punishment. I'm not going to draw this out. I won't build you up. No, I'm going to make you come fast and hard. Then, when we're done here, you can go back out and finish your sweet, innocent date for the evening knowing I'm the one that took this from you tonight. This orgasm is mine to take because you stole this opportunity from us." I slid my hand just under the waistband of her slacks and teased the lace of her underwear as her body vibrated beneath my touch.

"Look me in the eyes and tell me to stop, Holly. One word. This is your chance." I gave her an out, not because I wanted to but because consent is sexy. Sure, I get off on the fight, but I will be damned if I take something she doesn't willingly want to give.

I watched her as the corner of her plump, red lip curved up into a dangerous smile and she dipped her hips in one swift motion over my rock-hard cock. "Take it. I dare you."

This woman, does she realize what she's doing to me? What she's started?

My hand slipped under the lace of her panties as I slid one single finger over the smooth skin of her pussy, bare. Her skin felt like silk under the palm of my rough hand as I slid my finger into her fiery entrance. I denied every primal instinct of my body as her pussy tightened around the single digit of my finger, so wet…so tight.

My cock pulsed against the zipper of my pants painfully, and I couldn't help but imagine what she might feel like wrapped around my length.

I pumped my finger inside of her slick velvet twice, until a low groan left her lips. She's got about thirty seconds before she's on the floor of this elevator with her legs spread open…I fought to maintain control.

Dammit, that can't be what tonight is about. Tonight is about showing her what happens when she doesn't play nice. Rewards aren't for bad girls.

Wasting no time, I curled my finger inside of her so that I could massage the spot that I know will send her over the edge as she pressed further against me, looking for more, needing more. She pressed down into my palm fucking my finger as I continued to massage her g-spot.

"Say my name, Holly. Whose orgasm is this?" I grit my teeth as I spoke into her ear, a constant rhythm - slow and steady, not letting up on my assault.

"Fuck you." She bit back; she's fighting me.

"This pussy is mine, and you will say my name when you come. Only my name." I pressed the palm of my hand against her clit as I curled my finger once more and she came apart beneath me, screaming my name over and over again. Her words were outside of her control as her orgasm racked her body, and I continued to pump my finger inside of her slick pussy, drawing out every last drop.

I pulled my hand back, saturated with the moisture from her body, from her orgasm, and brought my hand up in front of her mouth. "Taste yourself, Holly. Taste what happens when you don't play by the rules." Not wanting to give me the satisfaction of hearing her words again she opened her lips just enough for me to slide my finger inside of her mouth. Her tongue wrapped around my finger in defiance as her teeth nipped at my skin and it was nearly my undoing.

Needing a taste myself, I pulled my fingers from her mouth and abruptly turned her body around, pressing her back to the wall, and my lips to hers, forcing my tongue inside with no pretense.

Sweet, just like I thought, with a slight aftertaste of sour that only makes me want to come back for more. She took what I gave and pushed back even further, sucking my tongue into her mouth and biting my lip until I could taste my blood on her lips.

I wasn't hungry earlier, but now I'm starved. I want to feast on her body, but tonight isn't the night for that. Tonight is a lesson, and I feel like my student passed with flying colors as I swallowed down her soft moans and saved them for later.

CHAPTER THIRTEEN
HOLLY

Every single nerve ending in my body was alight as I continued to rock my hips against Reid's solid cock, still not satisfied, even after the most intense orgasmic experience of my life.

I swallowed down the taste of blood from his lips, wanting more. When has blood ever tasted so sweet?

We've been in this elevator for just a few short minutes, and in that span of time, I'm so lost to this man he would probably be taking me against the mirror if it weren't for these damn pants.

For the record, I'm never wearing pants again.

"Look at me, Holly. Look me in the eyes and listen to my words." I gasped for air as he broke away from my lips, taking my source of oxygen with him.

I stared into his blue eyes, noticing for the first time tonight that he wasn't wearing his glasses. His eyes were sharp and held an intensity to them that mirrored our interactions as he looked into my eyes, searching. It felt as though he could see into the depths of my soul.

Maybe he felt it too and was also trying to understand the need that coursed through his body every time we touched, every time we shared the same air. Something about this man was consuming me, and yet I wasn't scared, not in the way that I was scared in my relationship with Chet. No, there was something very different about this.

"I know your story - your past and your present. To some extent, I might even say that I can see your future. What I can't put my finger on is why the story that I see in front of me doesn't play out the way it should. Your puzzle pieces don't fit together, and it's infuriating me. I want to strip you down. I want to learn your secrets. What happens between you and I is dependent on what I find out when I finally put your pieces back together. Only then, we might both shatter." I remained silent as he slid his hand around to my face and brushed his thumb over my swollen, abused lips as he spoke.

"You're pushing me, and testing me, and fuck if that isn't sexy as hell woman. I use and discard women, and yet, they continue to come to me willingly, begging for whatever I have to give, which is never more than one night – never more than one time. But you, you've bewitched me, and I'm going to take my time exploring your wicked ways. You can fight me on this, that's part of the fun, right? But, if you so much as think for one second that you get to play here and then go out there and play some more, you are sadly mistaken. Stay away from that man, Holly. You're mine, and I will say it again

– I always get what I want." With that he released me and slammed his hand over the switch on the elevator, allowing the doors to open.

Without another word, I watched his retreating back as he strode from the elevator and exited through a door on the right. All the while I stood there and tried to see through the haze that still surrounded me. My orgasm-rattled brain struggled to process what just happened and tried to understand the words that he said, unable to make sense of it all.

I stared at my reflection in the mirror and was barely able to reconcile this woman with the woman that I was when I walked into this restaurant tonight. My mascara was smudged at the corners and my lipstick was non-existent. My long silk strands of blonde hair were no longer without frizz or tangles. I look like a bear attacked me while I was in the restroom, actually that's not that far off from the truth, albeit not a believable alibi.

How long have I been gone? Ten minutes?

I'll be lucky if Duke's still sitting there at all when I get back.

Regaining some of my composure, I took a deep breath and attempted to pull myself back together.

Retying the ribbon on my slacks and straightening myself as best as I could given the circumstances, I turned and walked the opposite direction, down the hallway and back into the restaurant.

Back to an evening of false hope and gentle letdowns.

I was looking for a distraction tonight. Suffice to say, my distraction came quickly and without pretense in the confines of a small, private elevator in the back of a five-star restaurant. Unfortunately, it looks like the only way to get Reid Chapman out of my system is to play his game. I might not have gotten much from my egocentric, self-absorbed father, but it's safe to say I got his sheer determination and unwillingness to lose at anything.

I refuse to back down from a challenge, and who would have thought, Reid Chapman - a boring as hell insurance adjuster, just might be my biggest challenge yet. I will play his game, but we're using my rulebook.

-o-

REID

"Senior Special Agent Reid Chapman, to what do I owe the pleasure?" Director Alan Reynolds appeared in front of me on the screen of my desktop computer as I sat at my desk in my office at the Chapman Group.

"Cut the crap, Director. Why was Bennett on my case last night?" The more I thought about that slimy asshole's arrogant smirk as he sat across from Holly at dinner last night, the more my blood boiled. It took every ounce of control left in me not to hoist her over my shoulder and haul her ass out the back door with me when I walked out. But I'm already walking a thin line as it is, and a kidnapping charge wouldn't earn me any gold stars back at headquarters.

Director Reynolds steepled his hands under his chin as he tapped his fingers together in front of his face, contemplating how much he should tell me, I'm sure. I'm very aware that there are times in a case where information is withheld for the overall safety of the mission, but I don't really give two fucks what that reason is at this very moment. Bennett shouldn't be anywhere near my case without my pre-approval or at least a damn notification.

"Remember who you're talking to, Chapman. The better question is, what were you doing at that restaurant last night? Bennett saw you; he also watched Holly Adkins follow you into a hallway." I can't say I didn't see that one coming. Reynolds neglected to answer my question and instead turned the interrogation on me. I shouldn't be surprised, this is the way we operate, it's who we are. We find the truth in a sea of lies.

"This is my case, and Adkins is the daughter of one of my suspects. As the senior agent on this case, I have every right to perform my investigation as I see fit. I was given intel that she was having dinner at the restaurant, and that intel was enough for me to want to check in, make sure everything was above board. I understand that we've cleared her, but I can't help that my gut instinct has me keeping an eye on her just to be sure we haven't missed anything." I played with an ink pen that sat on my desk with my right hand, twirling it between my fingers and hoping like hell the director couldn't see through the holes in my explanation. While it's not entirely false, I will be the first to admit I'm stretching.

"And you're sure that you're listening to your gut and no other appendage of your body? I've seen some of the footage of your interactions with Ms. Adkins, Chapman. While I know you are an exceptional undercover agent, I can't help but wonder how much of those interactions are for this case and how much of them are for your personal benefit?" He pressed on as he questioned my motives, and that only served to piss me off further. This is my case, dammit. Who is he to tell me what is appropriate?

"All due respect, Director Reynolds…" I drew out the pronunciation of his name to drive home my point, as I spoke. "Our mission here is to take down one of the largest human trafficking rings in the country. I've already thrown my own father to the wolves for this case. We're sitting on enough to lock him up for years, and you want to question me about my interactions with the daughter of a known mafia boss. I think you're overstepping."

I stared into his eyes through the virtual portal on my computer and dared him to keep pushing, trying to convey the weight of my words even though we weren't physically in the same room. He may not be willing to tell me why Bennett checked into my case last night, but he sure as hell would understand that superior or not, I've earned my place on this case and within this organization, and I will not tolerate being disrespected.

His lips curled up into a satisfied smile as he leaned back into his desk chair and crossed his arms over his chest, kicking his chin up confidently. "I'm glad you feel that way, Chapman. We're pressing forward and making a move on your assignment. Have you or have you not been able to commandeer the Anderson House account through your current position with the Chapman Group?" His question a complete one-eighty from where we began this conversation.

"I'm still working with my father on some of the details due to his relationship with Wilks, but the claim itself has been assigned to me." I straightened in my chair as I waited to hear what possible move the higher ups could be making on *my* case.

"Perfect. Let me ask you a question, Chapman. Are you afraid of ghosts?"

CHAPTER FOURTEEN
HOLLY

"How many times are you going to check those bags, Holly?" Noel sat on the vintage black velvet sofa in my living room with her bare feet propped up and dangling from the end as she sipped on a mimosa mid-morning on a Monday.

Where in the hell did she get champagne?

I guess writing novels has its perks. Her laptop sat open and discarded on the glass coffee table to her right as she watched me with curiosity, no doubt contemplating whether or not she would use any of our interactions in her next book. It's not her fault, she just can't turn the writer brain off. She's been up since four this morning writing because of the jet lag she's still experiencing. Guess that's what happens when you spur of the moment decide to hop a plane to the other side of the world.

Talk about perfect timing. When I got home from my

date with Duke on Saturday night, I found Noel sitting on the floor in the hallway of my apartment building. She was wearing an oversized sweatshirt with a pair of leggings and was asleep, drooling on her hot pink suitcase.

When I woke her up, she mumbled something about needing to ground herself and cleanse her chakras as she stumbled into my apartment and made herself comfortable. She passed out in my bed before I even had time to get undressed from dinner.

The dinner that leisurely fizzled and died a slow and painful death after I returned from the…um…powder room with wild hair, smelling like a damn cedar tree, and my lady bits still tingling.

"I just need to make sure that I have everything I need to work remotely. I'm not so much worried about my wardrobe. I can't imagine needing to impress anyone on an active construction site, other than possible meetings with the client. But, according to my conversations with Laurel Chesire, Sylvester Wilks' personal assistant, it's highly unlikely I will need to meet with him. I pretty much have free reign over the entire renovation." I spoke without looking at her as I checked my laptop, tablet, and supply of no less than fifty ink pens for the fifth time before zipping that bag closed and moving on to the next one.

I'm leaving within the hour to head out to Anderson House for the first time. It's not like I'm flying or anything, the drive is only forty minutes or so, and that's with traffic. I can come back as much or as little as I would like, but I want to be prepared for any situation I might encounter. What if I get out there and I'm really feeling it? What if actually living on location feeds my creativity, and I don't want to leave the bubble I've created?

I'm definitely not checking and re-checking my bags because I'm nervous. I'm not at all worried about moving onto haunted property for six to eight weeks.

This is one of the most in-depth projects I've ever had the opportunity to design, and it's all mine. I'm about to rock the hell out of this renovation.

"Girl, you better rethink the words that just left your mouth." Noel stood from the couch and strode past me in nothing but a tank top and a thong, pulling back the curtain that acted as the door to my extended closet next to my bed in my loft style apartment. That's one downside to historical properties, closet space was never a priority. You would think that petticoats and formal gowns would have required more storage.

"Let's see…you definitely need these, oh, and these too." She scoured my hangers and drawers pulling out lingerie that I'm certain still has the tags on it and threw it at me as I stood in the middle of my living space.

"There is absolutely no reason why I would need lace or lingerie. Do you really have no concept of what I do Noel?" I questioned her as I dangled a pair of black lace garters from my hand.

"Oh no, I know what you do, and I heard you say something about construction crews. You don't think those men know what to do with lingerie in the bedroom? They use power tools for a living. They have thick calloused hands and worn-in muscles. They sweat and build shit with their bare hands. Please, you need to take lace. If you don't, you're wasting a golden opportunity. Trust me on this one."

I thought back, just two nights ago, to Reid's words about playing games and exploring. I haven't heard a single word from him since he walked out of that elevator with not even a second glance. Not a missed call, or unanswered text, and trust me, I would know. I'm ashamed to admit my phone has been glued to the palm of my hand. I've checked and rechecked, and every single time someone calls or texts me my heart races, only to stutter to a halt and crash land in the pit of my stomach when I realize it isn't him.

I've played out our conversation from the elevator over and over again, still unable to make complete sense of everything he said that night. What was he talking about, my past and the future? Maybe he was just as disoriented as I was, and his words weren't meant to make sense at all. It's highly probable that I'm overthinking the entire thing, but every time I shut my eyes or allow my mind to wander, I'm back in that elevator, allowing him to touch and take, fighting him, needing more.

"Wait a minute, I know that look, Holly Adkins, you're blushing. Is there a reason you would willingly pass on sweaty man sex? A specific reason? I've talked to Til, and I didn't think there had been anyone since that asshole we shall not name." Noel walked back into the living space, but instead of sitting her bare ass back down on my sofa, she sat on the floor, crossing her legs in front of her and leaning her back against the wall. I've seen her do this before, it has something to do with opening her mind to the vibes of the atmosphere or some nonsense.

"Other than the obvious? You just said the words sweaty man sex and it really didn't sound all that appealing to me, Noel."

"Don't knock it 'til you try it." She shrugged and leaned back into the wall, taking a deep breath and closing her eyes.

"For your information I was coming home from a date on Saturday night when I found you asleep literally at my doorstep. Remind me again why you're here?" *Why am I even bringing up my date with Duke? Oh yeah, right, so I don't open my big mouth and say something about Reid.*

"And yet you came home alone?"

"Til set me up with one of Kris' friends."

"Enough said." Her lips quirked up into a half smile that told me she knew exactly what that meant. Even if really in the grand scheme of things Duke wasn't really all that bad. Except for the obvious defect, he wasn't Reid and didn't attempt to kidnap me and make me come in the span of ten minutes.

"Really, Noel, what happened? How long are you planning to stay?" After that first night, Noel really didn't say much about why she flew here in the middle of the night and landed in front of my door. I didn't push, hoping she would willingly offer up that information, but I'm about five minutes from walking out the door for weeks and here she sits, half-naked in my living room.

She took a deep breath, preparing herself for whatever her explanation might be. "I was just getting ready to release my latest novel, and gah, it is so freaking good, Holly. I was handling the marketing and promoting the hell out of the release, not to mention I was already getting started on my next book, which will be a new series for me. I had a ton going on, and I was still living with Pablo. It wasn't serious or anything, but I kind of liked him, a little.

We were playing around, and yeah, so, maybe we did have shared visitors in our bed sometimes, it was fun, you know how much I like experimenting. But apparently Pablo was having a little too much fun while I was busy working. It just wasn't working out anymore, and the whole thing was messing with my head. I needed space. Tilly has the kids and the dog and the husband that studies feet, and I would rather watch Pablo fuck a giraffe than stay with mom and dad, so I came here." She shrugged as she hummed a mantra under her breath that I couldn't quite make out.

"And you're sure that you're going to be okay here? You can stay in my apartment as long as you want, barring you don't burn the place down or have an orgy in my bed." I shoved the random pieces of lingerie that Noel threw at me down into the side of one of my bags and zipped the last zipper closed. If I don't walk out that door in the next thirty seconds, I'm going to be late, and I despise being late.

"Dammit man, I was totally planning to film porn scenes in here later. The lighting through the windows in here is perfect for audiovisual." Noel laughed under her breath without opening her eyes.

"I love you, Noel. Call me if you need anything. I

might be in and out, or I might not. I'm not entirely sure how this is going to shake out, but I will have my cell with me." I grabbed my keys up from the entry table and put my backpack on, pulling my luggage behind me to the door.

"Remember what I said about the sweaty man sex, and wear the lace. Even the gruff men like a little midnight snack every once in a while. Love you, Holly." I rolled my eyes even though she couldn't see me and shut and locked the door to my apartment behind me for what could very well be the last time in weeks.

Or ever. You know, if I don't make it out alive.

CHAPTER FIFTEEN
REID

"You're going in blind; you do realize that? Old school mission." Alex's voice rang through my Bluetooth speaker, bordering on hysterics, as I packed up the apartment it seems like I just unpacked a few days ago. Oh, the joys of undercover work.

"You're being dramatic. It's not that bad, Alex. You're just twitchy because you won't have eyes on me 24/7. Yeah, the house is half toasted, possibly haunted by pissed off souls that never moved on to the afterlife, and the service out there is shit, but we are dealing with a multi-million-dollar industry here. If there isn't some kind of security already on that place when I get boots on the ground, you can kiss my mother." I pulled my t-shirt on over my bullet proof body armor and began strapping down my weapons. Left ankle, right thigh, two on my waistline…it's second nature to me at this point.

"Yeah, I'm not kissing your mom, asshole. Don't get

me wrong, I love a good MILF, but your mom saw me in diapers. That's just weird, even if her rack is still stacked when she bends over. I've got trackers on every piece of technology you own. Hell, I even have trackers on your weapons. Locate the security feed when you get in, and I will be live within an hour. Know better, do better. We use the technology that we have Reid. You'll be a hero with or without me in your ear telling you when the bad guys are planning to sneak up on your ass and put a bullet in your head." Bad guys; something about the way Alex says it takes me back to when we were kids. To all the summers we spent playing out superhero scenarios in our backyards. Sure, this was always our dream, but I never imagined we would really be here one day.

I snorted a laugh through my nose, "I would put a bullet in your leg if you kissed my mother. You know I was joking, stop looking at my mom's tits. I will be fine, like you just said, you can track the hell out of me without actually having eyes on me. I swear I will not allow a bullet to penetrate my skull without you. I promise to always watch my back and to locate the security feed in the crusty old mansion as soon as I possibly can. Scout's honor." I threw my bags over my shoulder and began pacing the apartment to perform a preliminary sweep to make sure I wasn't forgetting something. Knowing Alex like I know Alex, he's going to do a clean sweep of this place after I leave anyway.

The downside to my chosen career is that I don't have roots, my life is completely mobile. I can fit everything I own into a couple of overnight bags. That's also been the upside to my career, until recently. My life, this job, has always been enough. I've never considered wanting more because I had everything. I was accomplishing the goals I set out for myself years before I even considered them to be a reality. But now, I look at Alex, and I wonder if it's really worth it. I've had partners on missions before, hell, almost every mission that I've ever worked has been with someone else watching my back, and there have been situations that we've been in when I was damn well proud they were there.

What would it be like to have someone like that for life? In my real life, not just my career with the FBI, because no matter how much I like to prove I can keep up with the younger guys, the truth of the matter is I'm aging out. Unless I want to retire into a body bag, I've got to take all of my options into consideration.

"You were a boy scout for less than a month, they kicked you out because you didn't know how to share, and you lit a tent on fire."

"Says the man that was blowing oxygen on the flame." What can I say, we like to make things go boom, perks of the job.

"Listen Reid, I know Adkins is going to be there. I just, I don't know, something feels different about her. I don't want you to get distracted or some shit. I know we cleared her, but I need to know you've got your game face on in case things start to go sideways. These guys, they've been on our watch lists for years. This case is at its tipping point, and you're going in there alone. It's messing with my head." Concern laced every word that Alex spoke, and he's right, we're close – I can feel it.

"You're my brother Alex, so, off record, I'm probably

going to fuck her. I can't help it. You know this about me, and I've got to get her out of my system. But I can assure you that this mission is my number one priority. The safety of our team is paramount. The lives of each and every innocent that is currently facing their own version of hell, those are the faces I see when I close my eyes at night. So, yeah, I might have a little fun, but I will not allow myself to become distracted. We will succeed, because there is no other option." Alex has always been able to see through my bullshit, so I didn't bother lying to him.

Holly and I, we're inevitable. She's the oxygen to my flame, and we are one swift breeze away from igniting. But my priorities have and always will be the mission first; everything else comes secondary. I will lay down my life for this team and the innocents that we have sworn to protect, bar none.

"Yeah, yeah. Do me a solid and get that live stream up and running before you tap it."

"You're sick, Straton, and don't say *tap it* like you're some millennial. You're a grown ass man."

"Whatever, Em wants to watch. Who am I to deny my wife all the finer things in life."

"I will never understand either of you. Never."

"You hate us cause' you ain't us. Be safe, don't let the mafia boss find you fucking his daughter, and look for the damn connection."

"Love you guys. I'll see you on the flip side, and we'll have these assholes put away forever."

"Because hell if we aren't always winners."

"Hell yeah."

My lips curved up into a smile as I hit end on my cell phone and Alex's voice cut out from my Bluetooth speaker. Adrenaline pulsed through my bloodstream as I turned out the lights in the apartment, and I heard the soft snick of the door close behind me for the last time.

The director asked me if I was scared of ghosts. Maybe it's time they met the devil.

-o-

HOLLY

I slowed Ursula to a rolling stop at the locked gate that blocked the entrance to Anderson House from the rest of the world.

I didn't hit much traffic moving through downtown Carlton, so my forty-minute drive was actually closer to thirty. That might explain why there's no one here to unlock the gate yet.

Turning off of the main road, I drove for what my odometer said was a little over a mile but what felt like a lifetime, through dense, overgrown woods that blocked out most of the sunlight that is still very much overhead. We will have to hire someone to get the path cleaned up, the overgrowth is dangerous and doesn't give a very pleasant first impression. Less haunted spirit vibes, more historic plantation home.

Century old trees dotted the property behind the gate, their branches hung heavy and covered with a thick moss that draped off of them like a warm blanket. The house sits back on the property down a long tree-lined drive directly behind the foreboding gates that currently tower over me. Unsure of what else I need to do, I pressed the button to cut the ignition of my car. Slowly, I opened the door, stepping out of my black sports car baby in my favorite pair of lime green sneaks and a pair of black leggings.

That thing I said about pants? It doesn't apply to leggings.

Looking past the tall, rusted iron gates it isn't evident from first glance that the fire damage affected the exterior of the home. The house is a massive three-story mansion. It's a traditional plantation home with an expansive front porch that runs the length of the home, and a multitude of windows overlooking the property.

The white of the paint has dulled with age, but the stately columns still stand strong, and most of the original black shutters remain intact.

A quick breeze picked up and blew fallen leaves across the path on the opposite side of the gate sending a shiver up my spine.

I left my phone in the car, so I peek at the black watch I'm wearing on my left wrist to check the time. Laurel said someone would be here with a key. I swear, this place looks deserted.

This week there won't be any crews here, just me. According to the schedule in my contract, I'm to get settled in and do my own assessment of the damage. It's important that I separate the damage due to age and neglect apart from the damage that resulted from the fire. Laurel is supposed to be emailing me over the documents for the insurance claim so that I can set up a meeting with the adjuster, and get the ball rolling on getting Wilks whatever the applicable reimbursement is, but I won't have any of that information until I do my walk-through and assessment.

This project is my priority, so I've handed anything and everything else I was working on over to my team for completion. The commission on this renovation alone is more than what we usually gross annually at LGM, not to mention the unlimited budget on the reno and the fact that I will ultimately be able to add the finished product to my portfolio. This is huge for the company, so I'm giving it my undivided attention.

Taking a deep breath, I took a step back from the gate. Ok so, this place isn't quite as creepy as I remember it being as a teenager. It's daylight, and I absolutely do not believe in ghosts, so there's no reason for me to be concerned.

Ugh, I guess I'm going to have to call Laurel. I hate it when people don't do what they say they are going to do.

I turned back from the gate to grab my cell phone from where I left it inside of Ursula, and my heart stopped beating.

A scream ripped from my chest as I ran into a person that was not there mere seconds ago.

"Miss, are you okay?" A young boy dressed in a tattered pair of black pants and a stained white button-down shirt held onto my forearms. He can't be more than ten or twelve. The top of his head barely reached my shoulders, and I'm petite. His dark hair was oily with grease and dirt smudged most of the skin on his face and hands.

Where did he come from?

I turned my head frantically in search of a parent or

guardian that might explain why this boy appeared from thin air.

He continued to look at me expectantly, waiting for a response that was refusing to come from my mouth in the form of coherent words.

"Um, you…where…I'm meeting someone here." I choked out words, as if I was being held captive and not speaking to a little boy. It's just a kid, a child. Take a deep breath.

"Yes ma'am." He released my arms and dug his hand into the front pocket of his pants until a smile pulled at his lips, revealing crooked, yellowed teeth.

Pulling his hand from his pocket, he opened it to reveal a gold key, tarnished with age.

"Oh, you must know Ms. Chesire. You have the key to the gate. I apologize, I'm just a little jumpy today." I held my left hand over my frantically beating heart and reached for the key with my right. I'm not sure who I was expecting to meet here today, but it most definitely was not the young boy that stands in front of me with a knowing grin on his face.

My fingers brushed the metal of the key, still warm from the pocket of the boy just before he closed his hand and pulled back with the key still inside.

"Ma'am, this key is for that gate there. I heard the men talkin', and I know you must be the pretty lady that is movin' in over at the cook's house, or I guess it was her house anyways. It's been over a hundred years since the big house has had a lady, and we don't take kindly to visitors. 'Specially not ones like the men that keep stoppin' by to check-in on our place. This key will get ya' in, but well, it's up to you to get out."

Maybe this wasn't a good idea. Who is we? Who is he talking about? And why does his dialect sound like something from *Little House on the Prairie*?

His grin remained intact, now outwardly more creepy and less endearing, as he re-opened the palm of his hand presenting the key to me for a second time. Wiping the palms of my sweaty hands down the front of my leggings, I debated on running back to Ursula and getting the hell off this property as fast as I possibly can.

Man up, Holly. Your mind is playing tricks on you.

"Thank you…" The words tumbled from my mouth as I forced my hand to take the key from the boy, pulling back quickly with the key safely inside the palm of my hand.

This is my opportunity, dammit.

With our spooky game of hide the key over, and the key now in my possession, my heart rate began to slow and normalize. I finally relaxed enough to smile at the boy.

"What's your name?" I found myself asking him out of curiosity as I turned back toward the gate to unlock it so that I could drive through to the house.

I slid the key into the rusted padlock and rotated it, hearing the click of the lock release after years of rust and weather wear.

The padlock opened and I grabbed it with the key, turning back toward the boy after he neglected to respond to my question. I guess he's going to get shy on me now.

Only when I turned back, he was gone.

CHAPTER SIXTEEN
HOLLY

I wasted no time pushing the gates open and climbing back inside the safety of Ursula after my encounter with the young boy. Grabbing my phone, I picked it up to dial Laurel and noticed for the first time since arriving that I had zero cell reception.

Are you kidding?

What year is this? There are still places on this continent without cell reception?

We're not that far from civilization. I'm going to have to wait until I get a secure internet connection before I can contact her.

My mind began to race as the panic of not having cell reception began to set in.

She did verify there is internet available out here, right? I know we had that conversation; I've got to be able to do my job. I love ink, don't get me wrong, but I can't function with ink alone, and I most definitely cannot organize vendors and crews with no way to contact the outside world.

My eyes shot frantically to the key that sat securely on the center console of my vehicle, and I debated for a moment longer whether or not this was a good idea.

Was it really worth all of this? I mean, I have been doing a lot of research on this property over the last few weeks. I even watched the documentary that Olivia sent over. Suffice to say, I've freaked myself the fuck out, and it is likely that I'm just overthinking the history of this place, which is crazy if you think about it. Historical renovation is my jam, it's what I'm good at. I live for this stuff, but geez – am I willing to die for it?

No Holly, stop being dramatic – no one is going to die.

Deep breath. Regain your center. Control your thoughts.

I sat in my car and continued to debate with myself internally until I finally reasoned with myself enough to slip the car into drive and pull through the intimidating gates.

And nothing.

Absolutely nothing happened.

I wasn't swallowed into a black hole, I didn't hear blood curdling screams, I don't feel any ghostly spirits in the vehicle with me. I'm good. See, I was totally just overthinking it.

Without cell reception, I can't call Laurel for directions to the guest house, so I guess I'm just going to have to figure this out on my own. I still can't believe they sent a child out here to give me the key to get into this place, so strange.

I pulled down the long drive that ended at the stunning plantation home. I didn't think it was possible, but this place is even more beautiful up close. There's something about it that just feels, I don't know, stately. If you disregard the horrible things that happened behind these walls, it's easy to see why someone would want to restore it.

Turning right, I took a small dirt road path around the back of the home. I will have plenty of time to explore the house later, but I need to get unpacked and settled in first. Sure, I'm staying, but I don't know how much I plan to do around here after the sun goes down, and I would like to be settled in by then.

As soon as I finished rounding the corner of the plantation home a much smaller house came into view. The house looked miniature in comparison to the grandiose plantation house. It was one-story and was situated across a dirt path from the main home. The two houses were very obviously built together, as the siding was an exact match, and a small porch ran the length of the smaller home, a twin to its much larger counterpart.

The house was nestled into a wooded area to its rear. The woods probably haven't always been there, but quite possibly have overgrown and begun taking over the house due to years of neglect.

I parked Ursula next to the small house and said a prayer to anyone who would willingly listen that there was electricity inside.

Cutting the engine to my vehicle for a second time, I stepped out of my car with my useless cell phone in hand, like maybe I could use it as a weapon if need be and walked around to the front porch.

Once again, I don't have a key, and really, I'm just hoping the door is unlocked, because if another child pops up out of thin freaking air, I might just go into cardiac arrest.

I stepped up the single cement step and onto the porch as the worn, whitewashed wooden boards creaked and groaned under my weight in protest.

"Hello?" I called out for no other reason than to warn potential spirits or ghostly beings that I was coming. It's what all the pretty blonde girls do in the horror movies right before they walk into their utter demise, right?

Nothing. I stepped up to the door and turned the handle, slowly. Unlocked.

I'm having mixed emotions on whether or not I'm happy the door was already unlocked.

I'm just going to tell myself they unlocked the door because they were anticipating my arrival. I'm sure they cleaned it and maybe put fresh towels and linens in the home. Maybe even a welcome basket. That's exactly what they were doing. Definitely.

I entered what I'm assuming, from my knowledge of this era, is the main living quarters and was pleasantly surprised. Sunlight filtered into the living area, bringing the room to light and highlighting the minimal – period specific décor. The furniture looked original to the time, although more elaborate than would be expected for *the help* and was in pristine condition.

The room was large, given the size of the house and held a brick chimney, a small, wooden dining table, and kitchen area – which did appear to have been updated to provide access to running water.

I walked into the house through what was surely once the heart of this home. There was one bedroom off to the left of the larger room and a small bathroom next to that. The bathroom would have been a luxury not afforded to most individuals, of the time.

If this house truly did belong to the cook, as the boy said, it's likely the cook held some sort of social status or significance to the family, possibly a favorite mistress – which, I mean, if he killed her that might mean this place is haunted too. *Don't go there.*

This house is in immaculate condition, but everything appears to be just as it was over one hundred years ago. It's like inside this house time stood still, it's baffling.

Walking back out to the main living space, I searched for signs of modern technology anywhere at all, any freaking where. I was beginning to panic again when my eyes finally landed on a large black box stuck behind a woven, wicker sofa adorned with oversized white cushions.

Walking over to the sofa, I bent down to get a better look.

The house doesn't have electrical outlets, we will have to change that the minute we can get an electrician out here, but this beauty…aha! Civilization, I see you. This box is my new baby daddy, we're getting married and are going to bond for the next few weeks over the project of a lifetime. Relief washed over me immediately.

Yes! I'm no tech expert, but if this box does what I think it does, it's my ticket to the outside world and…blowing my hair out.

Surprisingly satisfied with my living accommodations, given the circumstances, I stood back up and walked back out onto the porch to grab my belongings from the car and prepared to make myself at home for the next few weeks.

It's not a penthouse suite, but considering the start of this journey, it could have been much, much worse.

Things are looking up, and I'm choosing to feel all the positive vibes…you know, instead of the scary ones that I'm sure are lurking around every corner if I look hard enough – which I won't. Nope. Not looking.

-o-

REID

I sat at my desk, feet propped up on the glass top, and made a quick phone call over to a Miss Laurel Chesire, personal assistant to Sylvester Wilks, to let her know the Chapman Group was in possession of keys for the Anderson House project, and she didn't need to worry about sending anyone out to let me in.

Hell, my bags were packed and ready to go in the car already.

It was at that point that she informed me, although I was already well aware, that Holly Adkins was also on her way to the property and would be staying for the duration of the renovations as part of her contract.

At the close of my debriefing from the director, I spoke with my father about *next level service*, my dreams for the future of the Chapman Group…blah, blah, blah. He fed right into the idea that I would stay onsite for this particular claim and perform our damage assessments and paperwork while staying at Anderson House – not that it particularly matters, it's all funny money anyway.

After wrapping up all of my loose ends at the office, I grabbed my keys and headed out to my SUV, having given Holly ample time to get to Anderson House and get settled in. According to Alex, Holly should already be there. She left her apartment earlier in the day.

From what I understand, there is currently no one occupying the main house, and the guest house has been converted into living quarters for Sylv and his guests, whatever the fuck that means, while he is on the property, which he won't be for the next few weeks.

According to Alex, we're starting to hear some chatter about the possibility of a shipment coming in. Rumor is we're less than a week out. These tunnels are a big deal for the North American trafficking industry because they allow direct, underground access to the railroad tracks, which lead straight to the harbor. Direct access to the waterway is golden. The easier the transport, the less hassle, the greater the profit.

This question is, why not wait for the renovations to be completed before they attempt a transport?

I need to get there and see what condition the tunnels are in. Is there a holding area already set up? I can't imagine they plan to use the house…unless they are planning some sort of onsite brothel. Actually, that makes sense, I need to ask Alex about that.

And why require Holly to move onto the property to complete the renovations? If she's not involved, I would think that would only make her a liability for their operation. If she is involved, what exactly is her part?

I turned my SUV off of the main road and onto an overgrown path that I know leads to the old plantation home just as the sun was beginning to set behind the horizon.

The drive through the forest was dark, the dense canopy of trees not leaving much space for light to filter through.

Just as I was beginning to think the drive might go on forever, the forest opened up, and I slowed to a stop at the entrance to a long drive as I approached a large iron gate.

I stepped out of the vehicle long enough to find that the gate was only pushed closed and not actually locked. A horrible sound of rusted metal against metal burned my eardrums as I pushed the gate open wide enough to drive through. I stopped just long enough to close it back before driving up a long, straight drive that led to the steps of the plantation house.

The house held no lights, and I didn't see Holly's car, so I continued around a side path that led behind the house until her vehicle came into view.

A tiny replica of the main house sat just back into the woods, and I could see a light flickering in the front window.

Parking my SUV next to her car, I left my bags for now, I can come back for them later.

I haven't seen Holly since the night in the elevator. The night she proved to me exactly what I knew all along, she is dangerous.

I wanted to call her, I craved her with every breath I

took.

I had vivid dreams of breaking into her apartment in the middle of the night to find her asleep in her bed wearing nothing but those damn boy shorts.

I fucked the palm of my hand an indecent amount of times to the soundtrack of her screams.

The fact that I want her so bad is the very reason I've kept my distance. I'm all for mutually using each other until we're both satisfied; until we can both move on from whatever this sick obsession is, but I'm not about feelings. And calling her again would mean that I'm feeling things, and that is shit I'm just not going to allow.

So, I step outside of my SUV in a pair of worn, black jeans, government issued combat boots, and a black t-shirt – sans glasses. I gently closed the door with a soft snick behind me, careful not to make too much noise. The corner of my mouth turned up into a smile as my blood began pumping faster with anticipation. I want to catch her by surprise.

I want to scare her.

I want to see her fight.

And then, I want to watch the fear in her eyes turn to hunger.

CHAPTER SEVENTEEN
HOLLY

I nibbled on a granola bar as I tried for the twenty-seventh time to relax on the wicker sofa in the main living room of the house.

After about thirty minutes of fighting with the black box in the corner, I finally figured out how to plug my laptop in and gain access to a satellite signal that allowed me to call Laurel and gain internet access, the signal strength is weak but it's working, for now anyway.

First world problems. I never even considered food for this evening. Where do you eat when you live in a haunted house in the middle of the forest? What am I supposed to do? Forage in the woods? I think not.

My self-preservation skills are lacking so I can only imagine that I would either a) get lost in the woods b) become a midnight snack for a mountain lion (wait, do you have to be in the mountains to get eaten by a mountain lion?) c) mistakenly eat one of those poison berries that kill you instantly like in that book the *Hunger Games* – that was a hell of a book, but I'm not trying to volunteer as tribute.

So instead, I found a company that was willing to deliver groceries to the main access road for an exorbitant fee tomorrow morning. It is truly ridiculous the amount of money these people charge for delivery. God forbid I ask them to meet me at the gates, oh hell no, that's too much to ask.

Unfortunately, that meant I was left to starve to death this evening. I guess I could leave and drive back into Carlton, but that would mean getting out of Ursula to open and close the gates in the dark, and I'm not really about that life. Thank God for the emergency food stash I always keep in my purse. This granola bar expired a couple of months ago, but it didn't smell funny, and it's only marginally stale, so I call that a win. If I'm feeling extra adventurous later, I've got some double bubble I can pull out for dessert. It's five-star cuisine around here, really.

The sun was setting before I realized that light was going to become a problem, and quickly. I managed to find a pack of matches on the bedside table and lit the oil lamp in the main living space, since I have to actually be plugged in to get enough signal strength that anything works. My cell phone is still pretty useless, but I was able to text through my browser to check in on the apartment and Noel, who said my building was still standing, and she wasn't having sex in my bed…yet.

I didn't get the chance to explore the main house tonight, but I plan to get a start on that in the morning once the sun is up.

The first thing I need to do is assess the fire damage. It was difficult to see from the exterior of the home, but once I get inside, I will be able to get a much better look. I'm actually a little excited, now that I'm here, and I've seen this miniature version of the house. If the main house is even remotely in a similar condition, we will have a good starting point to work from.

None of my contracts specify what the house is to be used for, which is pretty atypical for a renovation of this magnitude.

Sylv Wilks has a large, modern residential estate in the city. I've never been there, but I know my father spent some time there, just from overhearing conversations growing up. Word on the street, or you know around the country club, is that his wife is very similar to my mother, status is of the utmost importance to her. She believes herself to be among the elite, and everyone else is just a peon meant to worship her every move. My mother would drop dead before moving into what she would consider a *used* home. She would be mortified at the thought that someone else might have lived there before her, so I cannot imagine Mrs. Wilks is planning to move in and make this their new permanent residence.

I, personally, think this would make a phenomenal bed and breakfast, especially given the history behind it. However, Mr. Wilks doesn't strike me as the innkeeper type.

When I brought it up to Laurel, she was very adamant that I not ask questions that are none of my business. So, I promptly shut my mouth and referred back to my contract that explicitly stated I am to restore the plantation house to mimic the original home, imploring the historical details that are period specific. Got it.

Taking a break, and desperately wishing I'd brought a book to read, I sat my laptop down on the edge of the sofa and stretched out, allowing my muscles a moment to release the tension from the day. Reaching down, I grabbed at the thick, white blanket that lay at my feet and froze on the spot.

Um.

I heard a heavy booted footstep drop onto the porch, followed by the pained sounds of the old, wooden slats just on the other side of the door. Those old boards have survived over a century of wear and time, but they don't sound like they take kindly to visitors, and well, right this moment, I can't say that I do either.

I quickly scanned the room for weapons, coming up empty handed. Unless you count the oil lamp, but then what happens if I miss while trying to throw it at my intruder? I could potentially burn the house down. Or worse, I botch the throw and end up in the dark, blind, with a serial killer.

Because who else would be at an abandoned haunted house this late?

It's not the boy from earlier, the footstep was too heavy for that. And ghosts or apparitions or whatever don't have audible footsteps anyway, right? RIGHT?!

They appear and disappear.

Kind of like the boy. Ugh, do not think about that right now.

Another heavy footstep. I stood, quietly, from the

couch. If this is fight or flight, I'm about to turn into a damn F-22 Raptor. I know when to stay and when to run, and that foot belongs to someone a hell of a lot bigger than I am.

The door is locked, but this house is so old; I don't trust it to protect me from whatever is on the other side. There is an exit at the rear of the house that heads back into the woods, which now sound surprisingly appealing, if I can just get to the door...I heard the door handle move as my intruder attempted to enter the house and that was enough to kick my ass into gear. Turning on my sock covered feet, I tore through the living space with tunnel vision...but I wasn't quick enough...or my intruder already had a key.

-o-

REID

She heard me. The moment I stepped onto the porch she was alerted to my presence. She doesn't realize it's me...yet, but she knows someone is here.

Her heart is racing, and her bloodstream is filling with adrenaline and endorphins.

This house was built decades before insulation and sheetrock meaning I hear her jump from a spot that I'm making an assumption she was sitting, in the front room.

I wait her out as I stand on the porch; I'm curious, I want to see what she does.

She can't escape me. I'm the predator, and tonight, she's my prey.

What can I say?

I like to play with my food a little before I eat it, and

I'm fucking starved.

No movement, she's quiet, and that's interesting. I don't know what I'm walking into and that's exciting.

Taking one more step toward the door, I decide to turn the knob to see if it's unlocked. It's not, good girl.

Doesn't much matter to me because I have a key.

She's running, I heard the sound of her bolting from the room as I slipped the key into the lock and let myself into the dimly lit home.

This is going to be fun.

She's fast, but my legs are twice as long, and her cute little fuzzy socks aren't giving her much traction as she races for the exit at the rear of the house.

She doesn't turn to look, but a scream rips from her lungs the moment she realizes that tonight isn't the night she gets away. No, tonight she's mine.

The front room was lit by a small lamp, but it's dark at the back of the house, affording me a few more seconds of anonymity as I slip my arm around her waist and my hand over her mouth to cover her screams.

"We keep ending up like this, don't we princess?" I leaned over into her ear and spoke quietly as I spun her around and pressed her body against the door that was supposed to be her escape but has now become her prison.

Fuck, this woman, it's cold in this house and yet her skin is on fire. And there's so much skin, she's the culmination of every fantasy I've had about her over the last few weeks.

A tank top stretches over her breasts, barely holding them in as they threaten to spill over from the top. Her legs are completely exposed in her tiny boy shorts. It's too dark for me to see what color they are, but dammit if I don't want to know.

I want to remember every detail about this night. I need the memory of her like I need my next breath, because when this is over, and it will end eventually – it has to, I want to replay this night over and over in my mind. I already know I'm going to need to use her memory while I fuck every woman that comes after her.

I watched her chest heave, gasping for oxygen, but I didn't give her time to breathe as I covered her mouth with mine and swallowed down what was left of her air. Her lips bruised mine as we slammed together in an explosion of skin and teeth.

There is nothing slow or gentle about tonight, this is our battlefield and neither one of us is prepared to lose.

I pinned her hip against the wall with one hand and gripped her jaw with my other, as I took what I needed with zero remorse.

She bucked her hips under my firm grasp as she fought me, but she wasn't trying to get away, no she was pushing to get closer…harder…more.

A small gasp escaped her lips as I bit her plump bottom lip, and she opened for me on command. Sliding my tongue into the warmth of her mouth, she fought back sucking…hard, swallowing my tongue down her throat and taking every bit of my saliva with it. She's tasting me, and that's sexy as hell.

My cock reacted instantly, throbbing painfully against the zipper of my jeans. I squeezed her jaw harder, wanting her to feel what she was doing to me, forcing her to release me long enough for me to slide my tongue back out and begin my descent over her jawline. I held her in place as I bit and sucked over her jaw, moving to her neck and collarbone.

My body convulsed with need as her hands flew to the waistline of my pants, and she attempted to pull me closer with surprising strength.

"Reid." My name came from her mouth in a growl when I didn't give her what she wanted, and it did nothing but make me want to take more from her.

When I'm finished tonight, there might not be anything left of either of us.

"I'm going to fuck you, princess. I've been waiting for you, I've been watching, but my hand just isn't doing the job anymore. I'm going to take what's mine, and tonight you are mine. Do you understand?" I pulled back far enough that I could gauge the reaction in her eyes as I spoke.

Her eyes blazed with a fire that mimicked my own. "Don't. Call. Me. Princess." She didn't attempt to move, her face was made of stone, but her lips receded exposing her teeth as she clapped back, and her words came out in a snarl.

She's not a princess, no, she's a fucking warrior.

CHAPTER EIGHTEEN
HOLLY

I was overcome with strength as I stood my ground in front of Reid, and his blue eyes watched me with an intensity I felt all the way to my toes.

I've never felt this way before, this empowered in front of a man.

How can I hate him and want him all in the same breath?

He acts like he's the one in control, but in reality, he just handed me the power.

I'm not even sure he realizes he's doing it, but I see it in his eyes, I feel it in the forceful way he holds me. His force is laced with protection, it's controlled – his actions calculated and precise.

I know the difference, and that feeling alone is enough to allow me to trust him.

So, when he tells me that he's going to fuck me, well, I don't back away. I don't ask for forevers and promises.

This is my chance. My one chance to wear that damn pair of one-off Louboutin's, even if I can't keep them forever. Who am I to pass up a chance like that? So, instead of backing down, I step the fuck up and take control of the power he's given me.

His words break the silence of our stare. "Tell me what you want – princess. I want to hear you say it."

Princess, he's testing me. It's ok, he doesn't think I will speak. Maybe he thinks I'll be submissive. Yeah, I might submit, later…after I have a little fun. Because right now, I'm still a little pissed. He walked out of that elevator and didn't look back, and that was days ago. He left me to wonder, and I didn't like the way that made me feel. Not one single bit.

I arched my back against the wall to give myself some leverage, pressing my engorged breasts forward against Reid's chest, hoping he could feel the stiff peaks of my nipples through the thin tank top that I'm wearing. "Reid, I want you to fuck me. I want you to take everything I have to give you and then, when you think I've had enough, I want you to take some more. I want you to make it hurt, and then I want you to make it feel so good that I scream your name until we summon every damn spirit in this place. I want to wake the dead."

I watched a vein in Reid's neck begin to throb, his nostrils flared as his breathing intensified, and I felt his cock pulse through his jeans against the fabric of my underwear. Underwear that was already soaked with my need for this man.

"Last question." His words were raspy and laced with a tight-leashed desire.

I tilted my chin up, just slightly, my silent plea for him to continue.

He leaned in closer, so close that his nose touched the very tip of mine, and his lips barely hovered over my own. If I leaned in just a centimeter, they would be on mine again. I'm desperate for this man's touch.

"Are you scared?" He whispered, and I felt the ripple of goosebumps as they skated down my spine.

"Never." One word. With that one word I threw kerosene on the kindling and finished lighting the fuse.

My feet were swept off the floor from beneath me as Reid carried me back to the main living room and laid me out on the white cushions of the wicker sofa.

I sat up, aligning my spine with the tall back of the couch, and let my golden hair hit my shoulders in waves. Reid towered over me as he stood with the toes of his combat boots touching the front of the couch, and I moved my legs to encase him, spreading them open for him to see what he was doing to me, placing one leg on either side of his.

A slow, seductive smile spread over my lips as I confidently spoke the words I knew he was waiting for. "Take what you want, Reid."

That was all it took, he dropped to his knees in front of me, his eyes wild with hunger as he ran the rough palms of his large hands up my bare thighs until he reached the hem of my ocean blue boy shorts, almost an exact color match to Reid's eyes.

"Dammit, Holly. These shorts are my kryptonite. You're soaked." He used the placement of his hands to spread my thighs even further as he bent his long frame until his nose ran over the damp fabric that separated my skin from his. God, did I want to feel him. I want to feel all of him.

"I'm breaking all the rules, but I can't focus. I can't think straight, and when I lose my focus people die. I refuse to let that happen. So instead, I'm taking a risk, and allowing us to give in to whatever this is between us, and I'm hoping that we all come out on the other side alive." He spoke out loud like his words were more for himself than for me.

I tried to comprehend his words, tried to make sense of what he was saying, but all was lost when his teeth bit down over the fabric of my wet shorts and he pulled the fabric into his mouth. His fingers dug harder into my skin, and I welcomed the pain, anything to distract my mind from the pulse of my heartbeat that was thrumming low in my belly.

A low animalistic rumble came from deep within his chest as he pulled my shorts down my thighs with his teeth alone. Lifting my legs, I placed them over Reid's shoulders as he pulled my underwear the remainder of the way off and slid them into the pocket of his jeans.

I shivered as the cold air hit my moist, bare skin. A cold sweat broke out across my chest and stomach in anticipation of what was to come.

Reid looked up into my eyes once more, a sly smile crinkling the corners of his eyes. I watched as he leaned forward and involuntarily licked his lips, the action causing my hips to jerk forward, but he continued to hold me in place, his hands back on my thighs.

I was starting to think I might come from this torture

alone, because that's what he's doing, he's torturing me by prolonging what we both know I want, what I need.

Finally, after what seemed like a lifetime, he lifted my hips and ran his warm tongue over the line of my ass all the way to the top of my clit, and my eyes rolled back into my head with -instant satisfaction.

Holy shit.

My hands grabbed at his thick, dark hair, pulling him in closer as he spread the lips of my pussy and devoured me with his mouth.

The harder his hands dug into my thighs, the harder I pulled on his scalp. We were at war, but dammit if it didn't feel like I was winning this time.

This pleasure is like nothing I have ever experienced, it's consuming me.

"So good, you taste so damn good." Reid's words rumbled over my clit, and I shook beneath him, my body completely at his mercy.

I pressed my hips toward him harder, needing to find a rhythm. "Fuck my mouth, Holly. I want you to give me everything." His words pushed me higher and higher as my impending orgasm continued to build and taunt me.

Releasing my right thigh, Reid slid his hand to my swollen pussy and slid one finger inside, anticipating what I needed. "Come for me, Holly. Come now." He curled his finger and bit down on my clit as I came apart to the sound of my own voice screaming his name. The words burned as they were physically torn from my chest.

I couldn't think, I couldn't breathe, I could only feel.

-o-
REID

I didn't give her time to bask in the aftershocks of her orgasm. My insides felt like they were being ripped apart as Holly screamed my name over and over again.

I was overcome with the need to feel her, the need to mark her as mine.

So, instead of allowing her time to come down from her high, I allowed myself to channel my inner caveman and picked her up over my shoulder, carrying her to the bedroom that I knew sat just off to the side of the main living space.

I took advantage of the haze she was still in from her orgasm as I threw her down on the bed without protest and watched as her golden hair splayed across the comforter.

So fucking beautiful, she's a seductress.

Reaching behind me, I pulled my shirt up and over my head and then reached down to rid myself of my boots.

Her honey-coated words surprised me as I worked to get my boots off. "This is my job."

Having recovered from her initial shock, Holly scooted forward on the bed on her hands and knees until she reached the edge. The proximity of her mouth to my cock was enough to almost bring me to my knees a second time tonight for this woman, and I get on my knees for no one.

If she was curious as to why I was strapped down with enough artillery to go to battle, she didn't mention it. I disarmed myself, placing weapon after weapon on the armoire that sat against the wall to my right. I'm going to have to come up with some way to explain this shit in the morning, but right now my only priority is getting inside the woman that is currently looking at me like I'm her next meal.

I kicked my boots off one at a time and waited for her as she reached forward, her hands so small in comparison to my own. She looked up at me as she popped the button on my jeans and attempted to slide them down my thighs, the skin of her hands surprisingly soft against my legs.

She cursed out loud as she struggled to get my jeans over the muscle of my thighs. Her anger was cute, but I was becoming impatient. Reaching down to help her along, I finally got them kicked off, leaving me standing in front of her in nothing but a pair of black briefs.

"You're a masterpiece, Reid Chapman. Your body was carved from stone by the ultimate artist. Are you sure you aren't an apparition?" She gently ran her fingers across the V in my lower abdomen that led from my abs to my dick. My cock jumped, aching for her touch, begging her to release it from the confines of the material that was barely holding it in.

"I'm about two seconds from showing you just how real I am." I flexed my hands at my side, trying to let her have some control, but she's not playing fair, and hell if patience didn't fall off my list of priorities somewhere around the time I got the first taste of her on my tongue.

Pulling her back by her hair, I grabbed the waistband of my briefs and pulled them off, letting her see all of me for the first time.

She sat up on her knees, unphased by my demeanor

and smiled a smile that nearly split her face. Her eyes lit up like Christmas morning as she took me in. Something strange shifted in my chest watching her excitement.

Making a conscious choice to shake off the strange feeling, I instead focused on the painful, constant pressure from my cock that bounced, rock solid, between us.

"Like what you see, princess?" I nudged her knowing that my words would force her into action, and she didn't let me down. Wasting no time, she leaned forward again, reaching around to grip my ass and pulled me into her mouth, sucking me all the way down her throat, mimicking the way she sucked my tongue, what…how long has it been? Maybe an hour ago? Not long enough and so long at the same time.

There was no pretense, no lead up, I didn't have a chance to acclimate myself. She's lucky I didn't cum down her throat on contact because her mouth felt like I was bathing in fire.

"Shit, Holly." I barely got the words out as I gripped the back of her head and tried to hold on, but she wasn't slowing down. She refused to let me breathe as she continued to suck and lick my cock, digging her fingernails into my ass trying to pull me closer and sucking harder as she became frustrated that I couldn't get any closer than I already was, her tiny mouth unable to contain all of me at once.

I wrapped her hair around my hand and braced myself, trying anything I could think of to get my mind off of the mind-numbing pleasure that was threatening to engulf me with every swipe of her tongue.

I was standing on the edge of the cliff, but it wasn't up to me whether I jumped or not because she was determined to push me off.

I gave up trying to hold myself back and released what small sliver of control I had left. "This is what you wanted, Holly. Show me how much you want this." The words sounded harsh as they left my mouth, but I meant them, she begged for this. I used her hair as leverage, and I allowed her to pull my hips toward her as I filled her mouth over and over again until I couldn't take it anymore.

Tears ran down her face and smeared her mascara as she looked up at me once more with those big blue eyes. She curled her lips back, skimming the sensitive skin of my cock with her teeth until she hit the base, the tip of my cock touching the back of her throat, and I exploded.

I didn't ask permission, I let stream after stream of my cum shoot down her throat as my cock pulsed in her mouth, and I held her to me with her hair. My body was rigid with the force of my orgasm as she swallowed up everything I was willing to give her.

I needed more. I released her hair and slowly pulled out of her fiery mouth as she licked her lips, clearly proud of her performance. She should be, if I had some gold stars, I would give her every fucking sticker on the sheet. She deserves an Oscar for that performance.

I blindly reached for the pair of jeans that lay discarded next to the bed, grabbing a strip of condoms from the pocket. Maybe Alex was right. I wasn't a boy scout for long, but I came prepared tonight.

"Are you ready for me?" I asked, not really caring

what the answer was. I could look at her and tell she was ready, she was dripping. I held the condom with one hand and ripped it open with my teeth.

"The real question is…are you ready for me? So quickly?" She raised an eyebrow as she leaned back on the bed and pulled her tank top off over her head, leaving her completely naked in front of me.

"That question doesn't even justify an answer." I looked from her to my cock that was still standing at attention ready and waiting for round two, like she didn't just rock my world with the best blow job I've ever experienced, as I slid the condom on over the head that was still sensitive from my orgasm.

She giggled, and I pounced, unable to wait a second longer to feel her skin pressed against mine, all of it. The sound of her laughter turned from sweet and light to deep and throaty in an instant as I took her lips with mine, sliding my tongue in and tasting what was left of myself in her mouth.

One time isn't going to be enough. I thought I could fuck her out of my system, but one time isn't going to do it. I haven't even had her yet, and I already know I'm going to need more.

She arched her back against the bed as I moved my lips down to her breasts; sucking her soft, pink nipples into my mouth one at a time until they were both stiff and swollen. Her body was a live wire of sensation under my touch.

"Reid, I need to feel you inside of me. Now." The fire was back in her eyes as she reached her hand between us and touched my cock rubbing the tip over her sensitive clit over and over again as she rocked against me, demanding my attention.

"Enough." I couldn't take it anymore. I grabbed her tiny wrists and pulled them above her head, encompassing them with one hand as I used my opposite hand to guide my cock to her entrance.

I could feel the heat radiating from her before I ever even slid inside. Lining myself up, I held on to her hands and looked directly into her eyes as I slammed inside of her. A reminder to us both of what this really is. This is primal and raw. This isn't a fairytale. The only happy endings for us are short-lived and repeatable.

"It's not enough, it's never enough." Holly's words were a plea for more as she leaned up and grazed the stubble that lined my jaw with her teeth.

I remained still inside of her, filling her, holding out for as long as I possibly could because I knew the moment I started moving there was no turning back.

"Tell me who you belong to Holly. Whose pussy is this?"

"I belong to no one." She enunciated the words as she bit down on my jaw so hard I know I will be marked tomorrow, but I don't care. Let her mark me, the fire inside her only makes her that much more sexy.

"I guess we're done here then." I slid my cock out to the very tip. She and I both know this isn't over. The laws of the universe wouldn't allow it.

"Fuck me Reid, dammit." Fighting against my hold she bucked her hips forward again and again, fucking herself on my cock as I watched her take what she wanted.

I leaned my body weight back into her and slammed my hips over her again as I felt the tingling sensation already beginning to build again at the base of my spine.

"Who. Do. You. Belong. To?" My voice was thick with need as I barked out every word. I don't know why, but something inside of me needed her to just answer the damn question. The answer paramount to my ability to breathe.

She hesitated. I could see her mind turning, working through her answer and debating what and how much she was willing to say.

"Tonight, I'm yours, Reid." Her words were softer and held a truth to them that I understood. Tonight. We could have tonight.

I gripped her wrists and began a punishing rhythm, giving us both what we needed as I took her again and again. Deeper. Harder. Sweat dripped from my hair onto her breasts, but I didn't stop, I couldn't. "Come for me baby, come now." The words left my mouth, a demand and a prayer, as I felt her begin to tighten around me instantly setting off a chain reaction that caused my orgasm to barrel forward, unleashing inside of her and filling the condom.

"Fuck, fuck, fuck." Holly chanted the words over and over again as her orgasm continued to pull mine from me.

"Not my name, princess." I choked out a laugh as the aftershocks continued on endlessly, and I attempted to hold my body weight over her without collapsing on her and suffocating her. I need her to live through this so we can do it again. And again. I need to fuck her out of my system. I need more.

"Dammit Reid, stop calling me that." She rolled her eyes, pushing me off of her, and I slid out from inside of her as I finally collapsed next to her, not yet ready to move from the bed.

We laid in silence, side by side, both completely exhausted and yet not fulfilled. I don't know if I will ever be fulfilled when it comes to her, and that thought terrifies me.

"Reid." She whispered my name in the darkness as I felt her shift in the bed to turn and look at me.

"Yeah, Holly."

"Why the fuck is an insurance claims adjuster locked and loaded like Arnold Schwarzenegger in the movie *Terminator*?"

CHAPTER NINETEEN
HOLLY

I watch Reid's eyes as he watches me, and for the first time since meeting, him I see a brief flash of uncertainty. He's always so sure of himself, so arrogant, and honestly that's part of his charm. But the moment I ask him about the artillery he pulled off of his body and placed on the armoire next to the bed, I feel every muscle in his body turn rigid, and he falters.

No kidding, there are at least fifteen different weapons in this room at this moment. Not to mention some kind of bulletproof undershirt deal that I watched Reid pull over his head earlier and the combat boots that I've never seen him wear before tonight.

It's interesting because honestly, I was partially joking about the *Terminator* reference, but as I watch him and the haze from my second mind-blowing orgasm of the evening clears my mind, the more curious I am. He hasn't spoken yet, and that's troubling enough in itself. He's normally so quick to respond, but he stares at me and the skin between his eyebrows crinkles as he thinks. I watch the vein in his neck begin to pulse, and I know in that moment that he's preparing to lie to me.

So instead of allowing him to lie, I change tactics.

"Reid, what are you doing out here?" I'm not angry. My body is sated, relaxed, but my mind is moving a thousand miles an hour as different scenarios continue to play out in my head.

I'm not scared of Reid. It's like somewhere deep inside of me I know that he's not going to hurt me. Actually, I feel safer here now that Reid is here than I have been since arriving earlier today.

His eyes shifted back into focus, this question is easier for him, this is a question he's comfortable with. "I spoke with Laurel Chesire earlier. My father is a business associate of Sylvester Wilks, and the Chapman Group is handling the fire claim on this estate. At my father's direction, I've taken the lead on the claim. She might have mentioned during our discussion that you were out here, as part of your contract on the renovations." He paused, and I could tell that he was struggling to determine how much more he was going to tell me.

"I wanted to see you again, after that night in the elevator, hell, after that day I met you in the café."

He huffed out a breath of pure frustration before he continued. "I fuck women, Holly. I don't do relationships; I fuck them, and I discard them. I don't think about them after the fact, I don't crave them, and I sure as hell don't dream about them. I know how that makes me sound, but it's the truth. It's just the way that I am; I don't bother with excuses for it because I don't have any."

His eyes searched mine as he spoke, and I remained silent, wanting him to finish. "Something about you is different, and I'm intrigued by it. When Laurel told me you were here, I might have mentioned to my father that I would be willing to work remotely. My things are in the back of my SUV outside." He paused, running his hand through his hair that was still damp with sweat.

"I don't know what the hell just happened between us, but one time isn't going to be enough for me." He glanced down at his growing erection, and a giggle escaped my mouth. He's ready to go again, and I'm game if he is, but first....

I know he's being serious right now, but I couldn't help the smile that continued to tug at my lips, "and the weapons, Reid? What's the deal with the weapons?" I don't care, whatever it is, I really don't, I just need him to tell me the truth.

"I might have heard this place is haunted by a woman scorned. I know a hell of a lot about scorned women, and I know that they're not to be taken lightly. So, I came prepared." The lie slid off his tongue, and I decided to let it ride, for now. He thinks he's so smooth, but I see it in the subtle shift of his blue eyes, and in the way that vein throbs in his neck when he isn't being entirely truthful.

"I hate to break it to you, but you can't kill someone that's already dead." I rolled my eyes as Reid placed the palm of his hand over my bare hip and the feeling made my chest tighten.

"But dammit if it doesn't make you feel better, doesn't

it?" I do feel safer. However, I think that has more to do with Reid and less to do with his artillery; although I don't think that right now is the time to mention that.

"I don't have any idea what you're talking about, I was never scared." I leaned forward and crossed my arms over my chest, the action causing my breasts to push forward and Reid's eyes to dilate as he watched me intently.

"Keep telling yourself that, princess." A laugh escaped from deep within Reid's chest and the sound was surprisingly warm, something about it was soothing to me. He's always so…I don't know…serious. I want to hear more of that sound, of his laughter. Somehow, I'm managing to break through the stoic walls that seem to constantly surround him. The more they fall, the more I want to see what else I can uncover behind them.

"So, you're staying in the main house then?" I know he's not, but I ask anyway because I want to gauge his reaction.

"And share a bed with old lady Anderson? I think not. No, I'm staying right here in this bed, snuggled up next to your perky ass in those boy shorts that drive me fucking insane." His grip on my hip tightened as he yanked me back down onto the bed and pulled me on top of him, very clearly ready for round three.

-o-

REID

My body involuntarily jerked forward, and my eyes chased imaginary demons in the night as I attempted to reorient myself with my surroundings and determine whether or not there was danger in my immediate vicinity or if my brain was just re-living the danger from my past.

My skin was hot, covered in a thin layer of sweat, and the room smelled like old cedar trees laced with something sweet. Sweet. I looked to my left, and instead of demons, I saw an angel; or a demon in a damn good disguise, the verdict is still out.

My eyes burned with the contacts I never took out last night as they adjusted to the darkness of the room, and I studied the woman that lay peacefully next to me.

Her body is cocooned into a small ball in the center of the bed, right next to me despite the warm temperature of the room. A thin, white sheet just barely covers her delectable ass, but the rest of her body is on display, and I take my time memorizing her.

I study the curvature of her spine and the way her delicate shoulders protrude outward as she hugs the pillow she's sleeping with. I notice the small line of freckles that run over her nose for the first time and the way her top lip dips in just the smallest bit right in the center.

It is such a contrast, seeing her so calm and quiet, as opposed to the loud spitfire I battled all night. And boy did we battle.

I think it's safe to say we both won. I lost count of the number of orgasms after number four. At some point we both collapsed from pure exhaustion, her ability to keep up with my stamina was astonishing. I've never been so satisfied in bed and yet left wanting more.

One more taste, one more touch.

What is it about this woman?

She should be untouchable, and yet all I want to do is touch.

Last night I was negligent. I put my own wants and needs over the needs of countless innocents. Never in my entire career have I been so careless.

But, I knew that this would happen coming into this didn't I? And yet, I made the decision to come anyway. It's like my decisions are being driven by some force that's outside of my control, but I can't stop.

Fact – Holly Adkins is the daughter of a known mafia boss. A man so evil, so sickening, that his spot in hell has been reserved for eternity. His blood pumps through her veins, irregardless of whether or not she's directly involved with this case.

I cut my eyes back over to the blonde seductress that lay next to me drooling on the pillow she's hugging like a damn teddy bear and tried to reconcile this woman with the woman that she is on paper, and it does nothing but continue to frustrate me.

For the first time in my life, I feel like I'm compromised; I'm straddling the line, and it's preparing to snap beneath me, but we're too far in. There's no turning back now.

I've been under too long, and if I step down, they'll put Bennett on the case. I don't trust Bennett as far as I can throw him. I sure as hell don't trust him anywhere near Holly, especially after that stunt he tried to pull the other night.

I've got to figure out a way to take down Wilks and Adkins and maintain my cover with Holly. I can't leave her here, not after last night. If she's not involved with the case, she needs protection just as much as every other innocent we protect in this line of duty does, if not more so. Why would Adkins allow his own daughter to be led into the lion's den?

Whether or not she thinks she needs me, I'm here for the duration.

The question is…will she be my downfall or my redemption?

CHAPTER TWENTY
REID

I wonder what time it is.

After staring at Holly's sleeping form for an excessive amount of time, I was crossing over into creeper territory. I finally rolled over quietly as to not disturb her and slid out of the bed. My feet hit the slatted wood floors, and I cringed as they groaned beneath my weight.

I slipped on my jeans, not even bothering with the button and grabbed my cell phone from its spot next to my array of guns and knives on the armoire. I briefly debated on whether or not I should leave them in the room with her. She is feisty, and I wouldn't put it past her to shoot me. But, I feel like she's the type that would need a valid reason to do so, and I haven't knowingly given her one…yet…so I think it's safe for me to leave them in the bedroom instead of risk waking her by moving them.

If I wake her up, she really may shoot me, and that's not a risk I'm willing to gamble with.

I walked out into the main living space and tapped the screen on my phone to illuminate it – five o'clock. I can work with that; the sun will be up soon enough. There is absolutely no cell reception out here, and I'm positive Emily has had to hold Alex back from driving out here at least fifteen times since I left yesterday.

That man, I would say his obsession is unhealthy, but really, it's not. We're brothers, and I'm the only one he's got. Other than Emily and his kids, he doesn't really have anyone. He knows the dangers of this job, he's seen them first-hand, so I get it. I understand, and that's why I need to get him connected out here before he does something crazy.

The fire from the oil lamp has long burned out, so I light the room with the light from my phone and begin the search for internet access.

Bingo. Lucky for me, I didn't have to look far. A discarded laptop lays open on the sofa in the corner of the room. I followed a cable from the laptop to a black box nestled behind the sofa, this is exactly what I was looking for. Alex was right, there is some degree of civilization out here, even if they can't find it in the budget to spring for proper air conditioning.

I opened the front door and stepped out onto the porch as quiet as I possibly could. The air was thick with fog and a heavy dew from the humidity. It's not quite summer yet, but winter has long left the area. Some sort of insect chirped in the background, awake before the sun, I feel you, buddy.

I don't believe in ghosts, but the damn fog doesn't do anything to tame the reputation of the haunted plantation home as it sits abandoned across the gravel path from where I stand.

Walking over to my SUV, I pulled out my backpack and walked back to the house, not wanting to stand outside in the dense fog by myself any longer than necessary. Pulling out the plug that Alex handed me before I left, I plugged one end into my phone and the other end into the black box and said a silent prayer this worked. I'm no IT guy, and I rarely have to be because I have the best of the best in my back pocket, but I need my wingman. If this doesn't work, I'm positive that I'm not qualified to fix it.

Instantly my phone lit up and began vibrating in my hand. I pressed the button to answer and held the phone to my ear.

"Good morning, jackass. Took you long enough, I could have knitted a damn sweater it took you so long." I held in my chuckle as Alex ranted through the phone.

"My apologies, I got pre-occupied. Then I was occupied again and again and well, now here we are."

"Why are you whispering? Are you in the bed with Adkins right now, Chapman? Your weapons haven't left their GPS coordinates for hours."

"Yes and no and yes. I'm safe. What do you need me to do?"

"What are you plugged into? Is there an adapter?" Alex immediately switched modes, his voice direct and thoughtful.

"By adapter do you mean an electrical outlet?" I questioned as I eyed the black box in front of me, needing Alex to speak English.

"Look in the side of your bag and pull out the small black ring, it has two prongs on it. It should fit over one of the outlets. Plug it in and then take the sheet that looks like it has stickers on it from the same pocket. Start strategically placing the stickers about eye level at your location. Those stickers are actually cameras and will feed images to me on a rolling time schedule. It's not perfect, the technology is still in the testing phases, but it will give me what I need until we can get more access out there." I did exactly as Alex said while he spoke, knowing how important these instructions were. We may joke around, but I know when to take Alex seriously, and right now he's serious.

"Done." I paused in the middle of the room, the cord on the end of my phone stretched as far as it will reach.

"Ok, let me just hit this one button and…oh, hey there handsome, you couldn't even bother to get dressed for me this morning?" He teased, and I could literally hear him relax through the phone.

"Why put my clothes on when I plan on taking them off again, and no, I'm not putting these stickers in the bedroom so you can go ahead and flush that idea down that toilet before it leaves your mouth. You can't live stream my sex life as porn for your nighttime activities, it's disgusting."

"I will let you be the one to tell that to my wife."

"Emily is terrifying. Yeah, no thanks, that's on you. What else do you need?" I asked knowing my time in private was limited and not wanting to test the boundaries of waking up my sleeping barracuda.

"I'm good. The box you're plugged into is only

temporary. The satellite signal is garbage at best, find the main internet source, and we can get a live stream up. I think I can get a signal from the sticker cameras anywhere in that house so place them in strategic locations until we can stream. I want live access within twenty-four hours Chapman, so don't get distracted." Like he was summoning a siren, Holly appeared in the doorway to the bedroom wrapped in nothing but the white sheet from the bed. She didn't speak, just leaned against the doorframe and observed.

"Copy that. Anything else?" I stared into her blue eyes as I spoke, knowing images of her were probably filtering across Alex's screen as we spoke.

"I see it in your eyes, Reid. Be careful, ok. I've got a briefing with the director at noon. I will send a text to your phone when I'm ready for you to call for an update." Alex's words were a somber warning.

"Mhmm." I grunted before hitting end on the phone and putting my screen on lock.

Alex keeps telling me to be careful, but careful is for insurance claims adjusters and accountants. Good thing I've never been one of those. I smiled directly into one of the cameras as I took a step towards my greatest risk in the hopes that by taking a chance I could get an even greater reward.

-o-

HOLLY

"Holly...wake up Miss Holly." The familiar, soft voice of a young boy broke through my solid slumber as a brisk chill swept up my bare spine. My eyes shot open remembering where I was, and I immediately searched the room, pulling the sheet up over my body to cover myself.

Only, the room was completely empty. Ugh, I'm having nightmares after my interaction with that kid yesterday, damn overactive imagination. My racing heart slowed as I confirmed there was no one else in the room, and with that the realization of my sore, aching muscles took over.

Even my hair follicles are sore, which brings up another question. Where is Reid? How long have I been asleep? A few hours? Thirty minutes? I don't even remember passing out. The last thing I remember is collapsing onto Reid's bare chest after I let him take me from behind while I held on to the frame of the large four-poster bed I'm currently sitting in, alone, still.

Huh, I glanced over to the window, it's dark out.

My eyes landed on his small arsenal of weapons that sit untouched over on the armoire. He couldn't have gone far, I can't image he would have left without whatever that is over there, guns, knives…I'm sure if I got up and took a closer look, I would probably find some sort of grenades or explosives. When I say the man was strapped down, the man was strapped down. And while on some level that is very sexy, it is also still very concerning because I know he lied to my face about why exactly he was so heavily armed last night.

Everything about this is new and overwhelming. I would like to say that what happened last night was unexpected, but it wasn't. I didn't understand it at the time, but I knew from the moment he walked into that café that we were inevitable, even if I tried to deny it. Something shifted inside of me, and last night Reid solidified what I already knew, I can't walk away from whatever this is, I need to explore it.

Pulling the sheet with me as I went, I stood beside the bed in the middle of the dark room and listened. The walls in this small house are paper thin, and the floors creak and give with each step taken.

I heard his footsteps first, and then I heard the hushed tones of his voice. "Why put my clothes on when I plan on taking them off again, and no, I'm not putting these stickers in the bedroom so you can go ahead and flush that idea down that toilet before it leaves your mouth. You can't live stream my sex life as porn for your nighttime activities, it's disgusting."

I covered my mouth with my hand and held in the giggle that threatened to escape. I don't know who he's talking to or how he has cell reception out here in the middle of the forest, but I concur, neither one of us need clothes for the day…yet. My skin tingled at the thought of Reid's hands touching me again.

But then I paused, my brain still sluggish from sleep, stickers? Live streams? What's he talking about? I looked around the room I was standing in like there was some sort of hidden candid camera somewhere, maybe a red light that would be a dead giveaway, but nothing.

Weird. I wish I could hear the other side of the conversation, I stepped closer to the cracked door. It's the middle of the night, or at the very least the early hours of the morning, who would he be calling at this time?

"Emily is terrifying. Yeah, no thanks, that's on you.

What else do you need?"

Emily? I swear to the good Lord above if this man is married, I'm going to blow him up with his own damn grenade.

He's not married right? I would have discerned that by now, surely. I mean, I know my history doesn't lend to my ability to judge someone's character, but come on, surely I'm not that blind.

I stepped from the recesses of the bedroom, pushing open the door and leaned against the doorframe. Reid's blue eyes locked onto mine as he stood in the center of the room holding a cell phone to his ear. The phone was hooked to some sort of black cord that appears to be plugged into the box I found last night. Apparently, Reid is more techy than I gave him credit for.

His eyes were clear, focused. They held no guilt or doubt, which confirmed my theory that it's unlikely that he has a secret wife.

He didn't hang up immediately, but continued to listen, never once taking his eyes off of me.

He grunted something in the back of his throat that I couldn't quite make out before pulling the phone away from his ear, effectively ending the call. He stalked towards where I stood wrapped in nothing but the thin sheet from the bed.

"Morning or night?" I asked as he reached me in nothing but the wrinkled jeans he wore last night. The button was popped, and a trail of dark hair led from his beautiful abs down to my own personal Disneyland.

"Morning. But I don't know about you, but I want to go back to bed." He brushed a stray piece of hair from my face and gently put it back behind my ear, the intimacy of action taking me by surprise.

I hummed under my breath as I thought about what my next words would be. I have so many questions, and despite how I feel about Reid, I'm strong enough to know that I need some answers before moving forward. I made that mistake once before, and if the way I feel right now is any indication, I'm not sure I would survive a hurt of this magnitude.

CHAPTER TWENTY-ONE
REID

"Holly, baby, what is it? Spit it out." I listened to her soft humming and watched the way her eyes shifted right in thought. I want to take her right back to that bedroom, but I need her fire, her fight, and right now it's not there.

"Who is Emily, Reid?" The question took me aback, and my insides momentarily seized. How much of my conversation had she heard? Every time I turn around, I'm making mistakes when it comes to this woman, and potentially compromising the case.

"The wife of a friend of mine." I answered honestly.

"The friend…is that who you were on the phone with just now?" She brought her eyes back to meet mine. Interesting, Emily was bothering her, she was jealous. The thought warmed my insides and made me want to tackle her onto the bed like a caveman, which is weird. I've never felt this way about a woman before. I don't know what to do with myself.

"Yes, it is." I answered and took another step closer to her until our bodies were almost flush.

"The weapons?" She asked hesitantly, but she didn't back away from my proximity. She isn't scared of me, just curious.

"For work. I need them for work." I didn't elaborate, I can't give her any more of my truths right now, not until I know more about our situation and her involvement in it.

She didn't speak, but she nodded her acceptance of my answer, for now.

"You have cell reception?" Her lips turned up into a smile, and I knew I was out of the woods, figuratively, because we sure as hell are still in the middle of the woods.

"I do as long as that cable connects my phone to that black box there behind the sofa." I lifted my chin and nodded towards the wicker sofa that sat behind us in the living area.

"Care to make a trade?" She pulled her bottom lip into her mouth and bit down with her teeth playfully.

"Oh, so we're bartering now?"

"Come back to bed with me, and we can play a game. I might even let you tie me up if you play your cards right. In return, you let me borrow your nifty black cable so that I can contact the human world later today."

I slid my hand under the fold of the sheet and onto her skin, gripping her hip and pulling her the rest of the way to me. "You know you can use anything I have whenever you damn well want, Holly. I take your body because you want to give it to me, not because you have to." The words came out a little more harsh than I intended, but I meant them all the same.

I'm not the man you want to bring home to meet your mother, but for some reason I feel like I need Holly to know that I respect her. I've never cared before, but the deep pull in my chest to make her understand is forcing my hand. We might fight, and I might take, but it's only because I know it's what she craves. I can read her body; I understand the language it speaks without a single word.

"Oh, I know, I was just being polite. If you decide to take without asking, I know where you keep your explosives." She shrugged as she smiled innocently, and in that moment, I saw the blood of a mafia princess as she pulled away from my grip, sauntering back into the bedroom, and I followed – the damn sway of her hips demanded it.

-o-

"I saw your backpack by the door, you really are planning to stay, aren't you?" Holly absentmindedly drew circles with her manicured fingernails on my chest as we lay naked in the bed watching the sun's full ascent into the morning sky through the window.

Two more times, I took her two more times this morning and am covered in dried sweat and in desperate need of a shower, but I can't move. I'm entranced by the woman that lies next to me.

I thought that Victor Adkins had the power, I considered him my biggest unknown threat to this case, but it turns out Holly may be the most dangerous of them all. For years I've fought for the good guys, I've been a part of a team. But the foundations of my world are shifting beneath me with every bat of her long eyelashes against her delicate cheekbones. My loyalties are changing with or without my consent. It's no longer good versus evil. She's ensnaring me from the inside out, but how far am I willing to go to feed the hunger that is eating my soul?

"A few days at the least, as long as you stop threatening me with explosives." I teased, hoping to lighten the mood and get out of my own head.

"Pot meet kettle. You're the one that brought the guns to the gun show. At some point we have to get out of this bed and get some work done, no?" She sighed, the sound easy and relaxed.

"Tell me, what is on the agenda for the day?" I asked genuinely curious. I want to know the details of what Wilks has employed Holly to do out here. We've only gotten so much information from the paperwork and our inside channels. I know what Wilks' intentions are, but I don't know what Holly believes she is doing here.

"Well, first things first, we have to venture into the haunted house. I was saving that gem for daylight hours. Oh, and I have a grocery delivery scheduled, so at some point I'm going to have to go out to the main road and pick up sustenance. I would have ordered more if I knew you were coming. But as it stands, we will have enough to survive for a few days." I smiled listening to her talk. It's so strange, I enjoy her when she's fired up and pissed at me, and I enjoy her when she's talking about groceries. The sound of her voice is becoming a comfort to me.

"Sustenance? You really did order groceries didn't you? You do realize you have a vehicle here that is perfectly capable of transporting you to and from the city?"

"Yes, but I didn't want to leave my design bubble, and driving back into Carlton will eat up half of my day. I need to be productive over the next few days and get everything in order for the fire claim, as well as set up contractors for the renovations. I only have a week to get everything lined up, and I have yet to step foot into the main house. However, central heating and cooling and a total electrical re-wire of both houses is going to the top of the list if this house is any indication of what's going on over there."

"I'm not arguing with you about that, this place could use with some air flow and high-speed internet, the satellite box out there only goes so far. I happen to know a guy that might be willing to make your life a little easier on the claims side, if you're interested." I curled my lip up into my signature half-smile, half-smolder and watched as Holly's skin turned an adorable shade of pink.

"Depends, what's he got to offer in return? The last claims adjuster I worked with was an arrogant asshole." She rolled her eyes in exaggeration, but her smile was still there, playful.

"An arrogant asshole, really?" I grazed her rib cage with my hand.

"Yes, really. He even called me in the middle of the night one night, and then proceeded to demand I have dinner with him. Can you believe the nerve of that guy?"

"I'm guessing you said hell no?"

"You would be correct. I'm not a puppy, I don't fetch just because some man throws a bone my way." Laughter fell easily from my lips as a visual of Holly fetching flashed through my mind. No, this woman takes orders from no one, but I have my methods of persuasion.

"Oh really? So, you're a regular ole' badass then, aren't you?"

"I mean, if you want to put it that way." She shrugged her shoulders and lifted her chin arrogantly.

"And what if I asked you to dinner?"

"I dunno, I should probably check my schedule. You'll need to email my assistant." A smile teased at her lips as her laughter threatened to escape her attempt at a serious face.

"Final answer, princess?" She shrugged again, and I used her nonchalance as an opportunity to tickle her ribs with my fingers, sending her into a fit of chaotic laughter on the bed. And this wasn't the cute kind of laughter. No, Holly Adkins is ticklish. This woman was jumping and kicking her naked ass all over the bed as laughter heaved from her lungs.

"Stop it Reid...stop it right now!!" She screamed at the top of her lungs as I continued my torture of her ribcage.

"Dinner, woman." I demanded as I smiled watching her struggle.

"I will shoot your ass." The words came out a jumbled mess, but I'm only half certain she's joking about that.

"Holly, dinner." I moved to her thighs, and her laughter mixed with moans.

"Agh, ok – ok, just get off my ribs!" She relented, giving me what I wanted, as I flipped her to her back, rolling over on top of her and hovering there as I watched her blue eyes dilate.

"Reid, what's happening?" Those three words said so much.

My hands were wrapped in the silk strands of her hair, and I felt her toes brush my legs as our skin touched all over.

I studied her as I debated on what to say, because truthfully, I don't know what's happening. I'm stranded on an island that I've never mapped, but I have an inkling that there's treasure somewhere if I just look hard enough.

"I don't know. When I told you that I always get what I want, well, it's the truth. I'm relentless and controlled, giving up is never an option that I entertain. I knew I wanted you from the start. But, you aren't at all what I was expecting. Now that I have you, well, I find myself not wanting to give you back." I played with the strands of her hair between my fingers as I spoke to her.

She looked into my eyes and hesitated before opening her mouth to speak. "You can keep me for a while…if you want." Her words were a whisper of hope and a question wrapped up as one.

I've been trying to fit her pieces into a puzzle since the beginning, but maybe she never fit because I was putting her into the wrong puzzle all along.

"Ok." The words I needed to say were lodged in my throat, words that I knew were too soon to be spoken. Words that didn't even make sense, but that I wanted to say all the same. So, I said what I could and showed her what I couldn't, as my mouth descended on her.

I kissed her hair, her forehead, her mouth, her neck.

I trailed my lips over her body claiming her as my own.

I wasted no time reaching for the strip of condoms beside the bed that was already almost gone and ripping one off.

"Let me." She grabbed the package from my hand and opened it, pulling the condom from the wrapper and sliding it over the sensitive head of my cock. Her gentle touch nearly sending me over the ledge before we'd even begun. I'm so strung out for this woman.

She laid back into the pillows when she finished, satisfied with her work. The sunlight streamed through the window casting a golden light over her complexion, she's stunning.

Placing an elbow on either side of her head, I let her guide my cock into her body using only her hips. We've danced this dance before. Her body accepted mine with no protest as she rocked her hips forward, and I bottomed out inside of her warm velvet pussy.

"Mine." The word escaped my lips, and she rocked forward in response.

I began a slow rhythm, pulling out to the tip and sliding back in, over and over again, savoring her.

I kissed her jaw, her lips, her eyes as I continued to rock in and out, and she met me stride for stride, slowly building the ache that barely sat dormant from the night before.

"Holly, tell me you feel this. Tell me I'm not alone." I needed to know that she was right there with me.

"I'm scared, Reid." Her voice shook, and I felt her fingernails in my back as she spoke, she's holding on.

"Trust me. I am so many things, but I need you to promise me something..." I stilled inside of her and stared into her blue eyes needing to say words that I couldn't.

"No matter what happens, no matter what you think you know, I need you to trust me. Give me your trust, and I will protect your heart. Always." I made a promise that I never intended to make, but that I knew I meant as soon as the words left my mouth.

"Reid, I trust you. Please don't hurt me." Her words lit the fire inside of me, and I began moving again. This time harder – more intense – I wanted her to feel what the weight of her words meant to me.

"Promise me, Holly, no matter what you see or hear you will trust me." She didn't speak as I continued to move inside of her, pushing us both that much closer to the edge.

"Say it, Holly." My words were a desperate demand, but I needed to hear her say it.

"I promise." Redemption.

I watched her eyes flutter and felt the tightening of her pussy around my cock that I've become accustomed to. I anticipated her movements and knew what she needed to get there.

"I've got you baby, come for me." I bottomed out inside of her and leaned forward, letting my body weight lend to the pressure she needed on her clit setting off her orgasm as I felt the rhythmic tightening of her pussy that I knew would pull me over the edge with her.

"Reid, oh God, Reid." She chanted my name and the final puzzle piece shifted into place.

"Mine." The word was ripped from my chest as I stilled over her filling the condom that separated us.

The pieces of her puzzle fit with mine all along. Good or evil, I will continue to protect the innocent, but I'm also fighting for something else now.

I'm fighting for so much more.

CHAPTER TWENTY-TWO
EMILY

"We're pulling him off the case, Straton." I saw red and my body vibrated with anger as I sat in my brown leather office chair in the home that Alex and I share with our children.

I was logged on ten minutes early for our video conference with Director Alan Reynolds, douchebag of the first order, and guess who was already waiting for me.

Don't get me wrong, he's a decent guy. We've been working together for over a decade, but he's lost the plot if he thinks he's pulling Reid from this case without some serious push back and one hell of a tantrum.

My fingers twitched as I gripped the arms of the chair with the need to shoot someone. I'm fucking pissed.

"I'm sorry, is there an issue with our connection, director? Did I misunderstand what you just said? You want to pull Reid from his own case? The case he's been building for years. He's more than qualified, and you knew he was compromised because of his father going into it." My voice shook with frustration, but I did my best to speak calmly. Blowing up isn't going to buy us any favors today.

I felt Alex's presence to my back, as he continued to pace.

Back and forth. Back and forth.

The pacing used to drive me insane, but after all these years, there is something calming about it. Just knowing he's there is enough to help me keep my anger on lock. Sort of.

"We offered him the case knowing his father was involved, yes. He assured us that there was no reason to believe he was involved with Holly Adkins, but Bennett presented some disturbing video footage from that night at the restaurant that proved otherwise." Fucking A, Bennett. I cut my eyes over to Alex who was headed straight to his wall of computer monitors that made my measly office setup on the opposite side of the room look like a child's pretend play office.

"Director, why exactly was Bennett at the restaurant that night? Why did he have access to this case? He should have never had access to Adkins to begin with." I tried to buy Alex time, as he searched our database for the footage that the director was referring to.

If the video has been uploaded to the system, Alex can find it, and he can get rid of it. The damage is done, but we can keep it from going further and posing a threat to Reid's career or the future of whatever is happening between he and Holly. I've waited too damn long to see that man settle down with a woman, I'm not going to let some low-def cellphone camera footage in an elevator go public and jeopardize my chances of becoming an aunt sometime before I'm eighty.

"This isn't up for discussion Agent Straton, a decision has already been made, now let me finish. We are pulling Chapman, but he is to remain undercover. He's distracted, but now he's a player in our game that we can't afford lose. Our sources indicate a shipment coming in, in forty-eight hours. The shipment is set to arrive at Anderson House at zero two hundred hours on that day. This is a trial run for the new property, and the tunnel system. We understand Wilks and Adkins will both be there; this is our one shot. Bennett was never supposed to be at that restaurant, we have reason to believe he's no longer working for us, so I need you to be careful. Alex will continue to liaison between you and Chapman. Reid Chapman is one of our best men, Emily, you and I and the whole damn bureau know that. We don't believe Holly is involved in this case, but as it stands, she's a liability and she's in danger. Make certain she stays with Chapman. The clock is ticking, and it's up to you to finish this. This agency as well as the lives of countless women and children are depending on you; your entire career has led up to this moment. Don't let us down, Straton." I sat shocked, as I watched the director hit end on the call and my screen went black.

"Alex." I needed my touchstone. I felt him as he stood up and walked over to where I was sitting. I felt his lean body kneel beside my chair, but my eyes remained locked on the screen as I processed the mission that was just laid out before me.

"Emily." I felt his lips brush the side of my face, and I heard the laughter of one of our children as they ran by the open office door.

"Let's end this."

"That's my girl."

CHAPTER TWENTY-THREE
HOLLY

"Twenty bucks says you wet your pants and run out of there screaming like a little girl within ten minutes." I stood in the main living room waiting for Reid as I watched him through the doorway to the bedroom finish re-strapping down his body with artillery.

Insurance claims adjuster my ass. There's something else there, I just don't know what it is yet.

"Do I look like a pants wetter to you? I'm a man's man. Emerged from my mother's womb knowing how to use the toilet, never once did I even have to wear a diaper as an infant." Reid pulled a black t-shirt on over his chest and slipped his cell phone in his back pocket as he walked towards me.

He's wearing another pair of jeans today, this pair a little lighter than the dark pair he wore last night, and he has on another fitted black t-shirt. His hair is still damp from the shower, and he's wearing the same light tan combat boots that look like they've seen a few years. I thought he was sexy in fitted slacks and polo shirts, but this is an entirely other level of hot. A whole other stratosphere, and I want to visit that galaxy every single day. One small step for man, one giant leap for mankind, or womankind, or whatever.

I met him halfway, leaning in and standing on my toes to sniff at his neck, "aha, there it is, the overwhelming scent of testosterone in the room is definitely coming from you." My words were dripping with sarcasm.

"Thanks, it's my new cologne, Chapman No. 5. Maybe I should bottle it and sell it if the way you are still sniffing me is any indication. You do realize you're still sniffing me, right?" Reid smiled conceitedly as he turned his face into mine and brushed his lips over my forehead.

"Whatever, you're deflecting now because you don't want to admit you're truly terrified to go into the haunted house." I took a step back, having to forcefully extract my nose from Reid's neck. He does smell freaking amazing.

"Absolutely not, I'm not scared of anything." His words came out cocky, but he flinched for just an instant when something about what he said registered in his mind. Huh, he's scared of something alright.

"Why else would you be strapping yourself with a half-ton of ammunition?" I looked over my shoulder as I turned to walk out the front door of the house holding my notebook and an ink pen. My laptop isn't going to do me any good without high-speed internet.

"I've learned to always anticipate the unexpected. Nothing is ever as it seems." His words sat heavy over us as he strode up beside me with his long legs and closed the door behind us.

We stood side-by-side in the middle of the gravel path that separated the massive plantation home from the small house we've been hiding away in. The sun was overhead, and the morning dew had long since evaporated by the time we finally pulled ourselves out of the bed and showered…together.

I borrowed Reid's fancy cord and praised the heavens when my phone lit up with enough service to call out and touch base with Laurel, who will be sending a crew out to finish hooking up the internet as soon as possible. Apparently that process had begun but had not yet been completed. She let me know where Reid and I could access the panels for the electrical power out here. All information that would have been valuable pre-arrival, but I'm learning quickly that Miss Chesire doesn't willingly give up information. Even when she does, she isn't fast about it.

Reid was able to call into the office or somewhere, I really don't know, I try not to intrude. I know he's hiding something, but I figure when he's ready he'll tell me. So instead of being nosy, I finished getting dressed and drove out to the main road to pick up the grocery delivery. Hello lunchtime.

It was early afternoon by the time we finally had it together enough to venture out.

I've put off the inevitable long enough. It's time to get the ball rolling on this project full speed ahead, and that means one way or another, we're going in.

"You ready, princess?" Sensing my hesitation, Reid

reached over and grabbed my hand, looking down at me with his blue eyes. Something about the sky made them look so much bluer today.

It's strange, I'm still surprised by the small, intimate actions of this arrogant man. For someone that can be so crass and full of himself, he's surprisingly sweet. I don't even think it's occurred to him yet that he's doing it.

"As ready as I'm going to be. Let's do this." I gripped his hand tightly and took a step forward as I led us around the gravel path to the front entrance of the house. If I'm going to enter a haunted plantation house, is there really any other way to do it than right through the front door? I think not.

I do not believe in ghosts. I do not believe in ghosts.

I inhaled one last deep breath as Reid handed me the key to the front door. Apparently, he has the keys to every door around here – thanks a lot Laurel - and I slipped it into the lock.

Ready or not, here we come.

-o-

"Oh my God, Reid. Am I hallucinating? Is this real life?" We stepped through the front doors of the historic plantation house and were instantly transported back in time.

The large, custom carved wooden double doors opened into a grand foyer. Dark cherry hardwood floors ran for as long as you could see. The ceiling was open all the way to the top, and an elaborate golden gas-lit chandelier hung down overheard.

A stunning white staircase wrapped the length of the second story and descended just a few feet to our right. But what was probably most shocking of all was the fact that everything remained untouched. Draperies, rugs, furniture, décor, all covered in a thick layer in dust, and what I expect is soot from the fire all remain exactly as they were years ago.

My love for history beats for this home, for the life it should have lived, not the life it endured.

The stale scent of smoke lingers in the air, but luckily the house has had some time to air out, so it's not overwhelming. I bet we could call in a specialty restoration team and have most of the items in here treated for smoke damage. It will be costly, but we should be able to save everything that wasn't directly affected by the fire, and this staircase – the things we could do to this entry – my thoughts were taking flight as I stood mesmerized.

"Your eyes are dancing, Holly. I thought you might be scared, maybe even intimidated, but you're in love, aren't you?" Reid's deep voice broke through my racing thoughts.

"Do you feel it? Can you feel the history here?" My heart raced, and for some reason tears itched the back of my eyes as I stood beside Reid in the massive foyer.

"I can see it, but I don't think I feel it like you do. You gonna be, ok?" He squeezed my hand, and I sniffled my noise, regaining my composure. The heart of this home beats strong, it's loud and resilient, but it beats to a broken tune. So much has happened behind these walls. How can a place of such beauty hold such heartbreak?

"I'm good, the smoke's just getting to me, that's all." I smiled, and Reid nodded, not pushing me to explain further.

"So, I thought design was your thing, but it's the history, isn't it?" He questioned me as we walked further into the house together, shifting the subject.

There were no lights on, but the large antebellum plantation windows that lined the front of the house brought in ample sunlight, illuminating each room as we went.

"Both, really. I started out with the drawing actually. There's just something about watching the ink as it comes to life on paper. As a young girl, I would sit up in my room for hours just drawing, adventuring into the recesses of my imagination. It was my escape from the real world, one that I found I needed desperately." He glanced at the pad of paper I held in my opposite hand.

"It wasn't until I was a teenager that I became obsessed with history. Funny story actually, I went to an all-girls private school, and most of the professors were crotchety old women. They were all absolutely dreadful, but my sophomore year of high school the school got a wild hair and hired a male professor to teach history.

Doctor Matthew Henderson, he was dreamy. It was quite literally a race to see who could get signed up for his class first. I might have been crushing, but I didn't fall in love with Matt. No, instead he helped me to discover that history wasn't just in books, it was something that you could live and breathe. History was something to be respected. It was then that I decided there might be a way for me to combine my love for drawing with my newfound love for history. I could have both and have a successful career doing something that I loved." We stopped inside of a large dining room that housed a table for fifteen. Glass china sat at each place setting, all covered in dark gray soot. I ran my finger over the edge of one of the plates, wiping away the grime to reveal the pristine bone of the delicate porcelain.

"Truly, Holly, that's a beautiful story, but I don't know, for some reason I want to go find Doctor Matt and kick his ass…then maybe shoot him in the foot." The tone of Reid's voice made me laugh out loud, and the sound echoed off of the walls in the expansive room.

"Down boy, Professor Matt was and still is very happily married to his *husband* of thirty years, William. Matt was a huge help to me when I was completing my dissertation during my graduate program in New York. I still call him from time to time and bounce ideas off of him or ask questions about a particular restoration." As we continued through the butler's pantry that connected the dining area to the kitchen, the signs of the fire damage became more evident. As we neared the kitchen it was easy to see where the fire originated.

"It's interesting that the reports from the arson investigation stated that they were unable to find a cause for the fire. You wouldn't expect for a fire in a home that has reportedly been abandoned for centuries to originate in the kitchen of all places." Reid stopped us just inside the entrance to what was once the kitchen of the plantation home. Everything in the room had varying degrees of char and burn. It was abundantly evident that the entire kitchen would have to be pulled out and rebuilt to the best of my ability based on historical timelines, everything in here is unusable.

"Now you sound like a claims adjuster. Just remember, the arson investigation is closed. We have to go by the report, regardless of what we think we know." I raised an eyebrow in his direction.

"Just making an observation." He smiled and squeezed my hand lightly, slowly walking us further into the destroyed kitchen.

"What's that over there?" I pointed to an entryway that sat just off from the kitchen.

"I'm not sure, but we're exploring, so we may as well check it out. It looks darker in there, fewer windows. Are you up for it?" Reid asked as if he were trying to taunt me, but I'm not scared. So far, although massive, this house hasn't been much different than any other renovation I've performed in the past.

"Shut up, ghostbuster." I pulled us forward, careful to watch for weak spots in the floor from the fire damage until we crossed into a dark hallway. Reid and I stumbled through the darkness until the room opened up into a library.

Hundreds of books lined wooden bookshelves that spanned the expanse of two walls of the room. A large portrait hung on another wall of a man that on instant I knew was Hubert Anderson himself. Bile rose in my throat as I considered the evil that man was capable of. Just standing in a space that I know he once considered his made the tiny hairs on my neck stand to attention.

Reid released my hand and walked along the bookshelves, running his fingers over each and every spine.

"What are you doing?" I eyed him curiously.

"Looking for something." He answered, distracted by his search.

"I didn't realize you were so into the classics." I watched on as Reid continued his exploration of the bookshelves until he stopped abruptly.

"Holly, come stand over here beside me for a minute." Reid demanded, the tone of his voice taking me by surprise.

"Stop being weird." I gave him my best side eye as I glanced around the room looking for signs of danger that I might have initially overlooked.

"Suit yourself." Reid pulled out a book, and the framed portrait of Hubert Anderson swung open from the wall sending my heart into a tailspin.

Reid smiled arrogantly as I sprinted to his side at the bookshelf not feeling as brave as I did just minutes ago.

My breathing came out erratically as I looked at Reid with shocked eyes. "What the hell was that?"

"Welcome to the magic show. Let's see what's behind door number one." Reid smiled as I scowled. There is a time for joking and standing in the middle of a library that was once inhabited by the creepiest of all creepy men while portraits swing off the wall mysteriously is not the time to for it.

"What? Were you deprived of movies as a child? You have to realize all haunted houses have secret passages, and all secret passages originate from the library with a book. It's a thing." I followed behind Reid and observed as he finished opening the door that was behind the portrait and revealed some sort of lever mechanism.

"Fine, smarty pants. Tell me then, what does the lever do? Is the floor going to open up? Is a giant concrete ball going to start chasing us through the halls like Indiana Jones?" I asked as Reid studied the lever.

"Only one way to find out."

CHAPTER TWENTY-FOUR
REID

The look on Holly's face as I reached for the lever that was behind the portrait of old man Anderson was everything, I knew it would be.

I called Alex earlier to debrief after he texted me about his call with the director. He was short but mentioned that we needed to be prepared to move within the next forty-eight hours, and that the bureau reconfirmed what I already suspected, Holly needs protection. I am to keep eyes on her at all times.

Fortunately for me, that isn't going to prove to be much of a hardship. I can't take my eyes off of her as it is.

I got the electrical switched over via panels located on the backside of the property, which allowed Alex to pick up some aerial footage via satellite. Using heat sensing technology and the blueprints my father had saved in the file for this claim, he located both a hidden elevator as well as the entrance to what we believe are the tunnels.

According to the conversation Holly had with Laurel, we should have a connection to high-speed internet by tomorrow at the latest, which will give him the access he needs to get inside visually. I could feel the anxiety rolling off of Alex through the phone, something is about to go down. I need for Holly and me to be prepared for anything.

Luckily, we've got time. A forty-eight-hour lead time in my line of work is practically unheard of, sometimes we only get minutes. This time is invaluable, and right now, while Holly thinks we're playing around and exploring for her design project and the insurance claim, I'm mapping and I'm teaching her in the process. While I don't believe this house is haunted, it does hold secrets; secrets that we need to know the ins and outs of before the final hour ticks over. When we move, we will have to be prepared to move fast and know every available route and passage.

I look to the only other wall in the room that isn't covered floor to ceiling in books as my fingers brush the cold metal of the lever. The hinges are rusted with age, but it pulls down without much protest, and I watch as the wall shifts.

Holly's blue eyes doubled in size as she looked from my hand to the lever and then to the wall that now appeared as a door.

"How? How, Reid? I've seen the blueprints for this house, I studied them. Nowhere in those blueprints did I see anything about secrets doors." Her voice rose in a panic, and I let her release it. It's not every day you find a hidden elevator.

"Who sent over your blueprints? Laurel?" I asked already fairly certain I knew the answer. The blueprints Holly received were modified.

"Yes, that's who I've been dealing with since the beginning. Why? Where did yours come from?" Holly crossed her arms over her chest. She's wearing a pair of high-waisted blue jean shorts today with a black V-neck t-shirt. She didn't bother putting makeup on after her shower, and to be honest, she's even more stunning without it.

"Wilks is a friend of my father's, he sent over the set we received personally. I think that's where the discrepancy lies." All true.

"But why would they send me a set of inaccurate blueprints?" I could see her mind working through her own questions faster than I could answer.

"I don't think it's that they sent you an inaccurate set, I think it's more that they wanted to keep you on a need-to-know basis, and secret passageways aren't necessary to the renovation."

"Like hell they aren't. How is that fair? What is this, some sort of boys' club and sweet little Holly gets left out in the dark because I don't possess a dick? Literally, hell, Laurel probably wouldn't have even told me where the damn electrical panel was if it weren't for you being here too. And what's with her not even bothering to mention to me that you were coming here in the first place?" The more she spoke, the angrier she got, stumbling over so much information and missing pieces but then putting them back together all at once. This is something I need her to figure out on her own, but it doesn't mean I can't help her along a little.

"Boys' club, huh, you might be on to something with that. I guess I didn't think about it that way." I planted the seed for her.

"You wouldn't, would you?" She rolled her eyes but then darted them right back to mine as realization hit her.

"Chapman. Chapman." She repeated my last name over and over again piecing bits of the puzzle together on her own. "Your dad, is he part of a country club? You said he was friends with Wilks?" There you go.

"Ah, yeah, I believe so. He and Sylvester Wilks have been acquaintances for a while."

"My father is friends with Wilks too. I swear if that man had anything to do with me landing this renovation project. The nerve of him to step in on a business I have worked my ass off to build from the ground up. Years, for years I have built my career with no help from anyone. I didn't even touch the damn trust fund, unlike Til and Noel. Oh no, because they couldn't wait to get their hands on that money, but not Holly. I did it the hard way, my way. This is my business, and if he thinks after all these years he's going to step in, well he's got another thing coming." Her thoughts took a right turn when I thought they were headed left.

"Your father? You're worried about your father's involvement?" I ignored the open door to the elevator and let Holly vent. This is the information I need. I need her to fill in the blanks for me, so I know if I'm protecting her or if we're fleeing the country as fugitives when this is all over. I handed over my father willingly, but I'm keeping Holly. If that means we end up on an island far, far away from here, well those are the options we're facing right now.

"My parents were…how can I put this…detached. Oh, they loved Tilly, she was the first born, the country club debutante they always wanted. She followed all of the rules and paraded around doing as she was told, she still does, married to her damn foot doctor husband. Then there was Noel, the wild one. She took her trust fund money and decided to travel the world writing sex with a storyline and calling it a novel. And then there was me, the forgotten, and that was fine; I preferred it. My father was always so busy with his investments and his associates, and then there were the women. And my mother, oh she wasn't much better with her dinner parties and fucking the pool boy and God knows who else. I was out of there the first chance I got, and I haven't looked back, well other than maintaining my relationship with my sisters. My father called me a couple of years ago and wanted to discuss my trust fund, but that conversation ended quickly when I told him where he could put his money. He can't buy my love, and he especially can't do it now.

I was a child, and he all but ignored me. I needed love and attention, and yet they shuffled us between nannies and piano lessons and etiquette classes, all for our own good mind you. And now he's sniffing around my business. Oh, hell no. Let me borrow one of your guns, Reid, I have some things I need to take care of." Holly dropped her pen and notepad down on the desk that sat in the center of the library as she paced the floor and continued to fume, her tiny fists flexing open and closed at her sides. Her anger was palpable as she began to realize that her father may somehow be involved in this, and he is, just not necessarily in the way she thinks.

-o-

HOLLY

"Holly, baby, breathe." Reid hesitantly approached me as I walked the length of the library overwhelmed as truth after truth smacked me right in the face.

Why didn't I see it before? How could I be so blind to something that looking at it now is so blatantly obvious?

"God Reid, you probably think I'm some spoiled rich brat, don't you? Using daddy's connections to land these large contracts. Jesus, I always thought Til was bad, but at least she married into money. She spread her legs for her spot on the fucking real housewives. I just look like a damn moocher. Shit, that's why you call me princess, isn't it? It all makes sense now." I backed away from Reid as I ran my fingers through my hair in frustration and held in the tears that threatened to spill over onto my cheeks.

All the work I've put in, all the sacrifices I've made, and for what? They're still controlling me, and what's worse? I let them. I unknowingly played right into their game. How many of my contracts has my father had his hands in? And why does he care? What's in it for him? Because I know he sure as hell isn't doing it out of the goodness of his heart. He doesn't have one.

Reid's patience with my meltdown lasted all of two minutes. Thoughts of contracts and hidden doors in haunted houses were all but forgotten as Reid pressed his body against mine, pinning my back against the wall. "Dammit, Holly. No, if you must know, that is not why I call you princess. Yeah, I made assumptions based on your background when I met you, but every single time I blink you blow each of those assumptions out of the water. You are not a country club debutante. You are not a product of your parents. And your business is yours alone. You are a badass designer with a killer work ethic and impeccable attention to detail. Your clothes are fancy, and you drive one of the sexiest sports cars I've ever seen, and yet you're weirdly nerdy. You are spiraling right this minute, and it's ok to fall apart sometimes. We can talk through it, but I sure as hell am not going to stand here and let you fall alone." I welcomed the weight of his large frame as he leaned into me. His breath on my face was a balm to my racing heart. When his lips touched mine, it was almost as if I could physically feel his lungs pulling the anxiety from my chest.

I felt the anger seep from my body as I pulled Reid to me and used him to heal the hurt and betrayal that I felt. I gripped his hips with my hands and felt the length of his cock strengthen against my abdomen. "I don't want to be that girl, Reid. My entire life I've fought against that life. I don't want to be her." My words came out in heaving breaths as I ground my hips against his, needing to touch him, to be closer to him.

"You aren't that girl, Holly. You are so much more. You are not a product of your name; do you understand me? I want to hear you say it." Reid's large hand gripped my chin as he pulled my eyes up to meet his.

"I am not a product of my name, dammit." The words

tumbled from my mouth and tears stung my cheeks. How long have I been holding that in?

Pulling my face to him, Reid kissed the tears from my cheeks one by one. "What do you need from me Holly? Tell me." His voice was raw as he spoke.

"I want to feel you, Reid. I want to feel you inside of me. I want to feel your words with my body." I reached out with my hands and unbuttoned Reid's jeans pulling his briefs down just enough to free him. Then I popped the button on my shorts, shimmying them down my legs, leaving me in nothing but a black thong. I momentarily thanked Noel for throwing my lingerie at me the day I was packing to come out here or I might be standing in a pair of boy shorts right now; although really, I think Reid couldn't care less. He seems to have an affinity for the boy shorts.

I felt him slide his hand to my thong and pull it to the side, slipping a finger into my opening. "God, woman, you're so wet."

"I want you inside of me now, Reid." I used the wall as leverage and climbed his body until my legs were wrapped around his waist, and I could feel his thick cock against my wet slit.

Wrapping my arms around his neck I slid my tongue into his mouth as I ground my clit down over his cock, letting him feel my warmth and building the pressure I so desperately needed.

Pressing his body into mine further, Reid gripped my hair and pulled his mouth away, gasping to regain the oxygen that I stole from him. "I don't have any condoms in here Holly, we can go back…"

"No. I'm on the pill, Reid, and I'm clean. I want you to fill me up with your cum. I want you to mark me, and when this is over with, I want to feel you dripping from inside of me." I watched his physical reaction to my words with fascination. I observed as his eyes widened and his pupils dilated. I relished in his grip that tightened around my hair pulling at the roots, and I felt his cock as it somehow hardened even further pressing up against my sensitive clit.

"You're going to get us both killed. Dammit, woman." Reid growled but didn't fight me. No, he gave me exactly what I asked for as he slammed his mouth over mine, bruising my lips with his teeth. I held on with my legs as he slid his opposite hand between us and lined the head of his cock up with my entrance.

"I. Need. You. Reid. Now." I spoke the broken words between his lips with gritted teeth, and he released my hair to grip my hips with both hands, pulling me to him until we were flush, and his cock filled me completely.

"So big, Reid. You feel so good. God." Using my hips, he pulled me to him over and over again. My back slammed against the wall behind me, but I didn't care, I welcomed the pain.

"Holly, I'm going to come inside of you baby. I need you to be ready for me." The zipper of his pants hit my clit every time he pulled me to him and nearly pushed me over into the abyss. I'm on the brink of insanity. I've never let a man come inside of me, but I want Reid to mark me. I want him to fill me. I felt Reid growing inside of me, stretching me, and for just a moment I wished I wasn't on the pill. I want this man to have all of my eggs, to fill them with his semen. I want his seed. I'm his.

"God, Reid, I'm coming." My body was throbbing from the inside out, pulling Reid down with me.

"Holly." He roared my name in the silence of the abandoned library as I felt my pussy swallow stream after stream of his cum. My legs became heavy, but I held onto him as I spiraled out of the most intense high of my entire life.

My lungs heaved and my head dropped down onto Reid's shoulder with utter exhaustion, but he continued to hold me.

"I don't know what to say." My heart was screaming words at me, but the words wouldn't come out, lost in translation somewhere inside of me.

"It's ok. You don't have to say anything. I feel you. I can feel your words, Holly. Do you understand what I'm saying?" Reid slowly pulled out of me and stood me up on shaky legs in front of him.

"Why does it hurt?" I asked as I bent to pick up my shorts and revealed in Reid's moisture that I could feel inside of me.

"Well, not all men are quite as large..." Reid smirked as I bent back up and hit his chest with my fist, only it was more like hitting a brick wall, so it hurt my knuckles more than it probably hurt him.

"Kidding, I'm kidding. I mean, it's still true. But to answer your question, the truth is I don't know. It feels like you can't breathe, right? Like you might suffocate?" He watched me as he zipped his pants back up.

"But then you kiss me, and my lungs fill with oxygen." I finished his thoughts for him with my own.

"I don't understand it." His eyes held truth as he spoke. "But it's too late, because now that I've felt it, I don't think I can survive without it."

I nodded, unsure of what else to say or how else to respond because I feel the same way. He's consuming me, and I'm letting him. I want to be devoured.

CHAPTER TWENTY-FIVE
REID

I was wrong. I was so wrong about her.

She doesn't even realize who she is. She has no idea the power she possesses with a name that she doesn't even want. A name she sure as hell wouldn't want if she knew the history behind it; the absolute evil associated with it. I don't know if I'm pissed at Victor Adkins for keeping his daughter so far in the dark for all these years that she doesn't even know who she is, or if in some way I respect him.

Was this his way of protecting her?

Does he even have that capability? Or is he using her innocence to manipulate her in some way? Is she a smaller piece to the larger puzzle that is his ultimate end game? I want to believe he has the capacity to protect his daughters, but I've studied these men, I understand their social profiles. Victor Adkins is a narcissist. I know better than to think he would sacrifice anything for anyone and not get something out of it in return.

Somehow, he's using Holly, and it just became my job to figure it out and make sure he doesn't get anywhere near her before we get to him.

I need to have Alex run some additional background cross references on her sisters. The initial reports showed no indicators that they were involved, but now I'm not so sure anymore.

I was so focused on the coincidences surrounding Holly that I easily dismissed the profiles of the remaining two sisters.

If they've tapped into their trust funds, it's likely they understand the monetary gain of what it means to be involved with the Adkins family. Greed drives people to do things they wouldn't ordinarily do. Throw in the genetics of a mafia family, and it's a recipe for bad decisions. We might also need to run a workup on Mistletoe's husband, if he's involved with the same group of men at the country club it's likely he is somehow involved in this case.

"Thank you." Her soft words broke through the runaway train that my thoughts had become and re-directed my attention.

"That's what all the ladies say." I harassed her with my words, but my smile said I knew exactly what she was referring to. I felt her anger in my bones, her tears burned my lips, like a compulsion - I needed to fix what was broken.

"You're a true asshole, you know that?" She turned away from me with a smirk as she ran her fingers over the door that was now exposed in the wall, turning her attention back to the secrets of the library. Her earlier rage abating and in its place a newfound curiosity for our surroundings.

Reaching forward I grabbed her wrist and yanked her back to me, breathing in the sweet scent of her blonde hair hoping that it would, if only for that instant, satisfy my never-ceasing need for her. "I'm always going to be an asshole, but don't for one second act like you don't like it." I whispered the words over the shell of her ear and watched the gooseflesh rise on her skin.

"Mine." One word, that's all she said as she leaned her neck back and nipped at my chin with her teeth before pulling away.

Always hers. I never intended for this to happen. I never intended to belong to anyone, but she stole from me. She ripped my heart from my chest without asking, and now it only beats to a rhythm that she possesses, the song of the siren. I'm a prisoner to the soft curves of her body, the drive behind her desire to be the best, and the quick-witted mouth that hides behind those plump lips I can't seem to get enough of.

"Ok, Copperfield, tell me, what's behind this door?" She leaned forward and peaked behind the opening of the door without touching it.

"It's an elevator to the master bedroom on the second floor." Reaching above her head, I grabbed the door, opening it to reveal a small service lift, barely large enough for two adults.

"The technology seems advanced for this time period, no?" She asked as she looked at the elevator curiously.

"Yes and no. It has been connected to the electric, I'm

not sure when that was added but if you look over there in the corner, you'll see there is a pulley system. It can be operated either way." I pointed to an old, rusted chain over in the corner of the tiny room that ran through a loop and up through the top of the elevator.

"Why would he need an elevator directly to the master? It's just one floor. It doesn't make any sense?" This woman, she's pure. Sure, she sees woodgrain and crown molding, but she easily dismisses the intricate details of this home that so vividly highlight its sordid past. She can't see the evil of the world. I want to protect her from it, but if I'm going to keep her in my world, she's got to have some level of exposure.

"This elevator was a transport elevator. It was used to allow the Master of the house, in our case Hubert Anderson, to transport women and children to his chambers undetected, or so he thought. Anderson was a sick man, often times he forced his wife to watch his misdeeds, that's common knowledge to the history of this property and led to his utter demise. However, there were many times that he moved to and from his library here to his chambers upstairs using this elevator. Take a closer look. Look at the walls." Holly leaned forward, pulling out her cell phone and using the light to illuminate the dark space, highlighting notched out markings on the steel walls.

"What is that?" She eyed the markings with interest as she leaned in to get a closer look.

"They're claw marks. Anderson would lock the children in the elevator while he worked in the library, disabling the pulley mechanism as he listened to their screams until he was ready to use them." I watched the blood as it drained from her face and wished I could shelter her from the reality that was this the history of this home. It has a reputation for a reason, and it isn't a good one.

"So, we're going up then?" She stepped into the old elevator shaft, shocking me as she maneuvered her body to make room for us both.

"You're serious? After all that you want to take a ride in the elevator instead of heading back out and taking the stairs?" I stepped in behind her, folding my long body to fit. Anderson was wide, but a tall man he was not.

"I mean, it's creepy as hell, but it's all part of the history of the place. If I'm going to properly restore it, I need to feel it. Feelings aren't always rainbows and rocky road ice cream, Reid. More often than not feelings are painful, they suck the life from our soul and chip away at our innocence. To truly understand our future, we must first understand our past, and sometimes, well, it's terrifying." The words she spoke held so much truth, and yet she has no idea the intricacies of her own past, of the past of her family, or the blood that runs through her veins.

The light from Holly's cellphone was the only light in the enclosed space as I pulled the door closed and hooked the old chain to the pulley. With the door closed, the scent of stale metal and dust was almost overwhelming. Pressing a button on the side of the wall, I engaged the electrical mechanisms meant to power the elevator and hoped that it worked. If not, I would be manually pulling our body weight to the second floor.

The elevator creaked and groaned to life, and just as I was about to give up and begin pulling us up it shifted, and we rose to the second floor. I waited for the grates to stop and then pressed on the door, but nothing happened.

"Oh hell, this was all my idea and now we're stuck, aren't we?" Holly groaned as I tried to engage the door again to no avail.

"It's fine, we'll go back down and take the stairs up." I hit the button to re-engage the motor and nothing happened.

Not wanting to panic Holly, I pressed the button again, and then a third time. Not even a flicker of life. "Just say it, Reid. It's not working, is it?"

"Doesn't appear to be operating. No big deal, I will lower us down with the pulley." I gripped the rusted chain and began lowering us gently, not wanting to jar the old mechanisms of the shaft too much.

"Ok, we should be almost…" I lost the words as I felt the chain go slack in my hand, and the floor fell out from underneath us.

Holly's screams rang through the elevator, and I heard her phone fall somewhere as the small, enclosed room went dark.

-o-

HOLLY

This is how I die.

I had grand dreams of passing away at the ripe old age

of eighty-seven holding hands with the love of my life as we pass over into the fluffy clouds and streets paved of gold in our sleep. Together, obviously. What can I say? *The Notebook* set my standards exceptionally high.

Never, not one single time, did I consider I would plummet to my death in a secret elevator shaft in the middle of a haunted plantation house. Not sure why, but you know, the thought didn't occur to me.

But here we are, and the feeling of death – the actual act of dying itself - it's different than what I might have imagined, surreal almost. It's like I'm having an out of body experience. I heard the chain break, and almost as if it were happening in slow motion, I felt the loss of gravity as I became weightless, freefalling through the air. I know I'm screaming, but I hear it as if it isn't my own voice, but the voice of someone off in the distance.

And then, after what feels like an eternity and merely seconds all at once, the world stops.

Silence. Darkness.

Except, am I dead? Really?

A plume of dust infiltrates the dark space and fills my lungs causing me to cough. Dead people don't cough. So, not dead, good.

"Holly, baby." Reid, thank you Jesus, Mary, and Joseph. I wasn't ready to go, I haven't had my worldly fill of this man yet…speaking of….

"Reid? Dammit, I can't see anything." Using my hands, I felt around on my body searching for injuries, but everything seems fine.

"Are you hurt, Holly?" Reid's voice was stern and filled with what sounded like concern. He's worried about me; would you look at that.

"I don't think so, but I can't be one hundred percent sure, it's possible I'm in shock. Where are you?" Reid's chuckle echoed through the confines of the elevator shaft.

"You're on top of me." What? I felt around in the pitch-black darkness and oh…there he is. Hey there, muscles.

"Whoops. Um, I can't really move. Where is the door? Are you ok, Reid? I didn't hurt you, did I?" If I landed on Reid, what did he land on?

"I'm fine, I'm pretty sure your phone is digging into my right shoulder though, hold on." Reid groaned as he shifted us.

"Let there be light." He spoke as he illuminated the dark elevator.

"I thought the elevator just went from the library to the bedroom. How far did we fall?" I asked as I moved my body to allow Reid access to the door that we could now see because of the light.

"Surprise. I know you did your research on this property, and while it wasn't included on your blueprints, I'm also fairly certain you're aware of the underground tunnel system below the property. This elevator shaft served a dual purpose. While the more commonly discussed and socially accepted rumor is that these tunnels were part of the underground railroad circuit, the truth is that Hubert Anderson had the tunnels constructed in the dead of night over a period of months as a secret passageway from his home to the train tracks that lead to the harbor. It was his way of disposing of the bodies after he was finished with them. I guess he got tired of burying them out back; who knows really." Reid reached forward, and leveraging his weight with his shoulder, he wedged open the door far enough that we could get out.

"Wait, there are dead bodies down here? Am I about to come face to face with a skeleton, Reid? I need to be prepared for this shit; you've got to stop with the surprises. It was cute at first, but now I am legit freaking out." I stalled in the entrance of the elevator, unsure as to whether or not I was prepared to step out into the underground tunnel that may or may not be full of the remains of dead women and children. Or ghosts. Or their spirits. Dear Lord.

"And yet you questioned me this morning as I was strapping up with artillery." I couldn't see Reid, but I could feel his smirk in the air as his hand reached back into the elevator and grabbed mine, pulling me out into the tunnel that was barely lit by the light of my phone that Reid held.

"How many times do we have to go over this? You cannot kill something that is already dead. Explosives are going to do you zero favors facing off against a centuries old pissed off spirit." I stood in the darkness of the tunnel surrounded by dirt and clay, the floor under my feet felt as if it were lined with bricks or some sort of stone. I was joking about the whole Indiana Jones thing earlier, but now the idea doesn't seem so far-fetched.

"And yet for some reason, the pistol strapped to my thigh gives me comfort. Follow me, my set of blueprints did, in fact, have a map of the tunnel system. If my sense of direction is right, we can head this way and there should be an escape hatch that will get us out of here without having to walk the length of the tunnel to the train track." Reid held onto my hand as I stumbled blindly behind him.

"Is it just me, or is this place way more put together than I would have assumed it would be after having been abandoned underground for years? I was expecting cobwebs and mice, maybe some human skeletal remains, but it's surprisingly clean, right?" I asked as I took in my surroundings from what I could see from the dim light of my cell phone that Reid held out in front of us like a lantern, lighting our path ahead.

"No, you're right. Someone has been down here recently. The chain system on the walls of the tunnel is new, no rust. They're preparing." Chains? I tried to focus on the walls, but it was too dark.

Yanking Reid's hand back I stopped our progress. "Who is preparing? What chains? Give me the light, Reid."

His eyes studied me, but he didn't give me the light. Instead, he released my hand and walked toward the hand carved tunnel walls holding up the phone to illuminate what I couldn't initially see. The light ricocheted off of the chains of silver that hung down, slack against the walls. Chain after chain with attached wrist cuffs, they all looked brand new, hundreds of them.

Reid stood in silence as I tried to make sense of what I was seeing. "What is this? Who has been here? No one was in the house, but someone has been working in these tunnels. Why?"

Reid took a deep breath before turning back to me. He walked toward me until the tips of his combat boots touched the toes of my sneakers. "Remember when I told you that things aren't always what they seem?" His voice was serious, and my senses immediately went on high alert.

"Yes, I know you aren't a damn claims adjuster, Reid. I might be blonde, but I'm not stupid." I rolled my eyes, but on the inside, I was panicking. I know Reid isn't an insurance agent, that much is obvious. But right now, I'm alone in a dark tunnel turned prison apparent with a man that is prepared to go to war, and I don't know the battle we're fighting.

My heart is calm because I trust Reid, but am I prepared to find out his truths?

Is he prepared to give them to me?

Once I know his secrets, there's no turning back.

Is my heart prepared for the magnitude of those consequences?

CHAPTER TWENTY-SIX
REID

I counted to ten in my head and practiced breathing deeply as I prepared to do something that would irrevocably change both of our lives forever.

I cut the light on Holly's phone and slid it into my pocket plunging us into complete darkness as I pulled her to me and buried my face in the top of her hair. She's covered in dust and dirt from our fall, but the faint scent of strawberries, the sweetness, is still there.

"Reid?" My name was a question, one to which I had all of the answers. I just wasn't sure that she was ready to hear them. Would there ever be a right time?

I ran the palms of my hands up her arms as I began to speak. "As a little boy, I always knew what I wanted to be when I grew up. I never once questioned it, it was just a part of who I was. I lived in an upper middle-class neighborhood, and I think my father was much like yours, except not." I chuckled, but the sound was dark and deep in my chest as it vibrated between our bodies.

"My parents had me later in life, and my father owned and was the active CEO of the insurance company that had been in our family for decades. He was removed and absent more often than not. However, my mother, she was amazing, still is. My mother devoted her life to making sure that I got the opportunity to chase my dreams, instead of being forced into a life of the family business just because that's what was expected of me as a Chapman. So, I forged my own path, much like you did. I went to college, I received my degree, and when that wasn't enough, I kept going."

"My dreams and my nightmares share a bed; they are one and the same. For over a decade that's been my way of life. As long as I could go to bed at the end of the night, no matter what horrors I saw when I closed my eyes and know that I was fighting for the good of the world, that was enough. Until I met you." I heard her audible gasp; she still doesn't realize the power she has over me.

"It's funny, how we tend to circle back around in life. I never anticipated I would sit at a desk at the Chapman Group. Then again, I never anticipated you, and here we stand. You made me a promise, do you remember?"

"Trust. I promised to trust you, and I do. Reid just tell me already, the anticipation is killing me, and I'm not sure how much more I can take today." Her skin hummed beneath my fingertips.

"I told you that if you would trust me, I would protect your heart. But in reality, I'm here to protect so much more than that. Holly, I'm an undercover federal agent."

She stilled in my arms as I dropped the first of many bombs on her.

"Good guy or bad guy?" I smiled into her hair at her question.

"Good guy, or at least I try to be."

"FBI, CIA, what am I dealing with here?" She's not running, and she's not pissed. So far so good.

"FBI as a division of the Department of Homeland Security."

"Is your real name Reid?" Her head jerked up as she tried to look at me through the darkness that separated us.

"Yes, I'm undercover right now as myself, which sounds completely bizarre but is true none-the-less." I laughed under my breath at the odd set of circumstances that landed us both here.

"Wait, you said something about protection. You're not here for the fire then? You're here for me. You're protecting me? Why? Why do I need the protection of a federal agent, Reid?" I could feel her heart begin to race against my chest, as her breathing picked up.

"Sylvester Wilks is a bad man Holly, kind of like old man Anderson. He's a high-level criminal and involved with some extremely dangerous people." I began painting the picture for her.

"I knew it! Sylv, ugh, what a creepy old man. He used to do this weird thing with his eyes when I saw him around the house or at the country club growing up when he was meeting with my father. Wait…my father. Does this have anything to do with my father?" Here we go. Prepare for launch.

"How much do you know about your family history, Holly?" I asked the final question that had been eating at me.

"Um, well you know about my relationship with my parents. My mother was estranged from her family because, according to her, they were trailer trash that we shouldn't associate with, her words. My father was close with my Grandpa Adkins, but they lived in upstate New York. They were immigrants, and both he and my grandma were killed in a tragic car accident a few years ago. We didn't see them very often growing up, so I can't say there was much of a relationship there. Other than that, it was just my sisters and I." I tried to make out her features in the dark as she spoke, my eyes adjusting slowly.

"Holly, your father is Victor Adkins, one of the most well-known and elusive mafia bosses in the world. He's more dangerous than Wilks, Holly. We've been watching your family for decades, but they're too good – too smooth." Her body turned to stone under my fingertips.

"What?" Her question wasn't gentle, it was a demand for more answers.

"Holly, you are the heir to a mafia crime family dynasty. I have been tracking the movement of his group and Wilks as they relate to the trafficking of young children and women for over a decade. I've been inside of his clubs, worked for his cartels, been a soldier. Your father is a murderer, and yet his hands remain clean of the blood stains of the hundreds he has led to their deaths."

"Princess. That's why you call me princess." She

brought her hand up to cover her mouth, her eyes wide with shock.

"There were so many coincidences. My father is involved with laundering money for this operation. I was presented with this case because of my specific skill set and my ability to go undercover as none other than, myself; albeit compromised because of my relationship with my father, who is going to prison for a very long time when this is all over with. When your file came across my desk and I saw you were Victor's daughter and were also working the café renovation, which was involved with Chapman, and your company had been recently awarded the Anderson House contract I knew you had to be involved. I was so sure of it that even when the Bureau told me to back off, I kept pushing. I've been building the case against your father for years. If there is anything I've learned during that time, it's that there are no coincidences." I tried to tell her the truth, but I knew how the words sounded as they left my mouth.

"You were using me? All of this, everything. Oh my God, you're using me to get closer to my father?" She jerked away from me, forgetting the promises that she made. This was my fear. I would rather deal with a gunshot wound than hurt this woman.

"Dammit, Holly, don't make me chain you to the wall and force you to listen to me. You made a promise." I gripped her wrist with my hand to keep her from running. She could get lost in these tunnels for days, and we don't have days, we're counting down hours.

"And you lied to me Reid!" She's angry, I get it. She just found out she's been lied to her entire life, but if the fault lies on anyone, it's Victor Adkins, not me.

"I was protecting you. Jesus Holly, I was consumed by you and I didn't know why. I was told to stay away, and I kept coming back again and again. I never should have been anywhere near you. I risked the lives of hundreds of women and children, compromising my entire case and decades of work for my own damn personal needs. My entire life has been about my career. I was a little boy that wanted to be a superhero. I wanted to make a difference in the world. You were my coincidence, the exception to the rule when I lived by the damn book. Do you think I planned to fall in love with the daughter of a mafia boss?"

The words caught me off guard as I finally released the feelings that had been boiling just below the surface for weeks. They hung between us, in the silence of the dark tunnel, as I felt her taut wrist relax and the pulse in the vein just below my fingers thump a steady rhythm.

-o-
HOLLY

One word. Reid spoke one word that broke through the rushing chaos of my brain.

My lungs seized in my chest as I searched to find my equilibrium.

"Holly, I love you. Stop running from me, woman." Reid pulled on my wrist, and this time I let him. I gave up a fight I didn't want to win as I collapsed into him in the darkness.

Everything I have ever known is falling around me. The ashes of my life are raining down on me, a reminder of the explosion I've been dealt. My entire life I was conditioned to believe a lie.

Who am I?

I considered the implications of everything that Reid told me. Where does the truth lie?

My father is a murderer.

My family is the blood of mafia.

And I'm in love with an undercover FBI agent.

I'm in love with Reid.

"You love Holly Adkins, the mafia princess, or Holly Adkins, the designer with a secret identity that, up until a couple of minutes ago, she knew nothing about?" I looked up at Reid as he held me.

"Both? Holly, yes, your father is an evil man, there is no question about that. For generations your family has been involved in the dark world. But you, you are pure, and God am I thankful for that. I'm so thankful that you aren't tainted by the actions of your family. I fell in love with Holly the *warrior* princess. The intelligent woman with a strength that outweighs some of the most badass female agents I've worked with, and I can assure you that I've worked with some of the baddest of them all. The woman that sleeps in only boy shorts when her apartment is fucking Antarctica. The woman that willingly agreed to live in a haunted house because of her fascination with the history and architecture of the structure. The woman that continues to go to bed with a man that claims to be an insurance adjuster but is armed enough to take down an army, because even though she's in denial right now, she loves him too." He brushed a stray piece of hair from my eyes as it fell in my face, and I leaned into the warmth of his palm, needing his touch.

"That's the woman I fell in love with. I know you are just now finding out that there is another layer to your history that you never realized, but I fell in love with all of you. Up until the moment that I walked into that café, my career was the most important thing in my life, but I'm risking everything for you on the off chance that you'll take a chance and trust me. I need you to trust me Holly, our lives depend on it." I could hear the desperation mixed with sincerity in each of the words that he spoke.

The truth of the matter is that the list of people I trust right now could fit on a sticky note, and not one of the regular sized ones. No. I'm talking the tiny little ones that are used to mark tabs. But I hear Reid, I feel his words. If I'm being honest myself, I felt his words long before they ever left his mouth, and I trust him. I've always trusted him, even when I was certain he was lying to me. Now I know that my gut instinct was spot on, and while I'm sure there is so much more for me to find out, I trust Reid to tell me. I trust him to maintain his promise to protect me, to protect my heart.

"Will you still chain me to the wall for funsies if I agree?" My racing heart began to level out as my brain finished working through everything Reid told me. I smiled at him through the darkness, even though I'm not certain he can see me.

Air burst from Reid's lungs in a laugh that echoed the halls of the tunnel, a release of the pent-up tension he'd been holding in. "Holly, baby, I will gladly buy you a set for home if you want them. But I'm kind of ready to get you out of these tunnels. It's my job to keep you alive, and I've already sent us careening down an elevator shaft once today."

"Your job? It's your job to keep me alive? But I thought you wanted me for my mind and my brave warrior spirit?"

"Don't forget about that ass in those boy shorts." Reid pulled my phone from his pocket and bathed us in a dim light.

"Aha, I knew there was more to the story." I said the words playfully, but the look on Reid's face as he turned back to grab my hand said that there really was so much more.

"Come on, let's get out of these tunnels, and we can talk more." I followed Reid in silence through the darkness of the tunnels until we located a ladder that hung down from a wooden trap door in the ceiling.

Reid handed me the light as he climbed the ladder and pushed open the door. It was dark outside at this point, but I could feel the cool air and the smell of humidity as it penetrated the dry air of the tunnel.

"Ladies first." Reid hopped back down from the ladder and hoisted me to the first rung that hung a few feet from the ground.

"You're watching my ass, aren't you?" I purposely threw in an extra sway of my hips as I climbed.

"Do I have eyes? Hell yes I'm watching your ass." I felt Reid's weight on the ladder as I ascended the last rung and my head popped out into the night.

I hadn't realized how stifling the air was down there until I was able to fill my lungs with the clean air outside.

Distracted by my thoughts I jumped when I heard the wooden door close behind me. "Geez, give a woman a heart attack. I wasn't kidding when I said I can't take much more today." I felt Reid's presence as he came up behind me, and the strength of his hands on my hips calmed me immediately.

"I'm sorry. Listen, let's head back in for the night. We've got a lot to go over, and it's dark now. We can head back over to the plantation house tomorrow to finish looking around and finalize planning details." Reid spoke as I tried to re-orient myself.

"Yeah, I'm not going back in that house until daylight. Where are we?" I asked still unable to gain my exact bearings.

"We're on the opposite side of the property, the cook's house is back that way. It's a little walk but at least we aren't underground anymore." Reid nodded his head in the opposite direction as we began our walk back under the open air of the night sky.

"The cook's house. That's what the boy said too." I thought back to my conversation with the little boy when I arrived. It feels like a lifetime ago.

"The boy? What boy? You've spoken to someone else out here?" Reid looked back at me, his eyes clouding with worry.

"Yeah, but it was a young boy. Maybe ten or twelve years old at the most. It was a strange conversation actually, but he was here when I arrived. I thought I was meeting Laurel for a set of keys, but when I got here there was no one here, and the gate was locked. That's when the boy arrived and handed me the key to the gate."

"We'll look into it. I haven't been made aware of there being anyone else on this property. We know they are preparing for a shipment, but I'm not sure why they would have sent a little boy out here to meet you. It doesn't make any sense." I could see Reid working through various scenarios in his mind as he thought.

"Reid, I know you're here to protect me, but how much danger are we in…really?" I asked hesitantly, nervous as to what his answer would be.

"Ever shot a gun?"

"Nope."

"Thrown a grenade?"

"Can't say that I have."

"You're about to learn. Welcome to level ten, princess. Shit's about to get real."

CHAPTER TWENTY-SEVEN
HOLLY

"Shut up, so you're telling me that Duke Karrington III was never a doctor? Who the hell was I on a date with?" I shoved another forkful of ramen noodles into my mouth as I sat on the wicker sofa on the opposite side from Reid, my legs tangled in his as we ate.

"Special Agent Anthony Bennett. Don't say the word date when you're talking about yourself and another man Holly. The only man you date is me." He pointed a plastic fork at me from across the couch, his voice serious but his eyes playful.

"Is that right, Special Agent Reid Chapman? You know, that's super sexy by the way." I ran my bare toes over his thigh and watched his eyes light.

"Not the first time I've heard that, and it's Senior Special Agent to you." He grinned adorably as he continued to eat.

"Watch it, same goes for you. I don't share, and

remember, you're teaching me how to throw grenades tomorrow, so don't tempt me into becoming a felon."

I watched Reid's face transform from light and fun to serious. "Look, Holly, we don't know exactly why they've involved you in their business dealings. All this time, they've left you in the dark. To bring you in at such a pivotal turning point is concerning. At best, you're a liability to them, which makes you dead. At worst, who the hell knows what Victor and Sylv are planning. Bennett wasn't working for us that night. Who did you say set up that dinner?"

"Um, well Til did. She said he was friends with Kris. She's been trying to set me up for ages though." Reid placed his styrofoam bowl down on the floor next to the couch and picked up a laptop that was hooked through some special plug in the black box behind the couch.

"What's your relationship like with Mistletoe? How well do you know her husband? Kristopher Trainor, right?" Reid's fingers flew across the keyboard in concentration never once looking up at me as he spoke.

"Stop saying Mistletoe, it sounds weird and awkward. She's the oldest and I'm the youngest, so we're different. Noel and I have always been closer. Tilly was the people pleaser, she's involved in the country club, even lives in the same neighborhood as my parents. I don't know Kris that well. He's a foot doctor, quiet, reserved. He comes from money, too. I don't know, I just always kind of ignored him, he seemed boring as hell." I tried to think back to the interactions I'd had with Kris in the past, but there just weren't that many.

"So, she's the oldest. Mafia is generational, but given

was hiding in plain sight this entire time, sipping drinks by the pool at the damn country club. They served you up to us on a silver platter, and while we chased our own asses they were working in the background. Shit, that's why Bennett was there, and he saw me too. That only further confirmed that their plan was working. They were playing us both." His hands gripped my thighs as he kneeled eye level in front of me.

"Oh God, so many things make sense now. I just can't believe, after everything we've been through. Wait, Noel isn't somehow involved in this is she?" My thoughts raced as I began questioning my relationship with everyone in my family.

"We're still fairly certain she's not associated. When has she ever followed the crowd? Her social makeup doesn't match the profile. No, I think she's been in the dark just as much as you have, but you were an easier target for them. You were the obvious choice." I tried to focus on Reid's skin on mine, tried to let the good outweigh the bad because now is not the time to become overwhelmed, even when I know I should be drowning right now. There isn't time for that. While I know Reid is more than willing to save me if that happens, I don't want to need a savior. I want to be strong enough to save myself.

"I just can't believe it, my own family. Why would they do this?" I pushed my hair back out of my face in frustration. I'm more angry than anything. I'm not hurt, I don't have the sense of loss you might expect given the circumstances. You can't lose something that you never had, and love wasn't something of abundance in my household growing up.

"Look at me, Holly. You can't question the actions of people like your father and your sister. The minds of people like that, they defy the laws of logic. That's something I had to learn the hard way a long time ago. The evil is everywhere, it exists all around us, I've seen it more times than I care to remember and so many times that I will never be able to forget. But then I see you, and you're my light in the darkness of the world. You give me hope that everything I've seen, everything I've had to do to get to this point, it was all worth it."

-o-

REID

I stare into Holly's blue eyes as I kneel in front of the small couch that she sits on, and I see the fight that burns so brightly inside of her. When so many would have crumbled under the weight of the news she's heard today, she sits in front of me fearless.

Victor Adkins unknowingly gave his daughter a gift, and what's better? He has no idea. He's oblivious to the fact that his youngest daughter will be the one to bring him to his knees. They thought they could use her and discard her, but she's so much stronger than they gave her credit for. They've underestimated her strength, and that's how we win this war.

Reaching forward, I pulled Holly's face to mine, wanting to taste her, needing to bathe in the light that surrounds her. She didn't hesitate, sliding off the couch and straddling my lap on the wooden floor, her body molded to mine, and exact fit.

"Reid." My name rolled off her tongue and onto mine as she slid it into my mouth and pressed her plump lips to mine. There was no rush, no sense of urgency, she was savoring me.

I pushed my fingers through the soft strands of her hair as I pulled her closer, inhaling her sweet, pure scent, allowing it to calm my nerves.

I have twenty-four hours to make sure Holly is prepared to fight a battle she was always meant to lose. But losing isn't an option. We will fight, and we will win.

Tomorrow will be hell, so tonight, I allow her to take me to church.

Effortlessly, I lifted Holly with me as I stood from our spot on the floor and carried her to the bedroom, laying her out on full display in front of me on top of the sheets.

The moonlight is bright tonight as it filters through the windows and illuminates her skin. She's glowing, her golden locks frame her face like a halo.

"I can't get enough of you, Holly. I told you when we met that I always get what I want, and I want to keep you. Forever." I stood at the end of the bed between her legs as she watched me, thoughtfully. She's wearing a pair of black boy shorts tonight with a matching black tank top that contrasts against the light shades of her hair.

"Love was never meant for me to keep. Love is timeless, and unyielding. I don't want you forever, Reid." My heart tripped over itself as I was held captive by her words.

She sat up on her elbows as she looked directly into my blue eyes before she finally broke the heavy silence that hung between us. "Death is just as inevitable as life.

No, I don't want to keep you forever because forever has an expiration date. Our souls, our souls live on for an eternity. Keep me for eternity Reid." Air whooshed from my lungs as she reached for the hem of my grey t-shirt, and I let her pull me down over her body.

She kissed my jaw, my lips, down my neck, until she got frustrated with the fabric between us and I lifted my shirt off over my head, leaving me in a pair of government issued sweatpants that I've had since my academy days.

Her hands roamed slowly over my abs and down the thin line of hair on my stomach. Sitting up on her knees, she pulled off her tank top, exposing her perfect pink nipples, but before I could reach for them her mouth was on me again. She followed the invisible lines she drew with her fingers over my chest with her mouth. When she reached my nipples, she swirled her tongue around them lightly biting down, the sting causing a low groan to escape from my lips.

My eyes were transfixed by her movements as I watched her hips spread and the curvature of her spine bend. She leaned forward and continued to follow the line down my chest until she reached the waistband of my sweatpants. Using her small hands, she pushed them down until they were halted by my thighs, my hard cock bounced between us, and she smiled up at me seductively before taking the head between her warm lips.

"Fuck, Holly." I let the tops of my thighs hit the bed as she sucked the length of my cock down her throat. Placing one hand on her head and using the other to grip one of her full breasts, I allowed her to set her own pace as she slowly pulled back until the tip of my cock was on the very edge of her lips. Wrapping her soft hands around the base she lightly squeezed and then slid her tongue around the rim of the head of my cock. My body jerked involuntarily beneath her touch as a deep pressure began to build in my lower abdomen.

She pulled back only to dip back in and swipe the tip of my cock with her tongue, licking the pre-cum before it could drip. "Reid, you taste delicious." She smiled, and I was hypnotized by the moisture on her lips. She drew me into her mouth once more and swallowed me down until I hit the back of her throat eliciting a soft moan that sent vibrations of electric shock down my legs.

I tried to hold out, I waited until I couldn't take it any longer. It took all of my restraint to pull away from her, pushing her back onto the bed until she was once again laid out in front of me, legs spread open. The moisture from her pussy soaked through her underwear and coated her lean thighs.

"No, I need to be inside of you when I come." I didn't even recognize my own voice; it was rough and tight with restraint.

I finished stepping out of my sweatpants and then reached forward pulling off her underwear and dropping them to the floor beside my bare feet.

Picking up her foot, I placed a kiss on the inside of her ankle, lightly trailing my lips up her calf until I reached the bend of her knee. She jerked as I placed kisses on the delicate skin behind her kneecap. Placing her foot down on the bed, I did the same thing with the other side until her legs were positioned, propped open, and she was fully exposed to me.

Mine.

I climbed her body, resting an elbow on either side of her head, allowing the tip of my nose to touch hers. My cock sat rigid in the moisture between her legs, painfully begging for entrance with each beat of my heart.

"I thought I was invincible until you brought me to my knees." My words were raw with emotion, my lips so close to hers as I spoke.

"I'm not your weakness, Reid. Find your strength in me. We were made to be a team." Her eyes watched me with wonder as she lifted her hand to brush her fingers over the side of my face.

I rested my forehead on hers and fisted the sheets on either side of her head. "I can't lose you, Holly. Tomorrow, I can't..." My words were broken as the reality of what we would be facing was suffocating me, stealing this moment from me.

"Find your strength, Reid. Believe in us. I love you, Reid Chapman." She pressed her lips against mine, and her words filled my lungs with hope.

My angel in the flesh.

My redemption from the evil.

I lined my bare cock up with her slick entrance and slowly, relishing every single inch I pushed inside of her until our skin was flush and she was full. "Say it again, Holly."

"I love you, Reid. No matter what happens tomorrow, my soul is yours for eternity."

"My soul is yours." I repeated her words back to her as I set a slow pace, sliding out to the tip and back in, touching the spot deep inside of her that I know she craved and tortured us both.

Her hands gripped my ass, pulling me closer, putting pressure on her sensitive clit as our bodies moved fluidly together.

"Please, Reid, I need you to come inside of me. More, I need more." I pushed us harder, further as my cock swelled inside of her impossibly tight pussy.

"Now, Holly, come on my cock." I slammed into her and felt her body contract as my name left her lips in a chant that set off the fireworks in my spine. I filled her pussy with my cum and held her to me, her body engulfing me. I buried my face in her neck as the intensity of my orgasm rocked me to the core.

"Eternity." I whispered the word into her hair as the last of my orgasm was rung out from my body.

CHAPTER TWENTY-EIGHT
HOLLY

Reid lay on top of me until my toes went numb, but I didn't dare ask him to move. This strong, arrogant man needs me just as much as I need him, if not more so. His vulnerability is captivating.

We laid together as Reid whispered promises into the night until exhaustion finally pulled us under, the intensity of the day finally catching up to us.

-

"Holly, Miss Holly." Heat burned my skin and a thin layer of sweat made me feel sticky all over as I stood alone and listened for the innocent calling of a familiar voice.

Standing in the grand entrance of the plantation house, my eyes finally landed on him at the landing of the second story, at the top of the stairs.

"Hey, you never told me your name." I spoke but he ignored me, his eyes transfixed on something behind me.

"Be careful Miss Holly. I tried to warn you." His face

held no expression as the words left his mouth, his stance somber.

Panic began to fill my chest as his words resonated with me. "What do you mean? What warning? Who are you?" He slowly shook his head back and forth, still refusing to make eye contact with me but acknowledging me none-the-less.

"You said it yourself, death is just as inevitable as life. I'm sorry." My heart raced as he turned to leave. Those words were never meant for his ears. How?

"Wait!" My breathing came quickly as I sprinted up the stairs, but when I got to the top, he was gone.

-

"Holly!" My name was a shout as it rang through the night and woke me from the darkness that clouded my mind in sleep.

"Holly, wake up! What was that?" My eyes adjusted to the darkness to find Reid standing over me with a gun firmly held in his right hand.

"What the fuck, Reid? Really? A gun?" I watched the heavy rise and fall of his bare chest as realization set in over both of us and he looked to his hand, setting the gun down gently beside the bed.

"You scared the life out of me. Your mumbling woke me up, and then your breathing picked up. Before I knew it, you were screaming for someone to wait. I didn't know what was happening, I reacted." He shrugged as if that should be explanation enough, glancing to the gun. I rolled my eyes and sat up in the bed, trying to recall the details of my dream from the haze of my memory.

"It was the boy. The boy I told you about, from the

gate. He was there, in my dream, but it seemed so real. He kept saying something about a warning and apologizing. I was scared, but it's ok. I'm fine now, it was just a bad dream." I grabbed his wrist with my hand, needing him to calm down. We're both on edge, and it's probably early morning at this point. We won't sleep tonight; we need to be rested.

"That's easy for you to say, my forever was just reduced by about twenty years. I'm going to make some calls and try to get some research done. There's no way I'm going back to sleep. You get some rest, and when the sun's up, we'll get started." Reid leaned down and placed a kiss on my forehead, running his hand through his disheveled, dark hair before he turned to leave and walked out of the bedroom.

I'm not tired, not anymore, but I didn't follow. I could sense his need for time. Reid thrives on being in control, and my being here means that his priorities are now split. Whether he realizes it or not, he's doubting his ability to juggle all of the balls he has up in the air, and this case is something he's been working on his entire career. So many lives are at stake, and it all ends tonight.

-o-

"Hold your wrist steady and lift your right elbow just slightly." Reid's firm body presses up against my back as he guides my hands with his gun, aiming in the distance towards a makeshift target he set-up for the training that he insists that I have.

I've never really had a reason to learn how to shoot a

gun. Although, given my family history, it's shocking that I can't even recall touching one in my lifetime. My family may be mafia, but I will give it to my father, he didn't leave weapons lying around the house.

I was hesitant at first, but the minute Reid slid in behind me and gripped my hands in his, I decided that learning to shoot might not be so bad after all. We've already shot over one hundred rounds because Reid is adamant that I know what I'm doing. I'm a quick learner, and we probably could have stopped a while ago, but I might be playing dumb…just a little.

Shooting with Reid is an aphrodisiac I didn't anticipate, and I'm not ready for it to end yet. I know our time is limited, and I can only train so much in twenty-four hours, but I'm soaking it in. I'm trying to pretend that maybe this isn't as serious as I know it is. I'm trying to enjoy these moments with Reid before all hell breaks loose and things get dangerous.

"Focus Holly, you don't have to be exact. If your situation is serious enough that it requires you to point this gun at anyone, you always aim with the intentions of taking down your opponent. If that means someone dies, well, they shouldn't have been an asshole in the first place. If you felt like the danger warranted a gun, then someone was going to die anyway, and it's not going to be you. Shoot to kill." Reid's words were like sex on his lips as they raked over his dry throat. He didn't go back to sleep, neither one of us did, but I gave him the space he needed. I let him work while I tried to come to terms with the hand I'd been dealt yesterday. How has this become my life? It still seems so surreal.

We watched the morning sun as it rose over the trees of the forest. I fired shot after shot, the loud sound echoing through the abandoned property.

"When do I get to throw the grenade?" I turned my head slowly so that my lips brushed against Reid's stubbled cheek as I spoke.

"Handing you a grenade scares the shit out of me woman. I will show you how to initiate it, but we aren't playing with explosives today. We don't have the right equipment, and I need you not to be deaf when everything goes down tonight. If you have to use the grenade, things have gotten bad; if things are that bad, we're in survival mode. The grenade is your last resort."

"The rest of your team, will they be here?" I asked as I handed Reid his gun back and reluctantly stepped out of his hold.

"I expect them to be here. We're going to need backup. Everything I know is on a need-to-know basis right now, and according to my sources, it's better that we don't know the specifics. I know time and place, but if one of us were to get apprehended and questioned, what we don't know might save our lives. Or it could get us killed. Really, it could go either way. I'm counting on your sister and father having a soft spot for you, but we can't be certain. They are the ones that put you in this situation to begin with." I followed behind Reid, gathering up the remainder of the ammunition and headed back to the small house we've been sharing.

"Listen, Holly, I've been doing some research on your friend. The boy? My team sent over some images, and I want you to take a look at them." Reid pulled his laptop out after we walked into the house, clicking around on the keys and pulling up images.

"Wait, that one, right there." I pointed at the screen and paused as I took in the grainy black and white image that was pulled up on Reid's screen. It was the boy from the gate, the boy from my dream, but the photo was old and damaged. The black and white image was faded, and the edges of the scanned photo were torn and tattered. He stood next to a woman with similar features, both unsmiling, stoic.

"Who is he?" I asked as Reid's blue eyes searched my face.

"Holly, this photo is over a hundred years old. The woman was Hubert Anderson's mistress. And the head cook of the household. She was given this house to live in with her son. The young boy is her son. Better known as the bastard son of Hubert Anderson, the only child he ever fathered. That's why they were given this house, why they lived when so many others died. The cook, she claimed to be in love with Anderson despite his tendencies. When she got word of his murder, she killed their son and then herself in a fit of rage. This boy has been dead for over one hundred years." I stood frozen in the small living space of the house as Reid told me the story of my apparition, he chose me.

Why me? Why is he seeking me out? What is he trying to tell me? The warning.

"But, I saw him. He had the key! I felt the warmth from his body. Ghosts are supposed to be cold, Reid!" My words were a shout, but I wasn't angry. I just wanted to understand.

"I don't doubt it, I've seen enough to know that some things are unexplainable. The boy feels a connection to you for some reason. He sees what we can't see, he feel's what we can't feel. He's trapped between this life and the next, and for some reason he is trying to tell you something." Reid gently sat the computer down on the sofa and pulled me into his arms.

Taking a deep breath, I asked my next question, despite stories of spirits and souls trapped between worlds, we're running out of time.

"So, are you ready to go back into the main house?" I asked, knowing that our purpose has changed, or at least mine has. Yesterday I was studying for a renovation project that was never meant to come to fruition. I didn't even bother calling Laurel today. This project has always been a façade. Today our purpose is to finish mapping out the layout of the plantation house. Reid and I have both studied the blueprints, but the house has been damaged by fire, and like the elevator, things in that house aren't always what they seem. We need to walk through and map the layout with our own eyes in case we find ourselves lost in it tonight.

"The better question is, are you ready to go back in?" Reid raised an eyebrow as he pulled back from me and looked down into my eyes with questions.

"Yesterday you dropped us down a secret elevator shaft in the dark. My life flashed before my eyes. Now, I find out that a spirit from another century is trying to give me warnings. What's the worst that could happen?" I smiled as Reid rolled his eyes at me.

What else can I do but smile? I have a car. I could

easily climb in and drive far, far away from here. Maybe call Noel and catch the next flight out of this country. Instead, I smile because I'm very obviously losing it.

Maybe I'm a little insane, because I follow this man into the bedroom and allow him to strap a gun to my waist. I let him wrap a leather band around my calf and feel the cold steel of a knife blade as it lies against my skin. I let him pull a bulletproof undershirt that's too big over my chest, but he tightens it down over me anyway and inspects it with an intense scrutiny.

I watched Reid as he dressed, pulling on a pair of khaki cargo pants and a black t-shirt over his body that's armored far more heavily than mine. I stared at him as he pulled back on his combat boots and wondered how I was so oblivious to the truth of this man when I met him. Now that I've seen this side of him, I can't see him any other way.

But I guess that's why he's so good at what he does.

He's a trained chameleon, but I see through the front that he wears so easily.

I can see his heart because it was made for me.

He acts like a badass, and truth – he is. But he's so much more than that, he's also gentle and caring. He's a protector. That's what makes him so damn good at his job. That's how I know we won't die tonight. Maybe I'm naïve, but I refuse to believe that tonight is the night we lose the battle against the evil that Reid has fought so hard against his entire life. Despite my bad dream and the worry that I feel radiating off of Reid with every minute that ticks off of the clock, I feel it in my bones. Tonight, we win.

CHAPTER TWENTY-NINE
REID

"Everything ok?" I asked as Holly paused in the front entrance of the plantation house, her eyes locked onto the landing at the top of the stairs.

"I'm fine, just a little déjà vu. It's nothing." I stared at her exposed arms and watched the goosebumps rise to the top of her skin as she tried to deny being bothered by the memory of her dream last night. We both know she's not lying to me; she's lying to herself. She's bothered, but she's too damn stubborn to admit it, so we push forward, fear be damned. We don't have the luxury of time to devote to it anyway.

She scared the shit out of me last night. I'm no stranger to nightmares, I wake from them myself on a regular basis, but when the panic in Holly's voice registered in my brain, when I knew she should have been sleeping, I was immediately put on alert.

Her skin was cold and clammy, covered in sweat, and

the elevated panic in her voice rang through the quiet room, piercing my ears and my heart. My first instinct was to protect. My hand was on my gun before I inhaled a second breath. I could read the fear in her eyes when she woke, but it wasn't me she was fearful of as I stood over her with a gun in my hand. No, she was fearful of what she saw in the depths of her slumber. Evil is like that; premonitions, the unknown, it will find a way to permeate your subconscious and take over your mind.

That's why so few are cut out to handle this lifestyle. That's why I was always ok with the idea of not having a life partner. There are only so many Emily's of the world. And maybe, I might be concerned about bringing Holly into this life, but the truth is that she's stronger than both of us. She holds a power so few possess, and it radiates from inside of her. She is the light in the darkness.

"Where do you want to start? I might suggest the elevator, but..." I allowed my voice to trail off as I attempted to lighten the atmosphere that has followed us around like a dark cloud since I told Holly the truth about her background and my own.

I've spoken with Alex on and off since yesterday and kept him up to date on most everything as it unfolds out here, but things have been exceptionally quiet from his end. He's giving up minimal information, which makes me think that there is something the Bureau is holding back. I've been a part of this organization long enough to know that if they are holding something back, there is a valid reason. Alex is well aware of where Bennett's loyalties lie as well as the Bureau. Past that, I trust every other person on this team with my life. What's more than that, I trust them with Holly's.

I've been reviewing information with Holly non-stop over the last twenty-four hours and we've trained as much as is allowable in such a short time frame. Now we bide our time, and we plan escape routes and back-up plans. Plan A is easy, but in this line of work Plan A will fail, it's inevitable. It's Plan X, Y, and Z that we need to be prepared to initiate.

"You know, now that I think about it, every single time I've been in an elevator with you, something utterly insane happens. First with the kidnapping, then with the whole near-death experience. You really aren't to be trusted in a lift. I think we'll take the stairs." She brushed her jean clad ass past me, and her scent lingered as she walked, momentarily intoxicating me.

I let her walk ahead, until her sneaker hit the first stair and I was on her, hands gripping her hips and teeth grazing the skin of her delicate neck. "The kidnapping was fun though, no? You like to be chased Holly; you get off on the fear." She stopped her ascent as she leaned her head back onto my shoulder and gave my mouth more room to work.

"Mmmmm…" A soft moan escaped her lips, the sound bringing the sexual tension that constantly lies beneath the surface of my skin when I'm around this woman to life.

"Admit it, admit you like it when I scare you." I squeezed her hips, my grip hard enough that I knew it hurt. I was bruising, but she didn't fight my hold.

"Only you, Reid. Now get the fuck off me, and let's go look at the rest of this house." Her lips curled into a smile as she yanked her hips from my grip and swayed her gorgeous ass up the steps in front of me, leaving me to trail behind her. She might admit that she loves me now, but her mouth is still fire, alive with the sass that I'm infatuated with.

Turning a corner at the top of the landing, I continued to follow Holly to an open doorway, a room that we unsuccessfully attempted to enter yesterday before the elevator sent us plummeting into the tunnels.

-o-

"Oh my God. Do you think those are the same chains?" Holly stopped in the doorway to the grand master bedroom and covered her mouth with her hand, her smile gone.

"What do you think?" I asked, realizing the grave answer to my question before the words finished leaving my mouth.

Slowly, she walked into the room, examining it closely but careful not to touch.

The original four-poster bed sat in the middle of the room. The bedding was long gone, only leaving a mattress covered in dirt and dried blood. Stepping in front of Holly, I walked closer to the bed to get a better look. This blood is fresh, days old at most.

My eyes darted to every corner of the room, looking for things that appear out of place. Searching for the danger. I can feel it in the air like a living, breathing thing.

"Holly, be ready." I barely got the words out as I watched an old original vinyl record player seemingly shift on its own and come to life.

An old scratchy song played over the speaker, but it didn't take me long to recognize the familiar words…

Have a holly jolly Christmas
And when you walk down the street
Say hello to friends you know
And everyone you meet
Ho Ho the mistletoe
Is hung where you can see
Somebody waits for you
Kiss her once for me

"Reid." Holly's voice was solid as she spoke from behind me. Her hand brushed my hip, a silent warning. I held my hand on my gun, ready. They're here.

"It's time." I spun us around when I felt the floor shift beneath my feet, pinning Holly's back to the wall, knowing that if someone was going to get to her, they would have to go through me first.

"Til, what the absolute fuck are you doing?" Holly's shouted words from behind me momentarily stunned me. I'm not sure what I expected, but what I did not expect was her booming voice from behind me, seething with a pent-up anger that I could have never anticipated.

"Sweet, sweet Holly. Did you like my song? Cool trick, huh? I don't know, it just felt appropriate. Welcome to the fun house. I see you've met the playboy of the Bureau Reid 'I fuck everything with legs' Chapman. But then again, you're quite the *Ho Ho* yourself now, aren't you? See what I did there?" The smile on Trainor's face was venom as she baited Holly, and it worked, if the way Holly pushed against my hold to get to her sister was any indication.

"She's luring you, Holly. Stay levelheaded for me." My words were quiet as I spoke to Holly under my breath, but my eyes never left the blue eyes of her sister.

It's strange how similar two people can look, even share the same blood, same eyes, same hair, but how vastly different they are as humans.

An angel fights my hold at my back as I stare into the eyes of the devil in front of me.

"Aw, how cute. You're a team now? That's going to make this even more fun."

"What happened to you, Til? What about Kris? Your kids?" Holly spouted off questions rapid fire as she demanded answers from behind me, undeterred by her sister's psychotic behavior.

"That my cue? Baby, why do you always get started without me?" Kristopher Trainor walked into the room from the entrance to the elevator shaft wearing an outfit very similar to mine. Khaki cargo pants, black t-shirt, but he didn't try to hide his weapons, an automatic rifle slung over his shoulder as he reached his wife and leaned down to kiss her on the cheek.

"Well, I had that one pinned wrong." Holly huffed from behind me.

"I'm the heir to the Adkins family name, little sister. Don't you see? You're useless to our family now. Honestly, you always have been. Redundant. Noel was the backup, and you were just an accident. Kris and I are already molding the next generation, so really, we don't need you anymore." Holly stiffened from behind me, and my blood ran cold at the insinuation in the words that

Mistletoe spoke. The pure, unfiltered hate in her eyes.

"If I'm so useless, why am I here? Why me and not Noel? Why bother keeping me around this long?" Holly asked a question we both already knew the answer to as I tried to think of a way out of here. She's trying to buy us some time.

They're coming through the shaft, and the only other exit that isn't a window from the second story is the main door that Holly's sister is currently blocking.

"We were watching, we're always watching. We caught wind of your little fling here with our favorite agent. How long has it been, Chapman? Ten years we've been playing this game of cat and mouse? Just kids when we started." She picked at her fingernails as she spoke, as if the conversation was boring her.

"We need these tunnels; they'll change everything for our industry, but pretty boy here was getting too close. His damn father was always a liability, I tried to tell daddy that, but he wouldn't listen. This way we get rid of you both, and poof, no more problems. No worries, Reid, we'll fix it so your sweet mommy thinks you died doing something honorable." She shrugged, crossing her arms in front of her body as she stood across the room defensively.

"We aren't dying today Missile Adkins." I watched the small flash of panic as it passed her eyes, and then it was gone.

"I know who you are and so does the Bureau. This ends tonight." I tried to remain calm for Holly's sake, but with no way to alert Alex, it might be hours before our support shows up. We don't have hours.

"Who said anything about death? Oh wait, it was me. I did. But that would be too easy now, wouldn't it? How about we play first? Daddy should already be moving the first shipment downstairs as we speak. What do you think Kris? Wanna play?"

CHAPTER THIRTY
HOLLY

Everything happened so fast. One minute Reid was pressing my body between his and the wall of the master bedroom, and the next minute I was running.

The muscles in my legs burned as Reid yelled at me to move faster as we flew down the grand staircase in the plantation house. Shots rang out behind us, but I didn't dare turn around, I just kept moving. If we could just make it outside, we could get some coverage, but right now we fly through the halls of the house completely exposed.

I listened carefully for Reid's breathing behind me, I needed to know that chaos might be erupting around us, but as long he still breathes, we're going to make it – we have to. I should be terrified, but it's strange, I feel empowered. The adrenaline surge is renewing the energy in my veins and pushing me harder, faster.

Until we hit the first-floor landing and I am knocked

to the floor from the side, the air forced from my lungs with the impact as a familiar body uses his full force to tackle me to the ground. Duke, or I guess as Reid lovingly likes to refer to him, *fucking Bennett*, lands on top of me, restraining my body under his.

My eyes dart wildly around the grand foyer, looking for Reid, only seconds have passed from the moment I last heard his breath; his body lies limp next to the large double door entrance of the house. My heart seizes, and I kick out wildly, fighting my captor.

"Look at that, the youngest mafia princess. Don't tell your sister, but I always thought you were the prettiest. I knew you would end up under me eventually. I saw you in the elevator princess, I know you like it rough." I continued to fight his hold as his stale breath bathed my face and bile pooled in my throat.

"You don't get to call me princess." Looking into his eyes I spat in his face, causing him to reel back in disgust.

"What the fuck is it with you people and the spitting? Bitch." His bare hand stung my skin as he pulled back and slammed his palm across my face. I tasted the blood as it left my mouth, but it only fueled the fire that licked my insides.

"What did you do to him?" The words burned my throat as I swallowed down blood and fought for oxygen under the weight of Bennett's body.

"Who? Oh, your little boyfriend? Don't fret, I didn't kill him. I just put him to sleep for a minute. We'll let him get a nap, and then when he wakes up, if he's a good boy, he can enjoy the show. Now, let's get you back upstairs where you belong." Bennett wrapped my hair around his hand and pulled me to my feet as another man wearing a ski mask that covered most of his face, who I'm guessing is one of the soldiers Reid was telling me about, stepped into the foyer to hoist Reid over his shoulder and drag his lifeless body behind us.

I didn't make it easy; I felt my hair being ripped from my scalp, but I fought Bennett as he continued to force my body back up to the second-floor landing and into the master bedroom.

I remained conscious as my sister, a woman that I can no longer fathom that I share blood with, clasped cold, silver metal down over my wrists, chaining me to the large bed in the center of the master bedroom and throwing the keys at the soldier, leaving me defenseless.

Bennett nodded toward Til before stepping out of the room and disappearing into the hallway.

"Where do you want him?" The unidentified soldier spoke to Kris who tilted his chin towards the wall that sat directly across the room from the bed that had now become my prison.

The rancid smell from the mattress permeated my senses and made my gut turn with nausea.

Wake up, Reid. I need you, wake up.

"Where to start? Where to start?" Til walked back and forth in front of the bed, tapping her chin in exaggeration and pacing as she thought out loud.

"You think she's armed?" Kris spoke up as he kicked Reid's lifeless body that sat slumped on the floor.

"Soldier, whatever your name is, get over there and frisk her for weapons. You can touch, but don't get carried away. We have plans for her." I tried to prepare my mind and body as the masked soldier approached the bed I was chained to.

His face was covered, but his eyes, his eyes were visible, and there was something oddly familiar about them. Some memory tugged at my brain as I watched him come closer, but I couldn't place it.

He didn't speak, but he didn't hesitate to lean his large frame over mine as he began touching my body, and I waited for him to find the weapons that Reid so carefully placed on me just this morning.

He started at the top and worked his way down. He ran his hands over my arms and then slid his gloved palm under my shirt, touching my bare skin with slow, calculated movements.

A smile glinted in his eyes, but it wasn't evil, who is this man?

Why do I know him?

And why does my heart remain calm when he comes near me? I should be freaking out, but I'm not and that's strangely comforting given my current predicament.

His hand brushed over the gun at my waist, and he yanked, pulling it out, and throwing it behind him to Kris, who caught the firearm with ease.

His hands skimmed down my jean covered legs and over the bulge at the back of my calf, but he didn't pause. I saw a flash in his eyes, but he left my weapon. Reaching behind me, his hand brushed my last resort.

I made Reid two promises as we prepared to leave the house today.

One: I would not let myself get dragged into the tunnels. Under no circumstances would I go underground. Die first.

Two: Last resort is the grenade. Pull it, throw it, run.

The soldiers hand touched the grenade that was carefully strapped to my back and his eyes shot to mine in surprise. Lifting an eyebrow, I smirked at him. He took my gun, but he didn't rat me out for my knife. Let's call this a test.

I saw the tiny movements in his neck as he shook his head in disbelief, but he left it alone. Instead, he reached his hand up to my blonde hair and pushed the lose strands behind my ear. He hovered over me on the bed, and a low chuckle rumbled from his chest. All the while I ignored the show he was putting on and my brain tried to place him. I have seen this man before, and he doesn't scare me. Where?

"Enough! Back off soldier, she's not yours. Maybe we'll let you play when we're done with her, but not yet. Come over here and secure Chapman before he wakes up. The tranquilizer Bennett used should be wearing off any minute. Disarm him as well. We don't want him dead…yet." Tilly barked orders at the soldier who I could swear was trying to speak to me with his eyes alone as he pulled away and climbed off of the bed; leaving me exposed and alone once again.

I tracked the soldier as he touched Reid's lifeless body and watched as he pulled rope from one of the pockets of his cargo pants and began securing Reid's arms behind his back.

I refused to speak, I would not beg, but in my mind, I was screaming as I pleaded with Reid to wake up.

Wake the fuck up, Chapman. You promised.

I thought we still had hours to prepare. Why are they early? And where is our backup? How much longer? And what if they don't make it in time?

"Ok Kris, give the kind agent here a few minutes to wake up, and then you can have your fun. I know how you feel about an audience. Bennett gets to go next because he's like a fucking chihuahua. I swear I can hear his cock barking from the damn hallway. If she's still alive after you finish, we'll toss her down below with the others. Unless you decide to share with this guy, and then he can get a turn before we hand her over." Tilly pulled a chair from the corner of the room and sat down, crossing one denim clad leg over the other. A sick smile pulled at her lips as the soldier kicked Reid in the ribs again to jar him from his sleep after securing his ropes and taking his weapons.

-o-
REID

Spinning. Spinning. Everything around me is spinning like a fucking merry-go-round of death.

My mouth is dry and chalky. It tastes like something metallic mixed with ass right now.

I tried to recall my last memory through the fog that is currently the state of my brain, but I keep coming up short.

Where am I?

What do I know?

I was on a case. Drugged. Have I been drugged? I'm trained to recognize most of the side effects of the more commonly used drugs and dissociative anesthetics. This is different though. My eyesight is so blurry, like I'm not wearing my contacts, but I must be. They feel itchy and burn, definitely a side effect of some sort.

God, if the spinning would just stop.

Bile rose in my throat, and I heaved to my side, vomiting on the floor; the relief was immediate. So much so that I was able to focus enough to regain some of my memory. Holly.

If they got to me…

"Hold still, bitch." A man's voice rang in my ears as a loud slap echoed through the room, and I continued to fight against the side effects of whatever I've been given. The evening sun streaming through the windows burned my eyes, but I forced them open and attempted to focus, finding myself in the same room I ran out of on Holly's heels earlier.

We didn't make it.

My shoulder burned, but it wasn't a bullet. No, the burn was different, almost like my bone was on fire inside of my body.

"I will kill you, Kris Trainor. I will rip your testicles from your body with my bare hands and feed them to you just like old man Anderson if you come near me." Holly, her words were fueled with hate and intensity. My vision focused enough for me to finally see her location in the room.

Her arms are in chains, similar to the ones we found in the tunnel, spread open and attached to either post of the master bed. Her shirt has been cut open at the front and exposes her breasts as Kristopher Trainor kneels on the bed, over her legs, in front of her with a knife.

I've trained for every situation, every scenario. The Bureau never trained me for this shit. For watching the woman that I love be attacked by another man as I sit helpless on the floor with my damn hands tied behind my back. Slamming my combat boots on the floor I bucked forward, making my presence known and garnering the attention of every other person in the room, including Holly.

"Reid, you're awake. About damn time." Holly smiled sweetly as she leaned forward and spit in Kris' face, drawing a smile from me, despite our dire situation. That's my girl.

The more I was able to focus my vision, the more I could see her. Her face was bruised, and blood smeared her arm and shoulder. But, she was smiling like a damn psycho even as Kris slid his blade over her thigh cutting through the denim she wore and drawing blood.

God, I love this woman, but I'm about to kill a son of a bitch.

Pulling on my wrists, I noticed that the end of one was fisted in my palm. Why? All I need to do is pull, and I'm free. My eyes searched the room again for clues until they landed on a man dressed as a soldier standing guard in the corner of the room. He's covered from top to toe, but his eyes darted to mine, and in that instant, I knew. Alex.

Relief washed over me as my chest filled with a renewed hope I didn't have moments ago. Holly might perch on that bed like a badass, but that doesn't take away the fact that she's still in chains and her sister sits in the chair to my left with an assault rifle draped across her lap.

As it stands, in this room it's two on two. I'm not underestimating the skills of Missile or Kris despite the fact that Alex and I are both trained agents. It's interesting the Bureau has him in the field instead of behind the computer. In all the years we've been doing this, Alex has only physically been in the field with us a handful of times.

There is only one reason why he would be in this room. Emily has to be here somewhere; my best guess would be that she's handling the situation in the tunnels. If they're moving a shipment down there, she's able to blend easier than she would be up here.

They must have received word that the shipment was coming early. I don't know any other reason they would already be here. Unfortunately, it looks like Holly and I were the last to know.

"Jesus, Kris, stop playing around and take what you want. We don't have all day. I need to be at the harbor by nightfall." Missile spoke up from her spot in the corner, hurrying her husband along and fueling my desire to accidently take her out point blank when the time comes. Sometimes accidents happen, what can I say, it's just a hazard of the job.

I looked over to Alex again, who held up three fingers behind his back.

A third person.

It's ok. Alex and I have been training for this day since we could walk. He might not actively work in the field, but he's been my ride or die since we defended the universe from evil more than twenty years ago. If we can somehow free Holly, we're still on an even playing field.

"Reid." My head felt heavy with the aftereffects of whatever drug they used on me, but my spine stiffened in an instant at the sudden terror I heard in her voice.

Kris' legs straddled either side of Holly as he sat his knife down on the bed beside her and unbuttoned the button of her jeans, smiling. "No one in this room is going to save you, Holly. I've waited for this day for so, so long. You've always thought you were so much better than us. I'm just a foot doctor, right? Stare at feet all day? So damn boring. You were wrong. How does that feel? You were wrong about Chet, and here you are, wrong again. Come to think of it, I miss that guy, he put you in your place, didn't he?"

He continued to taunt her as the oxygen in my bloodstream worked overtime to fuel the adrenaline that pulsed in my veins.

Not today asshole. My eyes landed on Alex who read the fire in mine.

He knows. He understands because he's been there too. He feels the inferno engulfing me just as sure as I do.

I've been in a lot of tense situations and have been able to remain calm, but fuck if I'm going to sit here and let this man touch what's mine.

I looked back at Missile, who was momentarily distracted by the show her husband was putting on, and then back to Alex who now held up five fingers, four fingers, three fingers…countdown…two fingers, one.

CHAPTER THIRTY-ONE
HOLLY

I stared just over Kris' shoulder and watched the exchange happening between Reid and the soldier in the corner.

Every other person in the room was completely oblivious, but I saw it in their eyes.

I still don't know who he is, but my instincts were right about him.

I feigned attention as I pretended to watch the little show my brother-in-law was putting on, and not draw attention to the two of them from my sister, who sat in a chair in the corner like she was the damn Queen of England.

I kicked out against Kris when he reached for the button on my jeans, but I saved my energy, not putting up too much of a fight…yet.

I'm watching Reid for a signal, I see the way the tip of his boot tips forward, then again. A countdown. It's time to get the hell out of here.

Knife to my left. Knife on my calf. Last resort.

Kris leaned in, his body covering mine as his tongue swiped at my exposed breasts, and he let out a low moan.

The soldier moved first, pulling a gun from his waist, one shot. I held in my gasp as I watched my sister slumped in the chair in the corner. Oh shit.

Within seconds Reid was on Kris, picking up the knife that lay beside my leg and running it across Kris' throat as blood poured over the both of us.

"I'm sorry baby, I'm so sorry." Reid repeated the words as he looked at me with a mixture of horror and disbelief.

I watched the soldier grab my sisters' rifle and run to the bedside, unlocking my wrists that were now numb from loss of blood.

"Good guy, Reid?" I spoke as quickly as I could. We have to move, now. Bennett is still in the hallway, and God knows who else is out there.

"Good guy. Go. You two go. Get her out of her. Whatever you do, do not look back. I've got Em. Run. Remember, Holly, last resort."

"Last resort." I repeated his words as I leapt from the bed behind the masked soldier and followed Reid's instructions. With one exception, I looked back. I turned as the soldier pulled me forward out of the master bedroom. I turned back and watched Reid's descent into the tunnel until I heard a familiar voice echo through the hallway.

"Run, Miss Holly. Run. I'm sorry!" His voice was distraught, pained. Where is he?

I looked, but I couldn't find him. That's when the shots rang out. A slew of curse words left the mouth of the soldier as he pushed me forward and began firing shots from behind me as we continued to move. We flew down the steps and this time…we made it. Only it wasn't Reid I could hear breathing behind me. It was the voice of a stranger, the soldier.

"Where are you?" He paused just outside the entrance of the house and yelled into the night sky. He pulled his hand to his ear and pressed on an earpiece that I noticed for the first time.

"The helicopter? What about the tunnels?" The tunnels. Reid's in the tunnels.

"You got them out? The explosives. Fuck. Fuck. Reid's down there." He ran a hand over his head that was covered with a black knit hat.

"It's too late, I've got her. How long?" He let out a pained breath as his eyes darted to me.

"We're too close. Shit. Ok, love you Em." He gripped my hand and pulled my body forward, towards the dark forest.

"Wait! Where is Reid? Where is he?" My throat burned as I screamed the words into the night.

"It's too late, we've got to get you out of here. We're too close. We have to run. Now!" The soldier continued to bark orders at me as I pulled against him and fought to turn back to the house. Rationally, I know I should listen to him, but I lost all rationality somewhere back before I stepped foot on this damn property.

"I'm not leaving him here!" My tears mixed with anger as I shouted at the soldier, but he wasn't having it. He picked me up like I weighed nothing and groaned when he threw me over his shoulder just as he'd done Reid earlier and began running. Harder, faster, as he counted the seconds out loud. We moved further into the forest until he threw my body down behind a fallen tree and landed on top of me, covering me.

Instantly, the ground shook and the night lit up like the sunrise with a force that I've never experienced before and hope to never experience again. I felt the heat on my skin and my ears rang as an explosion detonated, surrounding us.

The soldier continued to curse as his body covered mine, protecting me.

His words made no sense. Something about brothers, death in the night, capes with red letters. It was gibberish, but I could feel the defeat as it seeped from his body and into mine. I could feel his fear.

The house - gone, Reid. Oh God.

Debris began to rain down around us. The wound on my leg throbbed, and I couldn't tell whose blood was where, but none of it mattered. None of it matters if Reid is gone.

I felt the first crack of my heart. Then, without warning, it ruptured.

Reaching around to my back, I grabbed the grenade. My last resort.

I pulled the pin and threw it, aiming toward the house that no longer existed.

"You promised me, Reid Chapman." The words were torn from the rupture in my chest.

My body heaved, and I convulsed with emotion as the

soldier picked me back up again and began running.

That's the last thing I remember before everything went dark, and I welcomed the peaceful slumber.

-o-
REID

"Thirteen!"

I strained to hear through the headset I pulled on as the loud noise of the propellor blades cut through the black ink of the night sky.

"What?"

"Thirteen times I have saved your ass, Chapman." I smirked at her sassy response as I looked out over the property down below as it burnt to the ground.

"I know you secretly love me Em, that's why you keep saving my arrogant ass. Don't worry, your secret is safe with me." I joked with her, but the mood was anything but light.

Straton isn't exaggerating, she saved my ass. The tunnels were abandoned when I finally made it to the bottom of the elevator shaft, but I saw the carefully placed explosives, and I hauled ass. I ran as fast as my legs would take me to the ladder that Holly and I used, and prayed it was still there.

Where was everyone? Where was the shipment?

I could hear the noise from the helicopter as soon as I opened the hatch in the middle of the field that was my escape route. We barely made it off the ground before the first explosion went off.

Emily was talking to Alex over her radio when I got in. He has her. I know that he's protecting her with his life but that doesn't stop my heart from seizing in my chest as I watch a second explosion detonate on the property that surrounds what's left of the old plantation house.

"Check in again, Emily. What the fuck was that?" The urgency in my voice carried through the microphone in my headset.

I listened to her voice ricochet through the line over and over again as she tried to make contact with Alex and simultaneously pilot us further away from danger. Further away from the other half of my heart.

"Check in, Alex. Check in." Nothing.

"Alex, dammit, check in." Silence.

My eyes met hers in the reflection of the glass, and I could read the words that she wasn't saying.

The last resort.

EPILOGUE
REID

"Thanks director, we appreciate everything, but I think we'll stay out here and enjoy our R&R a little while longer." I wrapped my arm around her exposed waist and pulled her to me on the covered lounge that overlooked the ocean. Her laughter echoed around us, and I soaked it in.

I hit end on my virtual meeting with the Bureau and shut down my satellite laptop, pushing it to the side. I ran my hand over the curve of her hip, brushing my fingers over the red tie of her bikini bottoms.

"I love you so fucking much, Holly Chapman." My words were rough with emotion as my eyes caught hers from across the lounge.

I'm still recovering.

Recovering from the unknown, from the moment I thought I lost it all.

It seemed like a lifetime before we got a frantic call

from Alex that he had Holly and needed us to pick them up. They were further into the woods surrounding the property than we expected. Alex lost service at some point before he was finally able to re-establish the connection and contact us.

Ryan Walsh had a private jet waiting for us that we boarded as soon as we set the helicopter down on the tarmac.

Walsh and his wife, along with their long-time employee Eliza, were keeping the Straton children temporarily while we sorted through the disaster this case had become. It wasn't safe for them yet. We couldn't return until we were cleared of all charges and all of our major players were apprehended.

We had to leave the country until we got clearance from the Bureau to return.

According to Emily, their raid was unsanctioned. They weren't given a choice; they had to make some tough decisions and move quickly.

The red tape was taking too long, and Alex had picked up some insider knowledge that the shipment was moving in earlier than we initially anticipated.

Given the evidence we were able to compile in such a short period of time, our team got Wilks in his home and arrested him. The shipment never made it to Anderson House, it was intercepted in transit by our guys.

Emily located Victor Adkins at the harbor, where she shot him once in each leg, disabling him, before calling him into our guys and leaving a sweet little note for them pinned to his chest. Something about not being able to run away in prison with two bum legs. Who knows really when it comes to Emily.

The helicopter was already waiting for her at the harbor. She got to Anderson house in record time, carefully placing the explosives in the tunnels while Alex and I took on Missile and Kris upstairs.

According to the reports that Alex was able to pull down from the federal case file, they never made it out of the house. Neither did Bennett, his body was recovered in the remnants of the rubble, cause of death was ruled a blast injury.

Alex watched the bullet as it entered his brain, but bullet – blast, it's basically the same thing.

My father will spend the rest of his life in a white-collar prison cell. He got off lucky compared to Wilks and Adkins for the part he played in this case. For my mother's sake, I hope that she's finally able to live her life out from under the repression of his shadow.

"Say my name one more time while you hold another woman." Holly's plump lips curved up into a seductive smile as she lowered herself onto the lounge in nothing but a black string bikini bottom next to Emily, who was running her hand over the light dusting of hair on my bare chest.

"Or what?" I teased her as Alex walked up carrying a drink, wearing a black pair of board shorts. His shoulder is still bandaged from the bullet he sustained when Bennett was shooting at them as they ran from the house.

"Or she will pull a pin on a damn grenade and nearly blow your ass to pieces. I still don't know what the fuck you were thinking, woman. You almost killed us both! Then I had to carry you for three miles with a bullet lodged in my shoulder after you blacked out." Alex sat down on the end of the lounge and ran his had up Emily's leg to the juncture of her thighs with his uninjured arm.

Reaching over Emily's body, I pulled Holly down beside me and buried my face in her neck, breathing in her sweet scent. "I love you so fucking much, Holly Chapman." I repeated my words, and this time I whispered them directly into her ear. "Better?" I smiled into her neck as Emily groaned behind me under Alex's touch.

"So much better. I love you so fucking much, Reid Chapman. My soul is yours for eternity. Don't ever make me think you're dead again, and I promise not to throw grenades, mostly. I don't know, it was kind of fun…" The white of her smile contrasted her tan skin, glowing from the last week we've spent on the beach on an island at our safe location.

"Speaking of fun…we have to go back to the real world soon." Holly brushed her lips over mine as she climbed onto my lap, running her hand over Emily's exposed breasts as Alex elicited soft moans from her next to me.

"Am I seriously still the only one considering retirement?" Alex pulled the strings holding Emily's bikini bottom on as he licked his lips, hovering over her now naked body.

"Retire now? And let all the young kids have all the fun? What else would we do?" Holly squealed as I pulled her down on top of me and kissed her until her laughter turned into whimpers. She ground down over my hard length and Alex's hand skimmed over the thin fabric of her bathing suit bottom.

-o-
HOLLY

I guess I did get to keep those shoes after all.

Lies, deceit, the blood of a mafia dynasty runs through my veins.

But, the one thing I've learned for certain?

Evil is everywhere. It's all around us. Despite that, there are still men and women out there fighting for the light.

Those are the few men and women that are willing to sacrifice it all for the many.

When the lines become blurred and you can no longer see which way to turn, that's when it's better to trust the devil you know.

Carlton Harbor

Book 1 – Mirror Image

Book 2 – Surprise Reflections

Book 3 – For Always

Book 4 – Starting Over

Silent Hero

Book 1 – Devil You Know

Book 2 – Until Death

ABOUT THE AUTHOR

Nicole Dixon is a Forensic Accountant with an affinity for writing sexy novels. She loves data, coffee, travel, and making sure all the voices in her head get the happily ever after they deserve. She made the decision to begin publishing her work in an effort to teach her children to never give up on their dreams, nothing is impossible.

Made in the USA
Columbia, SC
10 January 2025